Choosing Love Namaste

Melody Best

SCAN FOR GIFT

TrueLoveWriters

ISBN 978-1-963074-36-9 **& ISBN** 978-1-963074-15-4

Story creation, cover, and illustrations by Melody Noble & Harmony Curtis

To the girls labeled "too much."
Voices too loud, spirits running wild.
Minds overflowing with endless ideas.

To those told to hush, to conform,
to shrink themselves into neat little boxes.

This is for you, the beautifully outspoken.
The ones who refuse to dim their light.

May you forever stand tall,
Gloriously, unapologetically "too much."

For in your "too much" lies the passion
this world so desperately needs.

Choosing Love Namaste

Melody Best

SCAN FOR GIFT

TrueLoveWriters

Thank you for choosing this book.
We hope the story
brought you as much joy reading it
as we had in creating it!

We'd love to hear from you! Feel free to reach out via email at TrueLoveWriters@gmail.com, and follow us on <u>Instagram</u>, <u>Facebook</u>, <u>TikTok</u> at @truelovewriters for the latest updates and behind-the-scenes fun.

Get access to exclusive offers, bonus content, new release updates, and recommendations for more great reads.

Sign up for our e-newsletter at HarmonyNoble.com.

MEAGHAN'S
CHAI TEA LATTE

🍴 8 servings   🕐 5 minutes

Barista Meaghan's earth friendly, Chai Tea Latte is vegan and delicious!

ORDERING: "12 ounce hot chai latte with mac-nut milk."

INGREDIENTS

- 6 CARDAMOTHER PODS & 2 CINNAMON STICKS
- 1 STAR ANISE & 2 TSP. WHOLE CLOVES
- 1 TSP BLACK PEPPERCORNS & 1 PIECE FRESH GINGER SLICED
- 1/3 C. PACKED BROWN SUGAR
- 4 C. WATER
- 6 BLACK TEA BAGS
- 1 TSP. PURE VANILLA EXTRACT
- 1 OZ HONEY
- STEAMED MACADAMIA NUT MILK

DIRECTIONS

1. Bring all spices and water to a boil for 5 minutes, then remove from heat and add vanilla & tea bags (removing tea after 5 minutes). This is your homemade chai tea concentrate that lasts a week in the refrigerator.
2. Add 4 oz of warm chai concentrate to your 16 oz mug
3. Add honey to the mug
4. Heat & froth macadamia nut milk
5. Pour into your mug with the chai & stir together
6. Garnish with a cinnamon stick or a dusting of cinnamon

NOTE: This drink may be made cold by pouring the steeped tea over a cup of ice and adding cold milk. For full enjoyment, loudly explain the benefits of being vegan and how animal products are destroying the earth while you do your favorite yoga pose,.

Chapter 1

HOLDING ZEN-FORCEMENT STAY-CALM POSE

"Oh, my chakra!"

I slam on the brakes, and the front tires of my candy-apple red Mini Cooper narrowly miss a black squirrel darting across the freeway following Puget Sound's coastline.

Glancing in my rearview mirror, I gasp as my heart jumps in my throat. While my front tires avoided him, my back tires didn't miss the poor creature—so much for my "leaving more joy in the world" motto that I tell my friends and followers.

"This is not my fault," I say aloud to appease my new guilt, adding to my current pile of guilt as I throw down my cell phone filled with my mother's nagging texts.

The burned rubber aroma from slamming my brakes only adds to the aura of bad energy, making me blink back tears threatening to ruin my painstakingly applied winged eyeliner—I still haven't mastered its application.

I glance in the rearview mirror again, wincing at the lifeless black furball. *There's nothing I can do now.*

Taking a calming, centering breath, I selfishly think, *Thank goddess, I wasn't live-streaming.* My publicist, Brad, would have lost it. Not to mention my PETA-loving fans, who would've canceled me faster than I could say my tagline: "Namaste, Sparkle On."

My phone buzzes again, and another of my mother's texts lights up the screen.

"Seriously, Mother? Your timing is cosmically off," I groan, eyeing the device.

She's not sensing my vibes.

"Dr. Alex Peters can't wait to meet you. FYI, he makes his own kombucha!"

Since I turned twenty, her life's mission has been finding me the perfect husband—one who's "prestigious" enough to boost her country club wives' brunch bragging rights. In her world, a doctor fits the bill because she's married to a doctor, and marrying a doctor is needed to become a "proper lady" and to sip rosé at fancy luncheons. She despises my earthy vibe and kombucha, so I know the mention of it is her not-so-subtle bait.

Mother!

I shake my head, taking a calming breath. "Bad energy out. Positive vibes in. Sparkle on," I say, smiling through my lousy energy from the squirrel murder and my mother's terrible ideas.

I refuse to let this ruin my day. I reach for my phone, already spinning this squirrel catastrophe into a life lesson for Spreading Harmony, my yoga influencer platform. Because everything in life is a chance for positive growth, I'll turn this into a mindful driving tip or maybe a tribute to Mother Nature's unpredictability. That's totally on-brand and will increase my engagement.

My finger hovers over the record button. Wait—how do I tell my 500k followers that their zen-loving wellness guru is a squirrel's worst nightmare—without sounding like a psycho? #SquirrelSquasher feels like a poor choice.

#NamasteInYourLane, perhaps?

Before I can figure out how to spin it, flashing blue lights reflect in my rearview mirror.

Seriously? Is the universe teaching me a lesson?

Carefully, I pull over, inhaling deeply to channel my inner zen energy. "Namaste, Officer," I whisper to the mirror, practicing, before he approaches. I rehearse, trying to calm my nerves. "Care for some organic, cruelty-free breath mints? I promise I wasn't purposely aiming for the squirrel—I'd never intentionally harm an adorable forest friend!.. No, of course, I wasn't distracted looking at my phone," I coyishly murmur in the mirror, practicing to perfect the flirty vibe that is my fun-loving yoga brand and which my cutesy look oozes before he approaches.

As his boots crunch on gravel, I make a silent pact with the cosmos.

Tomorrow, I'll double down on my green juice cleanse, and I'll spread extra joy to improve my karma. Please, Universe, don't give me a ticket!

I crank down the window, inviting in a rush of pine-scented air and exhaust. My carefully crafted sweet smile and brown waves catch the breeze, dancing to *Zero 7*'s mellow beats drifting from my car's speakers. Eyeing my reflection, I roll my eyes at the fakeness of my "natural" makeup and the tightness of my "casual" attire. But the look works, and people love a carefree, fun yoga instructor.

My publicist's voice plays rent-free in my head, "Morning yoga live streams aren't about being real and relaxing. You must look casual chic, *not relaxed and sloppy*. Think about your calm *and* glamorous vibes. We're here to get sponsors—make money!"

Needless to say, my "love yourself and spread your joy" brand has changed since hiring Brad to manage my social media content and image. I miss my low-key, comfy yoga clothes and casual morning live streams without all the makeup, perfectly curled hair, and tightly stretched clothing.

But Brad is right.

Since hiring him, signing his crazy contract of rules, and following his advice, I've amassed half a million followers. And unbelievably, without college or marrying a doctor, I've started generating an income from my hobby. People love me and my brand, allowing me to spread joy worldwide. If eyeliner helps me do that, *I'll wear eyeliner!*

"Sorry, Mr. Squirrel," I whisper. "Your sacrifice isn't in vain. I promise."

I apply another layer of rose-petal pink vegan lip gloss as the Officer takes his time strutting to my door. My shimmery lips catch the morning light. Pasting on my irresistible smile, I inhale another centering breath.

Showtime.

A tall, muscular figure approaches, his chiseled jaw and aviator sunglasses making him look intense and mysterious as he nears. Despite my squirrel guilt, a flutter of excitement and warmth floods me. The universe is *giving*, in the form of a beefy, young policeman.

"Thank you, karma," I murmur.

As he draws closer, recognition dawns on me. His rugged, masculine features, the confident stride—*I know him.* But not in real life—from one of my online followers. Usually, in pics, he's dressed in a casual button-up and jeans, next to my new yoga follower, Bliss. Bliss' super-hot boyfriend is pulling me over. *What are the odds?*

"License and registration," he states in a crisp voice, devoid of any recognition of me.

Since I'm Insta-friends with Bliss—and I'm a pretty big deal—*he knows who I am.* Licking my sticky lips, an unexpected blush flares across my cheeks, and my stomach tightens. "Good morning, Offic er...?"

"Conner. Officer Conner," he replies authoritatively.

Widening my eyes and biting my lower lip, I lower my eyes, noticing the K9 dog unit emblem on his broad chest. His manly vibe is intimidating and oddly exhilarating. I bite my lip and debate if I should lead with outright flirting or explain that I'm Bliss' yoga teacher.

"Nice to meet you, Officer Conner," I start in a breathless voice.

"Miss, do you know why I pulled you over?" His tone is all business, with no playful banter attempt at all.

I'll change that!

I lick my lips and bat my eyelashes, handing him my license. "I'm Meaghan Mitchell. You might recognize me from Spreading Harmony. Did you stop me for an autograph?" I giggle, looking at my reflection in his mirrored glasses.

"Miss Mitchell, we aren't at a pub and this isn't a pick-up line," he states flatly. "I observed you driving erratically and using your phone while operating a vehicle. Both are serious offenses."

Smiling coquettishly, I ignore his tone and shrug. "This isn't exactly my best moment. But maybe the universe needed to bring us together, right?" I'm hitting on him so hard that he'll forget he has a girlfriend *and* forget to give me a ticket.

My heart speeds up–my parents will kill me and take back the car if I get another speeding ticket—even if this is partially my mother's fault for distracting me with her newest date setup for me.

His expression is unsympathetic. "Miss Mitchell, distracted driving is no laughing matter. I could take your license and tow your car right now. Using your cell phone puts lives at risk–*yours* included."

My heart pounds, not from the stress of a potential ticket but from how my name sounds coming from his tight lips.

"Yes, sir. Absolutely," I nod. His scolding gaze causes the wave of heat to spread from my cheeks to my chest and down further. I clear my throat and say, seriously, "I'm all about positive vibes and safety, Officer Conner. I promise."

"Positive vibes don't prevent accidents," he responds sternly. "I'll need your registration as well."

"Please, Officer Conner, surely we can talk and work something out. I appreciate you keeping me and everyone safe. Could you give me a warning and I could give you a one-on-one yoga session? Yoga is an amazing stress reliever."

He doesn't even crack a smile. "Miss Mitchell, attempting to bribe an officer is a criminal offense. I strongly advise against it. Now. Your registration. *Please.*"

I squirm uncomfortably, feeling like a butterfly pinned under a microscope. The summer heat suddenly is oppressive, and I resist the urge to fan myself as sweat trickles down my neck and into the curve of my pushed-up cleavage.

Officer Conner maintains his professional demeanor, showing no reaction to my discomfort. "Miss Mitchell. Your. Registration."

Reluctantly, I dig through my oversized Coach purse–Brad forced the name-brand monstrosity on me–and with all the complicated compartments and the slew of new makeup products, my trembling fingers fumble around. "Here you are, Officer Conner."

His hand brushes mine as he takes the document, sending an electric jolt through me. I gasp, quickly pulling back, and tell my heart to slow down. Taking a breath, I bite my bottom lip harder. He might not outwardly show that he notices my flirting, but his energy is giving it.

His jaw tightens.

I bite back my grin—*my bra top is working*—he feels the spark.

"This is expired," he states matter-of-factly.

I recover and flash him my most innocent smile. "Soooo Sorry! I must have my new one here somewhere. I hate wasting your time, Officer Conner. I promise that I do have it here *somewhere*."

His expression doesn't change. "Miss Mitchell, operating a vehicle with expired registration is a Washington state violation. It's not something I'd give a simple warning for."

My cheeks flush redder, and I've chewed most of my cute lip gloss from my lips.

Is he always this serious?

I shoot him my best doe-eyed, innocent look, then a syrupy, sweet smile—the smile that melts even the grumpiest customers when I work at Joy's Coffeehouse cafe.

"Maybe we could overlook it, just this once, Officer?"

He remains unmoved, lifting his sunglasses to meet my eyes. "Laws aren't optional, Miss Mitchell. They exist for everyone's safety, and I am tasked with enforcing them."

My flirting isn't working, but his eyes are simmering with more than the promise of a ticket. "Okay, alright. I'm very sorry. And I totally understand, Officer Conner."

Why am I so flustered?

He's just a cop. A handsome, stern-faced cop with piercing blue eyes that could make even a zen yogi lose their balance. I've admired his perfect features and chiseled abs from Bliss's Instagram, but I didn't realize he was a police officer. The uniform adds a whole new dimension to his hotness. "I do have the current registration, I promise."

Reaching for my glove box, I silently plea for the cosmos to cooperate. But because of the universe's wicked sense of humor, the glovebox erupts in a kaleidoscopic avalanche: papers, snacks, crystals, and various knick-knacks I've squirreled away. The colorful tornado of trinkets cascades everywhere.

Officer Conner's eyebrows react with an impressive arch, and he moves his aviators back–to cover his amusement, I hope—while he observes the chaos. I contemplate the cost of a "Driving While Disorganized" citation. This is all, *obviously*, the karmic consequence of the squirrel incident.

"Miss Mitchell, are you having difficulty locating the documentation?" he asks. His tone is as crisp as my homemade kale chips, which makes my stomach grumble.

Not only am I sweaty, red, and disorganized, but my loud stomach is going to make him think I have IBS! *My flirting is really not on point today.*

As he watches me search, I nervously chuckle and shrug at the mess, looking into his unreadable mirrored glasses. I'm glad he pulled them down because his blue eyes were mesmerizing. They are the same color as my favorite lapis lazuli meditation stone. My heart flips along with my stomach as I continue to fumble. Digging, I nervously giggle as my branded merch overflows onto the floor. I reach and grab a plush teddy bear wearing a tiny yoga outfit with my logo, a rainbow leaf with Spreading Harmony, and my yoga video QR code printed across its yoga bear booty shorts.

With no luck finding my registration, I hand him the plush bear in my hand. "Here, enjoy a lavender Spreading Harmony Yoga Bear. He keeps the good vibes flowing and gives snuggles, if you need them." I wink, hoping my sunny disposition will melt his cold resolve.

Officer Conner regards the bear with a look of bewilderment. "Miss Mitchell, I'm not here to flirt or take your weird bribes. I am issuing you a citation if you can't produce a valid registration."

"Everyone needs a Harmony bear. He'll keep your vibes calm with his lavender and coziness," I explain, offended. Under the bear, my registration appears. "Oh, here it is. Looks like Mr. Bear is already spreading good vibes. You'll need his energy while you protect and serve. Please enjoy. It's a gift."

He takes the bear, holding it like it contains a bomb. "I appreciate the gesture, but I can't accept gifts while on duty. It's against department policy." He shakes his head, his expression unchanging. "Now, about your distracted driving."

I wait for the universe to save me and pray to every deity I can think of.

Looking down at the paperwork, a flicker of recognition crosses his face. "Meaghan Mitchell from that yoga harmony thing?"

I laugh. He *finally* recognizes me. "That's what I was trying to tell you. I'm not a bad person. I'm trying to make the world, or at least Lakewood, a better place like you. I do it one yoga student at a time–spreading joy and Harmony," I explain, adding my tagline. The universe smiles at me, and I shimmy my shoulders to relieve the nervous tension as he finally relaxes his curled lips a little.

He nods curtly. "I see. My younger sister follows your channel. I think she's been to a few of your yoga classes. She's quite... enthusiastic... about your forest meditation-yoga-things and vegan recipes."

"Yay! Guilty as charged–I am vegan and passionate about yoga. You're a follower, too?"

Officer Conner's expression is not tense anymore, but he's not exactly friendly. "I don't spend time on social media. I prefer lifting weights to napping and doing stretches, but my sister certainly likes you."

I beam at his sideways praise. "Well, Officer Conner, if I can help your sister, then I'm doing my job." I hand him the blue meditation stone from my dash that matches his eyes. "Give this to her. I'm happy to spread more good vibes. Tell her it's a 'weird bribe' from Spreading Harmony, Meaghan." I pause and decide to stop and not creep him out by saying I've seen him online.

He purses his lips, trying not to smile, while juggling the smooth stone, the plush bear, and his notepad. He gives up, tucks his notepad into his front pocket, and tries handing the plush bear back to me.

"Ms. Mitchell, I appreciate your enthusiasm. But there is the matter at hand."

My eyes widened, and I deadpan him with my most innocent look while studying his chiseled form and my traitorous mind comes up with a few naughty scenarios on this quiet stretch of freeway. But my eyes land on the telltale circular outline in his pants pocket, distracting me.

Tsk, tsk, Officer Hottie. Don't you know chew is a huge yuck?

At the same time, my heart beats harder with his added bad boy, officer vibes. He's lucky he's in uniform, as he's looking yummier as each naughty second passes. I would love the challenge of introducing him to yoga and vegan meals. I shake my head and stifle a giggle at my silly horniness. I must be giddy with too much wheatgrass today.

I take a deep breath, trying to regain my focus. *Positive vibes, Meaghan. Positive vibes.* And I hear a low whine, followed by a sharp bark.

"Omigosh, is that your K-9 doggy partner?" I squeal, straining my neck to see his police cruiser. "What's her name? Can I pet her? Does she do doggy yoga?"

Officer Conner's expression softens, and he gives up on even attempting to be professional as he stuffs the odd assortment I've given him into his side pockets and grins at the bouncing form in his cruiser. "That's Rex. *He* is the best working dog the department has ever had. He doesn't do yoga and can't be distracted by beautiful women while he's on the job, working."

Officer Conner thinks I'm beautiful!

"Bummer. I bet he'd rock at yoga, especially downward dog," I giggle, my lashes fluttering. "My classes are 100% dog-friendly. Our fur friends need relaxation too."

Another low whine forces Officer Conner to glance back at his police car. "Rex is usually quiet and calm. He must sense your..." He looks me up and down, then adds, "energy."

"He's right about my energy. I absolutely adore dogs!" I gush, my hands moving over my heart. "The poor baby must be lonely and worried about you. Is he a drug dog? I might have something he could find, or my mom might have left a Xanax in here. He can sniff it out. Then, I can reward him by petting him and giving the good doggy my positive energy. Dogs really pick up and amplify vibes, you know."

Officer Conner gives up on his seriousness and wipes a hand across his face, turning away from me to mutter, "Why do you hate me, God?"

He looks back at me and gives me a tight smile. "I'm going to pretend I didn't hear that you might have drugs in your car. Rex started in narcotics detection and moved to bomb detection. Since his nose is excellent, the hospital even uses him for specialized detection programs. So no–he doesn't need any practice. No other dog can detect scents like him."

"Holy kale chips, that's amazing!" I say, dying to meet and give him a cuddle, even if Officer Hottie would frown on me doing that. "Rex sounds pretty special!"

Conner nods, a hint of pride in his voice. "He's exceptional. I'm lucky to be his partner and the department is fortunate to have him." Then, as if remembering himself, he straightens. "Now, Miss Mitchell, about your violations."

I gasp in mock offense. "Officer Conner, will you really give me a ticket after all our bonding and shared interests? After all we've been through, you can call me Meaghan." I give him a wide smile.

He doesn't crack a smile and ignores the request. "Miss Mitchell, I'm not sure what to do with you, but I certainly cannot let you continue driving distracted and with an expired registration. These are serious violations."

"Oh wait," I rummage again in the pile on the seat, and hand him a coupon.

He tries to hand the paper back to me. "I can't accept gifts... Err... *Any more gifts.*"

"It's not for you!" I smile, continuing, "It's for Rex. It sounds like he's pretty special. It's just a small thank you for keeping our community safe." I beam as he tucks the Joy's Coffeehouse Pup Cup coupon into his overflowing pocket.

Officer Conner sighs, pinches the bridge of his nose, and looks at his watch. "Miss Mitchell, I'm issuing you a warning this time. Please watch your speed, minimize distractions, and keep your registration handy. Let's keep the road and you safe."

Relief washes over me. "You got it, Officer Conner—eyes on the road, hands on the wheel, and all that jazz," I say, flashing him a smile and giving him my best jazz hands.

He grumbles and touches his forehead with a shake of his head.

"Thank you, Officer. I hope your sister keeps following. Maybe you'll catch a class or do my daily yoga meditation with her. I'd recommend my morning forest bathing, followed by a shot of wheatgrass to increase your positive chakra energy."

I feel his eyes roll behind the mirrored glasses as his full lips curve ever so slightly into a tight line, but I notice the slight smile as he opens his mouth. "I'll stick to the department-approved fitness regimen, thank you," he says, and as he turns, I see a flash of a smile with hidden dimples appearing. "Stay out of trouble," he adds with a wave.

"You, too," I sing back with a ridiculous salute. I watch him walk away, unable to tear my eyes away from his broad shoulders and confident stride. There's something about him that's infuriatingly attractive.

Maybe the universe is testing me or *rewarding me* with the morning eye candy. However, I'm too busy for flirting or a boyfriend. Besides being unavailable, Officer Conner is precisely my opposite type of person: stern, serious, lacking a sense of humor, and seeing the world in black and white.

He *does* inspire me to think about starting a yoga class for men in uniform. Maybe he'd come and give yoga a try with his sister, Bliss, or Rex.

I grin. *Challenge accepted, Officer Hottie.* I'll get you doing yoga and enjoying wheatgrass shots, faster than Rex can eat a Pup Cup.

Watching him drive away, I noticed his muscular frame filling the driver's seat. Despite his cold professionalism, I'm buzzing with his energy, and a spark ignites within me. His stern demeanor didn't fool me. His dimples really needed an excuse to shine, and I gave them that excuse.

Glancing at my phone, I'm late for my shift at Joy's Cafe. I quickly dial, and set the phone to hands-free, just in case Officer Conner sets another speed trap ahead.

"Joy's Coffeehouse, what can I do to make your day extra sweet?" Manager Sean's voice chirps through the speakers.

"Hey Sean, it's Meaghan. Sorry, I'm running late. I've had *a day,* and it's still morning," I explain.

"Girl, hurry up! The pup cup promo today is *fire,* and the cafe is bursting with dogs and sweaty post-morning-workout guys. *I love it,* but I need your upbeat yoga girl energy here, ASAP!"

I laugh, enjoying Sean's energy. Sean's the best cafe manager ever. After Officer Hottie's scolding, Sean's attitude makes me giggle. "On my way!"

Driving, I grin at my unexpected morning. I feel terrible about the squirrel, but between Officer Conner's dimples and Sean's vibe, my energy is buzzing. That's what my brand, Spreading Harmony, is all about: focusing on the positive and adding sparkle to everyday life.

I sparkle, turning the music back on loud and already planning my next social media post. "Namaste, Sparkle on, friends," I say into the mirror, testing it out. "Wait 'til you hear about this morning's cray cray adventure." I giggle, thinking about the sympathy and laughs I'll get from getting pulled over by a grumpy, hot cop.

"Everything turns out okay, if you relax into the universe's plan"—well, except for the squirrel.

I scrunch my nose, and promise, again to the cosmos and Officer Hottie, *I'll drive better and focus on the road.* I wink at my reflection and giggle, suddenly giddy for the day.

Chapter 2

CAFE CALM MEDITATION

The afternoon sun beats down on Joy's Cafe as I wrestle with the temperamental espresso machine affectionately named "The Beast." My earlier run-in with Officer Hottie—*I mean, Officer Conner*—keeps replaying in my mind like a playlist stuck on the same song set, "Handsome Cop Big Energy, Volume 1."

"Earth to Meaghan!" Sean's sassy comment snaps me back to reality. "That latte's not going to make itself, honey. Unless you've suddenly developed telekinetic barista powers?"

I roll my eyes so hard that it's a miracle I don't glimpse my past lives. "Sorry, Sean. Just, you know, caught up in deep cosmic thoughts. Like, what do dogs think traffic smells like? And is it possible to reach Nirvana while driving? My vibrations are *humming* today." I say, shimmying at him.

Sean shimmies back. He leans in, his lips curling into a cheeky smirk, and lowers his voice to a secretive whisper. "Are you just hot and bothered by that rude but irresistible cop you mentioned? The one who's 'chiseled by the gods,' with a jawline sharp enough to slice through glass and has 'mesmerizing ocean blue eyes.' By the way, that's not *positive vibes*. That's your animal *lust,* my dear."

"Sean! I did not say any of those things about him!" I hiss, my cheeks burn hotter than our overworked coffee roaster. "I mean, out loud."

"Oh, honey," Sean fans himself dramatically. "You didn't have to. It was written all over your face the moment you walked in. You look like you'd just seen Chris Hemsworth doing some hot yoga in a police uniform."

Before I can drop a clever comeback—one that'll hit me three hours from now in the shower since I can never think of snappy retorts—the drive-thru bell rings. I slap on my most totally-not-day-dreaming-about-a-handsome-cop smile and swivel to face the customer.

"Welcome to Joy's Cafe! Sip our award-winning lattes, or try a pastry that is a warm, gooey hug for your taste buds!" I say, reading the script left by the window.

Is this really our new cafe greeting from Joy, or is Sean messing with me?

"What sassy caffeinated adventure can I send you on today?"

Sean!

A police cruiser is at the window, and a familiar deep voice returns my greeting, making my heart perform a gymnastics routine worthy of the Olympics. The driver is looking down so he doesn't see me.

"Uh, yeah. Can I get a large black coffee and one of those... pup cup things?"

I grab the counter for support.

Holy organic kale chakra! It's him!

My face freezes in what I can only imagine is a deer-in-headlights meets I-won-the-lottery expression. "Officer Conner? Is that you, or am I hallucinating from too many espresso shots?"

There's a pause as his dreamy blue eyes look past the menu and meet mine with recognition dawning on his face like a sunrise—a very handsome, ocean blue-eyed, chiseled jawline, smoking hot sunrise. "Miss Mitchell? A second run-in with you? This must be my lucky day."

Sean inches closer, nosey with curiosity.

I shoot him an uncharacteristic do-not-say "I told you so" look.

He mouths, "The cop?" with enough glowing excitement to light up the entire block.

I nod, attempting to stay zen while my stomach does a full-on happy girl samba. "That's me! Your friendly neighborhood barista slash, troublemaker, slash joy-spreading, *safe* driver. Fancy meeting you here, Officer. Did you come to arrest our coffee for being criminally delicious, or maybe *a little bear* told you to stop by for positive vibes?" I flip my hair with a sparkle in my eyes. He must not be dating Bliss anymore if he's spending his Friday nights chasing me.

Come to think of it, I haven't seen him in her posts for a while.

"Just doing my job, ma'am," he replies, and I swear I hear a smile despite his cool demeanor. "I'm keeping the streets safe from distracted and caffeinated drivers, one day at a time."

"Your order is on the house, courtesy of the coupon," I say generously, adding extra whipped cream to the pup cup. I am enjoying my slightly bribery-adjacent flirty that is making him uncomfortable. "Quick question: does your furry partner prefer his pup cup with a side of 'I'm a good boy' or a 'Who's the most handsome K-9 in town'?"

He chuckles, giving Rex belly rubs, "Are you a 'good boy' or just 'the most handsome boy ever'?"

I can't help but think he's too soft-hearted to be a cop as I watch his sweet belly rubbing of his pup. Maybe Rex is the key to unlocking Officer Conner's smile.

Waiting for his answer, Sean sneaks up next to me, his eyes gleaming with mischief, and whispers, "Girl, what are you doing? All teasing aside, you can't date a customer. Especially one that's the opposite of your healthy, vegan yoga brand. Did you see all those fast-food burger bags on the floor? And he's a cop! No good comes from dating a cop." His straight-faced scolding dissolves when he adds, "The *dra-ma!* The potential for a *reallllllly* sexy handcuff situation!" He nudges me, makes a kissy face, and winks.

"Shh!" I hiss, my face heats up, and my heart flutters. "It's harmless. Plus, this is a little insurance. I don't want any more traffic tickets. I'm only flirting, not proposing marriage."

"Honey," Sean says, patting my arm like a naive child, "Cops are nothing but trouble. *Trust me.* They have no time for anything but their jobs—*workaholics*— and you'll never find one that's health-focused—*horrible habits from smoking to booger flicking.* I've watched every season of 'Brooklyn Nine-Nine.' I'm an expert, Sweetie."

Before I can remind Sean that TV isn't real life, an excited bark draws my attention back to the window. Rex, in all his furry glory, has his head poking out of the cruiser, tongue lolling and tail wagging as he tries to escape to greet me.

"You are a good boy! And the *most handsomes*t Police Officer in the *whole wide world*," I gush, causing the police cruiser to wag along with him. *Happy Rex balances out stern Officer Conner, for sure.* I can see their energy radiating glee. They are bathing me in glittery joy.

"Rex," he says, "Calm down, and you get your treat." Rex sits obediently, but his eyes stay on me, and his tongue lolls, waiting. "Sorry. He's usually well-behaved in the cruiser."

"Well," I say, grinning at the adorable dog. "It seems your partner likes me. He would *never* give me a ticket, and I bet he would even eat my kale chips," I tease.

Officer Conner's lips twitch, fighting a smile. "He prefers bacon, like me."

Rex barks his agreement and tries, in vain, to get his head out the window to sniff me.

Officer Conner moves his head and again orders him to sit. "I apologize for his enthusiasm. He's having a tough time controlling himself around you. Must be all those vibes you were talking about." He winks at me, unable to stop himself.

"Ah, yes," I quip with a grin. "Plus, I'm wearing my bacon perfume today, especially to attract dogs and bacon-eating men, if you know any?" I smile at myself for the great comeback–*I'm slaying the flirting game!* Giving him my doe-eyes, I ask, "Do you happen to like my bacon-ness?"

"Ouch, I better watch out for you, Miss Mitchell," Conner says. He clutches his chest in mock pain. "I thought this was a family-friendly cafe, but you wore irresistible perfume. How can we be professional and resist that?"

"You can't!" I laugh, nearly spilling his order in the process. "Officer Conner, are you joking around with me? Quick, someone call the papers–the headline: Grumpy Cop Finds a Sense of Humor!"

He grins, and his dimples appear.

The sweet dimples are even better than his mesmerizing eyes or chiseled features. His cute dimples forming are like watching the sun emerge from behind the clouds while a rainbow forms and unicorns prance in the background. I'm completely on the same vibration as him—big energy contained in a calm package. His rizz is *dangerous!*

"I'm full of surprises, Miss Mitchell. You might even say I'm funny *and fun* on the right occasions."

I gasp in exaggerated shock. "Be still my caffeinated heart! Next thing you know, you'll be telling me you do yoga and make kale chips."

"Let's not get carried away," he chuckles, a sound that does funny things to my insides. "I have a reputation to maintain. I wouldn't eat kale if it was cooked in bacon."

Handing him his order, I find my fingers brushing his, and there's that electric spark again. He sends a jolt through me, jumpstarting my heart. His eyes widen as he feels the swirl of energy between us.

"You know," he says, in a low tone, "I thought about what you said earlier."

My heart races faster than a squirrel on espresso. "Oh? Which part? The one about you needing to smile more or the one about you desperately needing a forest bath? Because I stand by both, for the record. And I have more to add to my original recommendations."

He runs his hand over his face, shaking his head. "No. Neither of those, actually. I was thinking more about getting coffee more often. In fact, Rex could be spoiled a little more often with a pup cup. Maybe I could see you again—you know, for research purposes. To better understand the mind of a lawbreaker. Also, I should follow up with my safety warning to make sure you're not as much trouble in the community as you are behind the wheel. I like to do my due diligence."

I laugh, and my mind reels from his straightforward coffee date invitation.

Is this really happening, or am I dreaming? How is a serious cop asking out a bad-driving, vegan barista?

"But, you... I... um..." I stammer, suddenly forgetting how to make words work with my numb lips.

Smooth, Meaghan. Real smooth.

Sensing my deer-in-headlights situation, Sean swoops in like my cafe guardian angel. "Sorry, Officer Hottie, but Meaghan's booked solid for the next century. Try your charm at the donut shop down the street. I hear they love men in uniform there. Especially ones who hit on friendly baristas with stale old one-liners."

Officer Conner's face falls slightly, but he recovers quickly, his professional mask sliding back into place. "Right. Of course. Thanks for the coffee, Meaghan. Stay out of trouble and in your own lane."

Watching him drive away, I turn to Sean. My vibes are a chaos of nerves, passion, and confusion. "What the heck was that? I was handling it." I bite my lip, disappointed I couldn't follow up with the cop or at least get his number.

"That, my dear," Sean says, crossing his arms, "was me saving you from making a huge mistake. Trust me, honey, you do not want to get mixed up with a cop. Think of how bad it would be for you. What would your new publicist say? You can't be dating that guy when your brand is about being chic and health-focused. Besides, you're too busy with your yoga and your mother's list of country club suitors."

I want to argue, to defend Officer Conner and his dreamy eyes. But all of Sean's points are right. Officer Conner's cruiser disappears into traffic, and my senses come back. Mars is in retrograde, so, of course, my emotions are topsy-turvy. I don't know Officer Conner *at all,* except that he is one of my followers' friends. His overly-male energy is a recipe for disaster. Plus, my new publicist, Brad, will have a meltdown if I date the opposite of my healthy lifestyle branding.

My mind flashes to Brad's reaction to me wearing a loose tank top and messy bun while streaming my yoga class. He made me toss out all my comfy clothes for the tight branded clothing I now wear. Then he lectured me that 'image is everything,' and I must 'project a polished, positive, fun vibe.' I am paying him to help my platform, and I agreed to follow his advice.

"Yeah, no," I say, trying to convince myself. "You're probably right. Thanks for the save."

But as I turn back to the espresso machine, my traitorous brain is already spinning ways to "accidentally" run into Officer Conner again. After all, a little flirty with him couldn't hurt. And if it comes with a side of his piercing blue eyes, cute dimples, and a furry, adorable sidekick, well, that increases my positive vibes.

I shake my head, clearing my thoughts.

What's wrong with me? He's too rigid, too severe, and probably thinks meditation is ridiculous. And yet...

"Hey, Meaghan," Tara calls. "Are you okay?"

I laugh, but it sounds as fake as a great-tasting decaf skinny latte. "Yeah, just thinking."

Sean shakes his head and tells Tara, "About the beefy cop who just drove away. He had enough testosterone for the entire male population of Lakewood."

Tara laughs, raising her eyebrows so high that they might crack her expert shading–*I need to hit her up for makeup pointers asap*. She says, "A man in uniform is an irresistable thing. I'm pretty sure if your followers saw Officer Sexy, they'd understand why you're eyeing him."

"No!" I protest way too quickly to be believable. "Maybe. *I don't know.* Ugh, let's change the subject. I need to get him out of my head."

Tara pats my shoulder sympathetically. "Nothing says you need a good shag like a tight ass by-the-book cop making you forget to hate bacon-eaters. He's Instagram-worthy. I think I've seen a pic of him online without a shirt. There were tattoos!"

"He was on Bliss' feed last month–working out with her at the gym," I groan. Then I shake my head, laying it against the counter, hiding from the conversation. "This is not going to end well, is it? I'm going to end up teaching downward dog from a jail cell, aren't I?"

"Probably," Tara agrees, way too cheerfully for my liking. "But hey, I'm not one to stand in the way of a good time. He may not have serious relationship potential, but he'd be a good side piece. A potentially disastrous but highly entertaining life choice for your followers to enjoy."

I lift my gaze just in time to spot a police cruiser cruising by the cafe like it owns the street. Instantly, my heart performs an acrobatic flip—and my hands start itching to do a ridiculous jazz hands thing.

Really! My body is betraying me. I moan softly at the universe's humor and bite on the grin it causes.

Oh, Officer Conner! What are you doing to me?

And how long do I have to wait for our next meeting? In this little town, we're bound to cross paths again—and now, I'm swirling in thoughts of handcuffs and yoga flow classes with a uniformed police partner.

No, Meaghan. Bad Meaghan!

I mentally slap myself. You can't go there. He's everything you're not. Oil and water. Yin and yang. Kale smoothies and whatever the opposite of kale smoothies is—probably donuts–bacon donuts atop a ribeye steak.

I take a deep breath, centering myself. Positive vibes. I am Meaghan Mitchell, Spreading Harmony with positive energy. I don't need a man, especially not one who chews tobacco and is a meat eater.

"You know what?" I announce to Tara and Sean, who are watching me with amusement. "I'm going to do it. I'm going to call Dr. Alex Peters."

Sean's jaw drops. "Wait, what? The kimchi guy your mom's been trying to set you up with?"

"Kombucha," I correct him. "Yep. He's perfect. He's a doctor. He's into health and wellness."

Tara raises an eyebrow. "And he's not a macho cop."

"Exactly!" I exclaim, perhaps a bit too enthusiastically. "He's exactly what I need. A nice, safe, predictable date with a nice, safe, predictable guy. Brad will be happy if I have a guy in my feed that is embracing a healthy lifestyle with me. No sparks, no drama, no handcuffs."

In unison, Sean and Tara exchange a smirk and raise their brows at me. They are doubling the don't-do-it, Girl–You're-making-a-mistake energy.

"Honey," Sean says gently, "Are you sure? I mean, I told you to stay away from Officer Hottie. But jumping right into a date with Dr. Kombucha with your crazy, whatever-is-going-on-here energy, doesn't seem like a good choice."

I wave off his concern. "It's perfect, Sean. It'll make my mom happy. This will be good for my brand–dating a health-conscious doctor—and most importantly, it'll get Officer Conner out of my head. I need good vibes."

"Or a good vibrator!" Tara chimes in, laughing, and Sean almost spits out his latte. She's lucky Crystal or Joy aren't here—she'd get written up for that super-inappropriate clapback.

I purse my lips but then smile.

Along with stealing makeup tips, I need some of her good comeback energy!

On cue, my phone buzzes. It's a text from my mom: "Meaghan, darling! Dr. Peters called me. He'd love to take you out for kombucha after work. Isn't that grand? He suggested a place close to Joy's Cafe!"

I show the text to Sean and Tara. "See? It's meant to be. The universe has spoken."

Tara shakes her head. "The universe has a weird way of speaking to you–through your mom."

I ignore Tara and reply to my mom: "Sounds great! Tell him I'm looking forward to it. "

Sending the message, I have more dread than excitement. *Or is it regret?* No, it's probably just my indigestion returning.

I plaster on my best influencer smile and flutter my overdone lashes. "There. It's done. Dr. Alex Peters, here I come. And Officer Hottie is out of sight, out of mind. My mom will be happy. Brad will be happy. And the universe will be all positive vibes from now on."

Just then, the drive-thru bell chimes. I turn, ready for my cafe customers, and find a minivan full of teenage girls who order five of the blended tie-dye Red Bull specials with the edible glitter—good for the afternoon caffeine fix and social media pics.

When I hand the multi-colored, dazzling concoctions out the window, my heart jumps in my throat, seeing a police cruiser in the busy traffic.

I exhale.

It's not him.

Working the cafe drive-thru is going to be a problem if every cop I see makes my heart leap into my throat.

Waving to the teens, I remind myself I have a date with a mother-approved, respectable doctor. I won't let myself get pulled into the gravitational field of an infuriatingly attractive cop with the strangely appealing vibe and cutest dimples.

Chapter 3

BUCHA BREW BALANCE POSE

I fidget on the barstool, trying to look casual and failing miserably. Buddha's Bucha's ambiance, with its zen garden decor and soft meditation music, usually calms me. Tonight, it's about as soothing as two quad-shot lattes.

I suggested the date location to Doctor Alex Peters, not only for the good vibes, but because I know that he likes kombucha. Buddha's is known for their delicious kombucha on tap. Plus, this gives me the perfect excuse to stage a not-so-accidental run-in with Bliss, my yoga follower and fellow health enthusiast.

I'm on a side mission to gather intel on Officer Hottie, partly for my own curiosity but mostly to satisfy the relentless thirst of my fellow baristas. They are buzzing about Officer Conner's dating status like he's the last iced latte during a heatwave.

Not that it matters since *I'm not interested.* But Bliss should know his status and that he's flirting with other women.

"Hey! I hear that being a fruitarian is on trend. Can you make any drink suggestions with raw fruits harvested within twenty miles?" I ask, catching Bliss' attention as she ties on her apron. Her blue eyes sparkle at my ridiculous question. It reminds me of a particularly serious officer from this morning.

Why can't I get Officer Conner out of my head?

"Meaghan!" Bliss exclaims, ignoring the other customers who are trying to get her attention. "I thought that was you. What brings our Lakewood Instagram-famous yoga goddess across the railroad tracks to drink at Buddha's Buchas tonight?"

I grin, raising an eyebrow at Bliss. She's like a human ray of sunshine, always bursting into the cafe with her infectious energy and leaving a trail of good vibes in her wake. Her social media is a goldmine of local hidden gems and her coffee orders are as quirky as they come–I mean, who else would dream up a Cherry Kahlua Flat White at seven PM on a Tuesday? She's popped up at a few of my nature-inspired yoga sessions too.

Part of me is dying to upgrade our relationship from 'casual acquaintances who share a mutual love for overpriced lattes and pretzel-like yoga poses' to actual friends. But between slinging espresso shots, contorting myself into Instagram-worthy yoga poses, and trying to convince the internet that I'm the next big thing in wellness, I barely have time to remember my own name, let alone nurture a budding friendship.

Still, Bliss is a good connection to bounce ideas off for all things social media. She's got this knack for knowing exactly what will make people double-tap faster than you can say 'namaste'. Maybe one day, when I'm not drowning in a sea of hashtags and almond milk, we'll finally get around to that girls' night out or any adventure outside of our jobs. Until then, I'll just have to settle for our current relationship of mostly Instagram stories.

"Oh, you know, just expanding my horizons," I say, nonchalantly. "I thought I'd see how the other half lives. The kombucha-drinking, dating half of the world." I say, lifting my chin and smoothing a stray brown curl behind my ear.

Bliss raises an eyebrow, taking my almost empty kombucha pint. "Dating? Do tell."

I lick my lips, trying not to stare at her perfectly tousled blonde hair.

Is it creepy that I stalk her online, envying her carefree university life, and now I'm totally jealous of her hair and kombucha serving lifestyle? Is it weird to ask her out on a friend date?

She has great energy and a vibrant aura. I wonder if she wants to chill out and grab a movie or walk in the park with me. I mean, I'd love to have a friend to make silly friendship bracelets with, like when I was a kid.

"Yeah, I'm supposed to be meeting a blind date here. I showed up twenty minutes late because I changed outfits five times. I am going for the casual-not-trying-too-hard look." My face heats up. "Of course, now, he's not here or answering my texts," I explain.

"Who is he? Maybe I know him."

"Dr. Alex Peters. I didn't get a picture but my mother says he's tall, dark and handsome and she's really into Sean Connery so I'm guessing he'll be a younger version of 007. My mother's been trying to set me up for months. But he's–" I checked my phone for the millionth time, "forty-five minutes late."

"Ouch," Bliss winces sympathetically. "Well, his loss—my gain. We can hangout and chill over local bucha. Now, I'm buying–what can I get for you? Something with an added shot to drown your sorrows, or are we sticking to the straight and narrow path of a Green Juice Ogre Special?" Her smile curves into full-on conspirator mode, and with those deep dimples, she looks more like she's ready to cheer at a high school football game than ace a university exam–which I saw on socials she did this morning—and serve drinks here.

I lean in to whisper a secret, saying too loudly, "Let's get wild. *Double shot me!* My chakras could use a little shaking up tonight."

Bliss grins and whispers, "I won't tell if you don't. Even the most health conscious person deserves to indulge. Spreading Harmony needs a little something something for the wait!"

"What happens at Buddha's Bucha stays at Buddha's Bucha, right," I say with a wink. "Unless it's really good content, then it goes on Instagram. Seriously, I'm getting close to getting a sponsorship as an influencer."

"Is that why you have been a bit more polished on your feeds? Just remember I liked you before the makeup and fancy clothes," Bliss winks at me.

"I'm using a social media marketer, Brad. I don't always like his ideas, but he has boosted my followers and has the connections with potential sponsors. Anything to bring Spreading Harmony to the masses."

"You'll go viral soon. You're stellar. You slay," she says. "Now, what can I make you?" She points to the special board that's impossible to read in the dim light.

"Make me something strong enough to make me forget about being a super-healthy positive yoga role model and having a blind date. I have a few other things disrupting my vibrations, too. Should we make it a triple?

Is that a thing?"

She giggles and starts making a drink. "Other things? Besides all that. Wow!" Bliss lifts a brow, and continues ignoring the other customer's making her coworker serve them, as she gives me her undivided attention. She reaches for the top-shelf tequila. "Come on, spill it. I'm legally obligated as a bartender to listen to your problems. It's in the job description, right between watering down sorority girls' drinks and emptying the trash. Listening is the best part of the job."

I sigh, watching as she expertly combines ingredients in a shaker. "Have you ever dated a cop?" I ask, hoping she doesn't say she's currently dating one.

"A cop? I have before," Bliss wipes her hands and shakes her head. "And cops are a whole different kind of trouble. Tell me what does a cop have to do with your blind date or is it the 'other things'?"

"A cocky cop pulled me over this morning," I explain, with my cheeks blushing at even talking about my hottie Officer Conner. "And pretended he didn't know me, then tried to give me multiple traffic tickets–that I didn't deserve, by the way. But, I gotta say, he was bursting with this crazy big energy even though he was so strict and wouldn't even flirt with me. He was so infuriating, and by-the-book serious that I tried to get him to agree to go to a forest meditation just to calm his vibes."

Bliss snorts, pouring my drink into a glass that looks more like a small fishbowl than a bar glass. "You couldn't find any sage to smudge his energy away? I can imagine you telling him, 'Officer, I swear, I'm not flirting with you, just trying to align your energy. Don't handcuff me, it'll ruin the positive vibrations!'"

I laugh, nearly snorting my drink. "What is it with cops and handcuff jokes?"

Taking a sip of Bliss's concoction, I'm hit with a flavor explosion that's part picnic on a freshly cut lawn, part 'oh god, what am I about to do?' It's like summer and bad decisions had a baby in my mouth.

Perfect.

"Wow, Bliss. You're definitely on my wavelength with this drink. It tastes like fun with a side of tomorrow's regret."

Bliss grins, looking pleased with herself. "That's my specialty. But seriously, about cops—" She leans in, her voice dropping to a conspiratorial whisper. "Aside from the handcuffs and the uniform—*which, let's be real, are pretty great*—there's no legit reason to date one. Most of them are so married to their job, they make workaholics look lazy. And don't get me started on how stern they are. They're like the physical embodiment of a party pooper."

She takes a dramatic sip of her own drink before adding, "Trust me, they're the certified killjoys of the dating world. I promise you, dating a cop is like trying to have a good time with a walking, talking 'fun police' siren."

"Exactly!" I lift my glass to her and take a giant drink. "But I can't stop thinking about him, which is ridiculous because he's a terrible match for me. He's not vegan and doesn't even do yoga."

"Opposites attract," Bliss shrugs, wiping down the bar. "Of course, meditation and yoga are becoming way more mainstream, thanks to people like you. I bet he's more spiritual than you think. Maybe the universe is trying to tell you something—your doctor isn't here and you seem pretty stuck on this cop. This could be the balance, harmony, yin and yang, and all that good vibes stuff you post about."

I roll my eyes and laugh. She's right, but there's no way my mother, Sean, Tara, or Brad would approve of Officer Conner. And really isn't it the thought of dating a bad boy, not actually kissing his bacon-eating lips that is exciting. I shutter with a chill dancing down my spine. "The universe needs to mind its own business. I'm here to meet a perfect gentleman who makes kombucha and would totally fit with my brand and image."

"Sounds thrilling," Bliss says, the words thick with sarcasm. "I can see why you're so disappointed he's late."

"No, really. I'm excited to meet him," I insist, taking another large gulp of my drink. "Dr. Alex Peters is perfect. He's a doctor. He's health-conscious. He's—"

"Not here," Bliss fills in, helpfully.

I groan, letting my head thunk against the bar. "Maybe he got lost on the way. Or maybe he's saving lives."

"What kind of doctor is he?"

"A dermatologist, but he met my dad working at the dermatology oncology clinic. I bet he's the kind of dermatologist who works emergencies." Now that I'm saying it out loud, it sounds laughable.

"Sure," Bliss nods sagely. "He could be performing an emergency pimple popping as we speak. You know, it could be life or death for a super model's career."

I giggle at her ridiculousness. "Oh god, what if he shows up with sunscreen painted across his nose, wearing trifocals?"

Just then, my phone buzzes. I snatch it up, hope blooming in my chest. I deflate when I see it's a text from my mother.

"Meaghan, darling! How's the date going? Isn't Dr. Peters dreamy? Don't forget to mention that you're looking to settle down and your parents are willing to pay for the wedding. Love you!"

I show the text to Bliss, who winces sympathetically. "Yikes, mom drama. Luckily, I miss out on that with my older brother raising me. Instead of setting me up on blind dates, he bought me a handgun and gave me shooting lessons."

I laugh and shake my head, "I'm sorry about your mom. You turned out pretty confident. It sounds like you have a good brother."

She smiles and nods. "Come to think of it, I'm single with no prospects. Maybe you *should* listen to your mom."

I giggle, "True! I wish I had siblings, but instead I get all their pressure and hopes, placed on my shoulders."

Bliss reaches to pat my hand, and she squeezes my hand, listening.

"Well, at least this non-date might save me from her next blind date set-up," I say with a weak smile and then refocus on my phone, typing out a quick reply. "I'm having a great time, Mom! Dr. Peters is indescribable."

"Not technically a lie," Bliss points out. "Can't describe someone who isn't here."

I'm about to respond when the door to Buddha's Bucha's swings open, and a familiar figure saunters in, like he's stepping out of a "Hot Cops Monthly" photoshoot.

Officer Conner approaches the bar, out of his uniform, but still radiating authority in pressed jeans and a shirt stretched across his broad chest. My heart does a somersault, and I briefly consider hiding behind the bar's potted plant.

"Oh no," I cry to Bliss as my heart thunders and my hands get sweaty wet. "That's him. That's the cocky cop."

Bliss's eyes widen, as she chirps, "Wait, that's the guy who pulled you over?"

As the words register, my cheeks heat with a blush easily visible since I'm make-up free. Did I make a big mistake talking with Bliss? Conner is her old boyfriend?

If I want to be her friend, I can't date her ex.

I swallow. Did I ruin our friend vibe? Does this mean I won't make matching friendship bracelets while listening to Taylor Swift's music? I was getting the energy that she'd be into that with me before Officer Wrong-For-Me walked in.

Officer Conner comes over and leans his large frame over the bar to throw his arms around Bliss in a big hug, that doesn't look like what you'd give an ex.

I glance at her and she opens her mouth but nothing comes out with his suffocating loving hug covering her face. I thought they weren't dating. anymore.

"How's my favorite little sister?" He bellows while looking around the bar. "No one's bothering you tonight, right?"

Sister?!

I freeze, and my heart pounds. Maybe he won't recognize me with my hair pulled up and in loose, comfy clothes.

"Not anymore!" she squeaks, slipping out of the embrace.

If I was a guy who wanted to flirt with Bliss, I'd be intimidated by him. This must be why she said cops are party poopers.

He sits one stool over. Officer Conner's eyes land on me, and he recognizes me even without the makeup. Giving me a smile with an intensity that makes my toes curl in my eco-friendly sandals, he lifts his chin. "Miss Mitchell," he says, his voice a low rumble that does funny things to my insides. "Fancy meeting you here." He knits his brows and looks at the large drink in front of me. "I hope you're not planning on driving tonight."

I straighten up, summoning every ounce of dignity I can muster. Which, after half a fishbowl of Bliss's mystery cocktail, isn't much. "Officer Conner. What a surprise. Are you here to arrest me for disturbing the peas with my overwhelming positive vibes?"

He quirks an eyebrow, the start of a smile, tugging at the corner of his lips. "The peas? No, not tonight. I'm off duty. I'm just stopping in to check on my sister and make sure there aren't any creeps bothering her."

"How nice of you," I say, aiming for nonchalance and sounding mildly rude.

Why am I so off around him?

"I'm here on a date. With a doctor. He's a pretty big-deal surgeon-type. He makes kombucha and likes kale. He is just running a bit late," I ramble, my words tripping over each other.

Officer Conner glances at the empty seat beside me, then at the half-empty fishbowl in front of me. "I see. And how late is your big deal date?"

I recheck my phone, wincing at the time. "Only an hour and seven minutes. But who's counting?"

"Um," he nods, sliding onto the stool next to me. My rebellious heart does a little jig at his proximity. "I'm sure he has a good reason. Traffic, perhaps. Or a kombucha surgical emergency."

I can't help but laugh. "Is that a thing? Do you get a lot of calls about rowdy kombucha and need to call a surgeon? Being a cop, I'm sure you've seen it all."

"Oh, every day," he says seriously, but I can see the laughter in his eyes. "Fermented tea-related crimes are a huge problem in this town. It's a real culture shock for people outside of Washington state."

I laugh with a smile remaining on my lips. "Officer Conner, was that a joke? I'm shocked. I thought your earlier joke was a fluke. Your jokes should be illegal."

He clutches his chest in mock offense. "Miss Mitchell. I'll have you know I have an excellent sense of humor. It's just very well hidden. I can't joke at work, for security purposes, of course."

"Of course," I nod, solemnly. "Can't have criminals knowing you're capable of laughter. It might ruin your street cred."

As we banter, I relax with the tension of the past hour melting away. Officer Conner, it turns out, is surprisingly easy to talk to when he's not writing me a ticket. We comfortably chat, like old friends getting back together, about everything from the merits of green juice—he's skeptical—to the best hiking trails in the area–we agree to disagree on whether 'forest bathing' is an actual meditation thing and not something I made up to lure him into the woods with me.

Only when Bliss clears her throat pointedly do I realize how much time has passed. "Another round for you two?"

I blink, surprised to find my fishbowl empty.

When did that happen?

"Oh, um, I should probably slow down. I'm still technically waiting for my blind date."

Officer Conner checks his watch, his expression softening. "Miss Mitchell–Meaghan, I think it's safe to say your date isn't coming. You don't need to go on blind date anyways."

The words hit me like a bucket of cold water, cutting through the pleasant buzz of alcohol and conversation. I've been stood up, and he thinks he's enough of a reason for me not to go on blind dates. "Oh. Right. Of course." My cheeks are burning with embarrassment. "God, I'm such an idiot. Who waits around for two hours for a blind date?"

"Hey," Officer Conner says gently, placing his hand over mine. "You're not an idiot. You're optimistic. Your positive attitude is sweet and refreshing, actually."

I look up at him, struck by the sincerity in his blue eyes. I forget how to breathe, and my heart stops beating for a second.

"Thanks," I manage to squeak out. "That's really nice of you to say." My brain says no to him, but my dissident body melts closer to him.

Darn, his big, attractive manly energy!

Just as I'm about to suggest we continue our conversation somewhere else—purely for politeness, of course—my phone buzzes. I glance down, expecting another text from my mother, but instead, it's an unknown number.

"Meaghan, this is Alex Peters. I am so, so sorry. There was an emergency at the hospital—a burn victim. I got called in to help. My phone died, and I've only charged it now. I feel terrible. Can we reschedule? I promise to make it up to you."

Staring at the text, I'm all over the place with emotions swirling. I inhale and exhale slowly, grounding myself from the increasing energy, and finding a calmer energy on the wooden barstool.

Thank goodness Dr. Peters is not a jerk standing me up.

But having Officer Conner show up and entertain me made me forget about my date. I'm enjoying myself, and guilt creeps over me, thinking of my actual date anxiously to reach me during his emergency. I blush deeper, glancing at Officer Connor.

I'm a jerk!

"Everything all good?" Officer Conner asks, cocking an eyebrow and drinking a Coke that he must have brought with him since they only serve local, organic products.

I nod and glance at Bliss. "It's my date. He had an emergency and couldn't call."

Officer Hottie nods, and his chiseled jaw tightens, his expression unreadable. "Sounds like he had a good reason. Are you going to meet him later to give him another chance?"

I bite my lip, considering. "I don't know. I mean, it's not his fault, but still, you shouldn't stand up a first date. I guess I should reschedule."

"Unless you have a better date option," he says with a hint of a smile playing on his lips.

I lick my lips and exhale heavily. "Not everyone has the handsomest dog to hangout with," I shoot back, pleased with my comeback.

With a chuckle, he nods. "No one compares to Rex," he grins with dimples, and I see the resemblance to Bliss when he's happy.

"He did apologize, and—"

Another text from Dr. Peters interrupts.

"Meaghan, I feel terrible. I've been looking forward to meeting you. Please, let me make it up to you. You name the time and place for our second date, and I will not miss it. Sky's the limit—unless you're into skydiving, in which case, I'll need some liquid courage, and you'll definitely have to push me out of the plane."

I chuckle at the text. It's sweet, and he's giving me all good vibes and energy. He's being apologetic and letting me pick the date. The little skydiving dig is unexpectedly cute from a boring dermatologist.

"Looks like I'm going on a date with him. I gotta give him a second chance–he's my *best* option," I say with a shrug, keeping my eyes averted from the blue hypnotizing eyes next to me.

"Okay then. Sounds like you're decided, Miss Mitchell," Officer Conner says with a smile that doesn't quite reach his eyes.

How did my eyes naturally go to his, even when I told myself to stop flirting with him? I look between him and my phone, torn. On the one hand, Dr. Peters was my original date and is vetted by my mom as a proper gentleman.

On the other hand, my body yearns to be near Officer Conner, *proper or not*. Despite making it clear who I'm choosing, somehow, my elbow is grazing his arm. The heat from touching him is making my insides syrupy. I have such an unexpected energy and magnetic attraction with Officer Conner, I pause, afraid.

"I think," I say, leaning away, "I should give my date a chance. After all, my mom set this up, and he seems like a really nice guy. Plus, he works with my dad."

Officer Conner nods, standing up. "Of course. It's the right thing to do and he is a pretty big deal, I hear. Plus, you can't disappoint your family." He lifts a brow and rolls his large shoulders back, filling the room with his masculine vibe.

"Thank you. For keeping me company tonight. And you actually seem nice, when you're out of uniform and smile."

He remains stoic, giving me a nod. "Anytime, Harmony Yoga girl. Just try to stay out of trouble, okay?"

"She's Spreading Harmony, bro," Bliss says, rolling her eyes, unfazed by her brother's dominant energy.

"No promises," I wink back at him, with a fresh thrill dancing down my spine. "I can't change who I am."

He waves to me and Bliss, swaggering out with his empty coke bottle. I glance at my empty fish bowl, and it looks like he is the health conscious one, not me.

My heart sinks as he leaves. I should have taken more time to talk with him and weigh my options. I want to chase him and forget all about Doctor Alex Peters. Regret floods me—I should have given the cop a chance, and trusted the vibes. Love isn't weighing the best options but following your heart.

I shake my head, remembering that everything is upside down with Mars in retrograde, and my head spinning from the drink.

Dr. Peters is the obvious choice. He is the safe, logical choice that aligns with my interests and lifestyle.

On the other hand, Officer Conner is a wild card. He would be an unexpected variable in my otherwise orderly life, but I don't see him fitting into my yoga group or at the country club.

Why am I even still debating the issue?

I shake my head, and the hot pulsing under my clothes starts to calm, returning me to my normal, calm energy wavelength.

I remind myself that a sudden physical connection between strangers happens all the time, and it doesn't mean anything. Hormones and contrasting energy fields caused the sparks.

Biting my lip, I admit I miss Officer Conner's sparks, and his big masculine. I'm tempted. However, I've made my decision. I look away from the door and smile at Bliss.

"Thanks for making me the drink and not telling your brother that I was calling him a cocky jerk," I say, picking up my phone. I add, "Hey, come to sunrise yoga tomorrow at the park, if you want. It'll be fun!"

"Okay," she nods.

I pick up my phone, inspired, and text Dr. Peters, "How about joining me for my sunrise yoga class tomorrow at 5:30 AM? Fair warning–most people think it's way too early for anything–let alone a date. But if you're up for it, I promise it'll be an unforgettable experience. " I hit send, half expecting him to decline politely. I mean, a pre-dawn yoga date is unusual. But to my surprise, my phone buzzes immediately:

"5:30 AM? Are you trying to test me? I'm in! At least you didn't pick skydiving, but I might be falling, anyways. I'll bring the coffee or kombucha? You bring your zen. Just promise not to laugh when I fall over trying to do a downward dog."

I giggle with a surge of excitement. He is funny, and if he's cute, then he's perfect for me. "Coffee and kombucha before yoga is a no-go. Oh, Dr. Peters, I have so much to teach you. A green smoothie, like a kale-banana-spirulina blend, pairs better with morning yoga."

"Kale-banana-spirulina? Okay. I have a juicer, and I accept the challenge, Yoga Goddess. I'm going to impress you, as long as flexibility isn't a factor."

I laugh. "Excellent! Don't worry, I'll go easy on you. It's all calm, good vibes in my class. You'll enjoy the simple sun salutations. It's the best way to greet the day."

"Sun salutations at 5:30 AM–the sun better appreciate our efforts. See you tomorrow, Meaghan. I'm looking forward to meeting you and learning yoga!"

Putting my phone away, I smile at the gentle, fun vibes he's bringing. Dr. Peters is turning out to be surprisingly sweet.

Who knew a doctor could stand me up but still make me smile with his playful texts? He does deserve a second chance.

Gathering my things, I find my eyes drifting to the door where Officer Conner disappeared. I wonder what it would be like if I had invited him to my yoga class instead. Would he show up in his police uniform with his notepad out, ready to arrest me for disturbing the peace? Seeing Officer Conner holding a complicated yoga pose, especially shirtless, makes me blush and blink hard. I wonder what his tattoos look like. I shake my head, laughing at my silly thoughts.

Nope, I made the right choice. Dr. Peters and I have a lot in common and the same energy. Plus, my mom will be ecstatic about me doing yoga with him.

Still, stepping out into the cool night air, I have a tiny twinge of dark energy clouding.

Regret?

Curiosity?

Lust?

I shrug. I'm sure it's the effects of Bliss's mystery cocktail and my unsettled stomach.

Either way, tomorrow is a new day. A new day that starts at sunrise with a first date doing yoga. That's the kind of date that is perfect and on-brand for me.

Maybe Dr. Peters will surprise me. Perhaps he'll be a natural at yoga. Maybe he'll make me laugh so hard that I fall out of tree pose.

Or, a rugged, serious policeman will be patrolling near the park at 5:30 AM.

Hey, a girl can have fantasies, right?

Energy crackles in my chest, as I stride to the bus stop, half hoping to see a friendly Officer to offer me a ride home and maybe more. I look at the clear sky and take a cleansing breath. Tomorrow, I have a sunrise yoga class to teach and a new connection in my life.

And if my dreams tonight happen to feature a beefy heart-throb officer, *and* a proper doctor, *I'm blaming Mars!*

Chapter 4

Sunrise Sway Salutation

A chill creeps over my bare arms from the pre-dawn crisp air as I set up my yoga mat in the forest clearing.

"Stunning," I whisper at the first hints of sunrise painting the sky in soft pinks and oranges. I take a cleansing breath to relax. Usually, I'm the picture of Zen before my sunrise classes, but today, my stomach is still temperamental, rumbling, and tight.

My super-tight, gelled ponytail makes my scalp ache and doesn't help. Plus, the new merch, branded "Spreading Harmony" yoga top and leggings, is a bit too snug, despite Brad's insistence that it's perfect and on brand. I sigh, missing my old, comfy hoodie and sweats I used to wear as yoga clothes.

This is for the brand, I remind myself. I'm *almost* an influencer.

"Deep breaths, Meaghan," I mutter, but then I remember Dr Alex Peters is coming, and my heart speeds up. "It's just a yoga class. With a cute doctor. At an ungodly hour. In clothes that look painted on. No biggie."

"Talking to yourself again?" a cheerful voice pipes up behind me. I turn to see Demi, her long blonde hair in a perfect fishtail braid, grinning like she knows all my secrets. She probably does since my life is broadcasted online, and she gets coffee at the cafe.

"Demi! You're early," I say, failing miserably at sounding like a relaxed, upbeat yoga instructor.

"Wouldn't miss this for the world," she says, rolling her mat up front. "It's not every day that you invite a hot date to the sunrise class—Bliss told me," she says with a wink. "Plus, this could be the class that goes viral, then I'll be Instagram famous too."

My cheeks flush from mentioning my "date" and the reminder of why I'm so nervous. "It's not a real date. It's just a guy joining our class. Who happens to be a doctor. And cute. And funny. But not a romantic date."

"Uh-huh," Demi nods, clearly not buying it. "And I'm here at 5:30 AM because I love waking up early. Face it, this is going to be a first date. A very public yoga date."

Before I can protest further, Bliss jogs up, looking annoyingly perky for being up all night with me at the pub. "Morning, ladies!"

I turn to my eager students rolling out their mats, "Ready for some sun salutations and selfies?"

"More like moon salutations," Demi jokes good-naturedly. "The sun's not even awake, yet. I should've grabbed a morning espresso."

"This will wake you up," I laugh, my nervousness dissipating with my student's friendly smiles. "Thanks for coming, guys. I really appreciate the support."

"Anytime, girl," Bliss says.

I pull out my phone and angle the screen with my bag on the bench to face us. "Everyone spread out your mat and relax, breathing in the coming day and gathering the morning energy."

"Now, let's get your daily social media photos done before your big-deal doctor arrives," Demi chirps, and I glare at Bliss for the details she shared with Demi.

"Brad wants three extra-special yoga poses and a video clip of class. Can you take those?" I hand my phone to Bliss, who knows the drill since Brad started sending me daily marketing assignments.

"Thank you both for tolerating this new social media push to get the real-yet-perfectly-posed pictures." I sigh, striking a strained pose in the tight clothes meant to look natural and fun. Sometimes, I wonder if I'm losing the joy of yoga with all this commercialization of my passion.

Demi looks at me sympathetically. "Hey, if it helps spread your message of harmony to more people, it's a good thing. You really are the real deal, Girl. Everyone needs a little sunrise yoga wake-up."

"I guess," I concede, trying to smile while balancing in the twisted stork pose. "It's just that my yoga used to be about helping people find inner peace and connection to the world. Now it's about clothing and accessories to have a Sparkle On lifestyle and look, you know?"

"Honey," Bliss says, snapping, "in this world, inner peace and stretchy pants are samesies. Now, give me your best 'I'm at one with the universe' face."

I roll my eyes but comply, grateful for my friends and students' understanding, with the uneasy situation clouding my aura.

After a thousand photos and ten minutes later, Demi's eyes light up. "Ooh, speaking of your mystery man, spill! We can listen to details while finding the day's energy. At least tell us his details."

I sigh, realizing there's no escape. "His name is Alex. He's a dermatologist. We were supposed to meet last night, but he had an emergency. So, I invited him to do morning yoga with me."

"Sunrise yoga class is the perfect punishment for standing you up," Bliss adds, arching an eyebrow.

"Morning meditative yoga is a treat, not a punishment," I say out the side of my mouth, demonstrating the lazy palm sway for the class to follow.

Bliss says, off-handedly, "I kinda thought you and my brother were hitting it off."

I shake my head and tell the class, "Hold this pose for five breaths and move to the other side." I look at her and rub my nose, then my face, forgetting that I'm smearing all my yoga-glamorous makeup. "Your brother needs an alpha female energy—my calming vibe doesn't match his, *at all*."

"You seemed to be vibing last night," she teases.

I try not to react at the mention of Officer Conner, but my traitorous heart does a little flip. "Oh?"

"Yeah, he's not funny ever. He is different around you—happy, even," Bliss says, not even pretending to do yoga as her eyes meet mine, searching. "It's the first time I've seen him smile like that in a long time. He's always been serious, raising me after our parents...then military and being a police officer. I worry, and I feel guilty that he missed out. Anyways, that was TMI. It's just nice to see him happy."

A muddled vibe swirls in me, and my stomach clenches. My aura is totally off. "Oh."

Not seeing Bliss's expression, Demi says, "But a doctor matches your lifestyle better, right, Meaghan? I mean, can you imagine a police officer doing yoga?"

I can, and *I have.*

Unfortunately, my imagination gives me a bonus mental image of Officer Conner in yoga pants, trying to do a downward dog, with his tight glutes straining his uniform pants. It's enough to make me snort with laughter. "Thanks, Demi."

A figure appears at the edge of the clearing, clutching a small cooler. His hair's tousled, and he's looking adorably lost—Dr. Alex Peters is here! He's tall, with long hair and strong features, like a cross between a surfer dude and a model. This is the doctor my mom picked for me? Maybe I should have been listening to her—*he's hot!*

"Ladies," I whisper, tugging at my yoga top and straightening my ponytail, "let's play it cool. And by cool, I mean, no giggling until after he leaves."

Bliss nudges Demi. "Twenty bucks says he faceplants in his first pose."

I roll my eyes but smile at the handsome sorta-stranger. *No pressure, right?*

"Dr. Peters!" I wave him over, my heart doing a weird little somersault. "You made it!"

He turns, his eyes lighting up in recognition, and wow—that smile. "Meaghan! I was starting to think I'd been pranked. This view and location—wow! Do you normally order up a perfect sunrise and an enchanted forest for your classes?"

I laugh, already liking him more than I expected. "Only when I'm trying to impress someone. Or give them an excuse to not run away screaming."

His laugh is low and warm, and the nerves I didn't know I fade. He says, "I don't run, except for emergencies. But I figured showing up would at least score me a few brownie points."

I grin, feeling bolder. "Definitely. I mean, it's Saturday morning, so just being here makes you a hero."

He smiles back with the warm and easy energy I felt in his text messages. I ask, "What's in the cooler—a load of ice bags for your sprains and strains if I push you too hard?"

"Oh that would have been a good idea," he smirks.

I eye the container suspiciously. "Please tell me that's not kombucha at this hour?"

He adopts an expression of mock offense. "I'll have you know that I make a mean batch of kombucha, but this is a kale-banana-spirulina smoothie. I made it special just for you, per your request. I may have added a splash of kombucha for medicinal purposes, of course."

I giggle back at his playfulness, "Of course. Very healing of you, Doctor."

I walk him back to the group, and I can't help but notice how at ease I feel with Alex. He makes everything feel light and fun. There's no nervous energy or tension.

"Alright, everyone," I address the class as the last of my students arrived. "Remember, there's no judgment here. Yoga is about connecting with yourself and the world around you, not about perfect poses."

Alex sneaks into the back of the class and spreads an extra yoga mat, pulling off his hoodie to reveal a fit body.

I catch Alex's warm eyes and add with a wink, "That goes double for any doctors in the class or girls that stayed out too late having fun." I hear giggles from Bliss and Demi.

As I begin the class, I'm pleasantly surprised by Alex's enthusiasm. Sure, he wobbles in tree pose—much to Bliss's delight—and his downward dog looks more like a confused giraffe, but he throws himself into every pose, enthusiastically trying them.

"How's everyone feeling?" I ask as we transition into warrior pose.

"I'm discovering muscles I never knew I had," Alex quips, his face slick with concentration and a grin.

"That's the magic of yoga," I grin. "It awakens all the muscles, sensations, and energy in your body."

As the class progresses, I find myself drawn to Alex's presence. It's not just his willingness to try something new or his rippling muscles as he moves into positions. There's something more, an easy energy and attraction I hadn't expected.

Alex closes his eyes during a more challenging position, breathing steadily despite the strain. When I move everyone back to the mountain pose, I catch him smiling softly back. His eyes glow as they move, taking in the sunrise breaking over the forest and warming us.

"Beautiful, isn't it?" Walking around the class, I quietly remark to him, assisting people with their positioning.

I touch his arm to adjust it in better alignment. He stiffens oddly at my touch. Then, his body relaxes into the solid form of the pose.

He shares his easy smile, his eyes meeting mine and making me tingle with positive energy at his kind vibes. "It really is. You know, in my line of work, I spend a lot of time searching for problems. But this natural beauty reminds me of why I live in the Pacific NorthWest. It's so beautiful and natural here. That is why I became a doctor to help people enjoy beauty like this, in themselves and in their lives."

His sincerity and passion strike me. It's evident that being a doctor is his calling, and he is trying to spread positivity in the world. This is the way I feel about teaching yoga. His spreading healing is like my Spreading Harmony. It's funny how well we vibe, and our life's passions are the same. Warmth spreads through my chest that has nothing to do with the physical exertion of yoga.

Moving into the final relaxation pose, I guide the class through meditation: "Focus on your breath. Feel the warmth of the sunlight on your skin. Focus on the connection between your body and the earth beneath you. Let go of any thoughts or worries. Just be present in this moment."

I watch Alex's face relax, the furrow between his brows smoothing. There's a peacefulness to him that I find incredibly attractive, not physically—although he is with his brown wavy hair and lanky frame—but in a way that resonates with my soul.

Alex approaches me after class as everyone rolls up their mats and chats. His long, wavy hair is adorably messy, and his forehead has a slight sheen of sweat. He looks like a yoga veteran, not a newbie, in his comfortable workout clothing with the required Washington style of Birks with socks.

"So, how'd I do?" he asks, grinning at me, his aura now sparkling gold.

"Well, you didn't fall over or pull any muscles, so I'd say it was a rousing success," I tease.

He laughs, then grows serious. "Thank you for this, Meaghan. I know it might seem silly, but this morning is the most peaceful and connected with myself I've felt in a long time."

There's a warm flutter in my chest at his words. "It's not silly at all. That's why I do this, you know? To help people find that peace, the connection."

Alex nods, his eyes bright and understanding.

We stand there for a moment, just smiling at each other, and I'm seeing Alex—*really seeing him.* He's not just a Pacific Northwest doctor with a sense of humor or a proper gentleman my mom thinks I need.

He genuinely cares about making a difference in people's lives and understands the importance of connecting with others on a deeper level. He's adventurous—willing to try yoga and meet a stranger for sunrise.

"So," Alex says, handing me a smoothie from the cooler, "How did I do making your smoothie?"

I laugh and take a big sip of the green concoction. It's delicious—I'm grateful he took the time to make me a special treat. "You did good, Doctor. Do you want to walk around the lake with me?"

"Lead the way, Meaghan," he says with a nod, taking my bag of yoga stuff for me.

I catch Bliss and Demi watching us with matching grins.

"Have fun, you two!" Demi calls out, giving me a not-so-subtle thumbs up.

I roll my eyes but smile back. Walking side by side, talking and laughing, with Alex makes the possibility of dating unfurl within me. I didn't think I had time to date, let alone a boyfriend, but he's making me reconsider. The feeling is not the heart-pounding, pulse-racing attraction I felt with Officer Conner, but it's a softer, warmer connection. I'm comfortable, and his energy feels right, mirroring mine.

I'm enjoying this moment, this connection with Alex, without overthinking it. After all, living in harmony is about each moment, and the present moment, walking next to this handsome Doctor is pretty enjoyable.

Walking, I realize I'm still wearing my tight branded yoga outfit. Part of me is self-conscious about the overly snug outfit that not only shows my brand but my body, too. I shake my head, wishing I was wearing my old yoga pants and cotton t-shirt. But then I catch Alex looking at me, not at my tight-fitting clothes. His eyes are on my face, with a warm, gentle energy that makes me forget all about my social media strategies and marketing.

"You know," he says, "I have to admit, I was a bit nervous about coming to a yoga class. I thought it might be all perfect poses, and I'd have to be really flexible. But it was relaxed and fun. I like it. Thank you for sharing your passion with me."

A soft warmth blooms inside me that has nothing to do with the rising sun. "I'm glad you liked it," I say softly. "I just want to create a space where people can be themselves and find harmony with the world."

He nods, his brown eyes meeting mine. "You've certainly achieved that. Though I have to ask, do you always do yourself up for early morning yoga? You look incredible but I can't imagine getting up so early to get ready." His eyes scan from my designer sandals to my tightly slicked ponytail.

I can't help but laugh, tugging at my branded top. "Ah, you noticed my branded outfit. Let's just say this is part of the less glamorous side of becoming a yoga influencer. My publicist insists I be picture-ready at all times. It's good for the brand."

"You'd look good in anything," he says and raises an eyebrow. "But what do you think?"

I pause, surprised by the question. It's been a while since someone asked what I thought rather than commenting on how good I look or my unique social media presence. "Honestly? I miss my old, comfy yoga clothes and messy bun. But this marketing helps spread my message of harmony to more people. So—" I shrug without finishing.

He nods, a thoughtful look on his face. "It's a balancing act, isn't it? Staying true to yourself and passion while growing your reach and influence. You're stretching and balancing like you teach in class. Uncomfortable isn't it?"

I blink, struck by his insight. "That's actually a really good way of looking at it."

Reaching the parking lot, the time walking around the lake went by quickly with him. I'm reluctant to end our time together. "So, Dr. Peters," I say with a casual grin. "Do you think you might want to try this sunrise yoga date thing again?"

"Please, call me Alex," he grins, his eyes twinkling. "And it depends if you'll let me pick the next date, and it must include kombucha."

I laugh and nod, and he hands me back my yoga bag. His closeness and male scent make me blush, and my lips have a funny tingle. I lick them to be ready if he wants to end our blind date with a kiss.

Chapter 5

Cosmic Egg Embrace

Stepping through the front door of my parents' picture-perfect mansion is like tumbling down a rabbit hole into an episode of Better Homes and Gardens. One minute, I'm drinking a mug of chai tea and getting ready in the warm chaos of my bohemian loft—complete with mismatched furniture and way too many yoga accessories—and the next, I'm enveloped by the floral boutique aroma from fresh-cut flowers, ready to be served French-pressed coffee in a bone china cup.

As I tiptoe down the gleaming marble hallway, my eco-friendly sandals squeak in protest against this level of sophistication that intimidates me despite growing up in this home. Every corner screams perfection and looks coldly modern instead of cozy warm. I chuckle at how mismatched my casual vibes are with the polished elegance—I'm a walking contradiction in flip-flops and a tie-dyed cotton jumper. Since I'm not in public, I wear a non-Brad-approved, slouchy outfit.

Besides, my outfit gives my mother something to complain about, so I can avoid the topic of my dating life.

"Deep breaths, Meaghan," I mutter to myself. "It's only Sunday brunch. With your loving, overbearing, parents. No biggie."

The sound of clinking silverware and soft jazz music reaches my ears, indicating that brunch is in full swing. I brace myself for the weekly inquisition by my mother, 'When Will Meaghan Finally Grow Up?' and 'Will I Ever Have Grandchildren?'

"Meaghan, darling, you're late," my mother remarks, waving me into the dining room flashing a new diamond tennis bracelet and her glossy French manicured nails. She's arranging a bouquet of lilies with the precision of a nuclear physicist, not bothering to glance up. "We're about to start brunch. Your father is waiting."

I sigh inwardly, mild anxiety and a tightness taking hold despite my calming strategies. My eyes land on my father, the great Dr. Bill Mitchell, who is engrossed in a medical journal with a plate of bakery items and coffee before him.

"Hey, Dad," I say, leaning down to give him a quick peck on the cheek. His eyes barely lift from the pages, but he smiles at my greeting, and his calming presence balances my mother's tightly wound vibes.

The cook made my vegan preferences of avocado toast, quinoa salad, and a colorful fruit platter alongside the usual Mitchell family fare of crepes, bacon, and eggs. It's a culinary border dispute between my plant-based lifestyle and my parents' French-inspired fare.

Settling into brunch, I find the conversation taking its predictable turn. My mother's country club agenda nudges the discussion toward my future as we chat. She delicately sips her chamomile tea, her eyes expectant.

"Meaghan, sweetheart," my mother begins. "Have you thought more about your plans? Maybe pursuing an arts degree or settling into a stable future?"

I poke at my quinoa salad, considering my response. "Mom, we've discussed this. My yoga business *is* a career. Plus, it's my passion, and I make a difference in people's lives—helping them."

"Of course, dear," she says, suggesting my business is as stable as a tower of champagne glasses on a windy day. "But you must consider settling down, starting a family, and beginning your adult life."

I nearly choke on my bite of avocado toast. "Mom! I'm only twenty-one. There's no need to rush into marriage or babies."

"Will you at least tell me how the date with Dr. Alex Peters went?" she continues, undeterred.

"It actually went really well," I admit, with an unwitting blush coloring my cheeks.

"Don't leave me waiting," she jokes, leaning forward and stopping mid-sip.

"He is very sweet. I actually was with him this morning."

"Meaghan!" My mother gasps, scandalized but beaming.

My father chuckles and looks up from spreading more butter atop his croissant.

"At my yoga class, Mom!" I clarify, "He attended my sunrise session, which by the way, you have an open invitation to go to and haven't."

"If I knew you were meeting him there, I might have set an alarm," she says, rolling her eyes.

"He even made me a green smoothie with his homemade kombucha."

"I knew he'd be perfect for you since you're both hippy-ish!" My mother's smile is triumphant.

My father looks up from his medical journal and croissant, adding, "Sweetheart, date whoever makes you happy."

I shoot him a grateful look. "Thanks, Dad. I do want to experience life and enjoy my youth. I'm not ready to settle down with one guy for the rest of my life. I want to enjoy meeting people and finding out who and what I like."

"Umph," my mom bemoans and steers the conversation toward the latest country club gossip... upcoming weddings, baby announcements, and upcoming club events.

Her agenda for me is straightforward and shameless.

I shake my head, imagining living the life she envisions for me: a trophy wife with a rich husband sipping mimosas at the club while a nanny takes care of my baby. Then shame clouds my face, because it's her life that I'm snubbing.

"Do you want to meet John for lunch tomorrow?" She suggests breaking me out of my daydream.

"Excuse me?"

She pats the corner of her mouth and explains, "If you're unsure about Doctor Alex then I met a great, single tax litigator. He's a bit dull but has a yacht and vacation home in France. You like to travel."

"No, Mother. One blind date a month is my max. I might go out with Doctor Alex again. Plus, I'm busy with my yoga classes and working at the cafe," I assert, trying to politely stop her from planning my country club wedding to John, the dull, wealthy tax attorney.

"It's good to keep your options open," my mother adds.

"Sandy," my father interjects, coming to my rescue, "You didn't marry me until you were thirty. Meaghan has plenty of time to find a man who is just as special as she is." My dad shoots me a wink and a smile.

"Pffft," my mother scoffs. "Yoga classes and social media junk isn't going to help to find a quality husband. You need to be seen at the right places and be mixing with the right people."

"Mom, things are different nowadays," I argue. "Spreading Harmony, my yoga platform is taking off and I'm getting a lot of followers. My publicist, Brad, thinks I'll be making a decent income by the end of the year, and I might even get some classy sponsor like Cartier or Rolex."

"Oh, that'd be great. Men would be tripping over themselves to date a Rolex model," she says sipping her coffee. "You could dress more sophisticated, too."

I take a deep cleansing breath and release it and the negative energy as I respond, "I'd still be a yoga teacher, Mother. I would just be teaching and streaming with a sponsorship from them. You know I can be successful without a man to support me. Besides, I like working."

"You are independent and driven, just like me, Sweetie," my father says, patting my hand. "We're very proud of you."

"Yes, we're very proud of your fitness, keeping your figure, and your ability to make a mocha-whatever," my mother concedes. "But we would be prouder if you got settled down and gave me a grandchild. Just think of the lavish wedding I'll throw you. It could be on a yacht," she says, her eyes lit up and her head tilted.

"I'll consider it, Mom," I say to appease her while my father grins and shakes his head.

"Speaking of social media," I say, changing the subject, "Can I take a picture for my site? I'm emphasizing Spreading Harmony through connection with family and friends to my followers this week. You know, focus on gratitude for your loved ones." I think of Bliss being raised by her brother not having parents to nag and have brunch with.

I'm quite lucky. I repeat my thoughts, "I am so lucky, and I appreciate you both."

My dad smiles, and my mom nods.

I set up my phone on the mini tripod I keep with me, and I grab my mom's cashmere pashmina to throw over my comfy clothes so Brad doesn't kill me. My mother touches her lipstick, and my father puts his arm around me, ready.

"This is just a quick family snapshot. Smile," I say between them as the phone flashes. "One more." And I do it one more time as they stay in position and smile next to me. We are the perfect happy family with the sun streaming in and the vase of lilies behind us.

My mother's hand on my shoulder stops me as I stand. Her grip is tight.

"Meaghan, hold on. Bill, have you seen this?"

My father leans over me, brow furrowing, examining something on my shoulder. "How long have you had this mole?"

I try to crane my neck to see, but it's just out of sight.

"What mole? I can't recall anything there."

"I don't like the looks of it," my father says, his doctor mode kicking in. He turns to my mother. "Sandy, hon, call the dermatology clinic and schedule her for the next available appointment with Doctor Peters. Tell them it's Dr. Mitchell referring."

My mother nods, already dialing.

"It's an emergency," she tells the person on the other end of the line.

I roll my eyes at her calling my blemish "an emergency," and even being able to get a hold of anyone on a weekend. But my father is the head honcho at the hospital, and I know better than to argue with my doting parents.

"Tuesday at four," my mother says, hanging up her phone. "That's your appointment with Dr. Peters."

I nod, already thinking about seeing Alex again, this time in a professional capacity.

I bite my lip. *Is this a good idea?*

"Thanks, Mother," I say instead, taking my last bite of quinoa salad.

"You're okay with being Doctor Alex's patient, right? He is the best," my dad asks.

I shrug, trying to appear nonchalant but wondering if I'll be taking off all my clothes for an exam. My blush returns, and my heart rate climbs. "I don't mind, Dad. If you trust him, I trust him."

"He's an exceptional dermatologist," my father says. "And I refer my regular patients to him."

My mother looks too pleased with this turn of events, and I'm starting to wonder if there is even a mole on my shoulder. Although my mother might set up an elaborate lie to get me to date a doctor, my father is too serious to do that.

"You wear sunscreen, right?" my mother interjects, her forehead not creasing despite her raised brows. I'm guessing she recently got Botox.

I pop a grape in my mouth, buying time before I answer. "Mostly. But the chemicals in sunscreen are really bad for the environment—it kills coral and causes sterility in ocean wildlife."

"Sunscreen saves you from wrinkles, and age spots," my mother argues. "Bill, Honey, tell her she must wear sunscreen."

My father concedes with a nod. "You should, sweetheart. With our fair skin, you need the protection."

"See. And you don't want wrinkles," my mother shutters and picks at her salad.

I grin, unable to resist pushing her buttons. "I actually like wrinkles. They tell the story of a life well-lived. The laugh lines lining a woman's eyes, the weathered face of a farmer who's spent years in the sun—it's a beautiful story etched on our skin, really."

My mother looks like she might faint at the mere thought of embracing her wrinkles. She shakes her head and takes the tiniest bite of sliced watermelon.

"Oh, before I forget," my father says, his eyes twinkling and paper down as he enjoys watching me teasing my mother. I've got a conference coming up in Hawaii. Your mother is busy with the latest hospital charity gala benefiting the Canines in Cancer Program. What do you think of joining your old man for father-daughter bonding time at the condo during the conference?"

My eyes light up at the idea of a vacation. "Really? That sounds amazing, Dad! But are you sure you want me to risk my porcelain, unwrinkled skin in Hawaii?"

He chuckles, "I'll buy you a large hat. You can relax, do your bendy poses on the beach, and I'll try not to bore you with my medical conference stuff. Plus, you get family pictures with me on the beach for your interweb stuff and I might even do some yoga poses with you. Father-daughter yoga bonding time?"

"It sounds great! Your charity function sounds fun, too, but we'll miss you," I tell my mother.

"You two have fun. I'll be working," Mom chimes in. "Without me to organize the catering and event planning, the CIC—Canines in Cancer detection group—would be a disaster. I'm going to raise money to fund more puppy training, and dog uniforms." She beams with pride, looking like she's solving world hunger, not drinking wine all night, and writing checks with her friends.

"I was just talking about doing a doggy yoga class. Maybe I can come help out the program when I get back from Hawaii?"

Mother shakes her head, grinning. "Dogs and yoga? I can't tell if you're serious or joking, sweetie."

"It's a serious offer, Mother."

"John, the friend I mentioned, does have a little Frenchie. Maybe you could do another yoga date since that worked so well with Doctor Alex," she prods and sips her coffee.

"I think you're busy enough without adding more classes, Sweetie," Dad says as he cleans his readers. "Besides, I don't think my respectable reputation could handle the blow of my daughter's career being puppy-yoga focused."

"Oh please," Mother rolls her eyes playfully, "Your reputation survived that Hawaiian shirt phase you went through last summer. I think it can handle anything."

I giggle over them, and a wave of affection for my parents fills me with blue soft energy. Sure, they drive me crazier than a cat in a room full of cucumbers sometimes, but their love and support shine through.

They may not fully understand my choices—like why I insist on doing headstands at dawn or my firm belief that avocado toast is a food group—but they support me in their own way.

I smile, content. My energy vibrations are humming with my family joy.

Chapter 6

MYSTICAL MOLE MEDITATION

I squeeze my red Mini into a lone spot in the crowded hospital parking lot, silently thanking the universe for small mercies. I'm five minutes late, but this is punctual for me–*even early*. Strolling into the looming medical plaza, I hesitate to walk into the sterile, white, energy-sucking building.

I gasp, assaulted by the artificial blast of arctic air conditioning and brightness. I swear, medical buildings are made to be unwelcoming. Outside, the late afternoon sun is fading but still warm. I tug my knit halter top down over my jean shorts, wishing I had my jacket for the AC coldness.

"Deep breaths. Positive vibes," I mutter to myself. It's just a routine check-up with a cute doctor. He's already seen me sweaty and disheveled in yoga class. "This will be fun."

The front greeters point me to Dr. Peters' office. Entering, I'm pleasantly surprised, as I step into his warm, inviting workspace, away from the sterile, fluorescent-lit purgatory. Prayer flags—similar to the ones in my loft—and artwork adorn the clinic walls. Even a Himalayan salt lamp, similar to my own, glows softly in the corner. My shoulders relax, and I half expect to hear the soothing sounds of a babbling brook at any moment.

I'm alone in the waiting room, so I admire the awards adorning the walls: humanitarian efforts, emergency surgery heroics, international diplomacy–Dr. Alex Peters is basically a medical superhero. I'm half expecting to see an award for kombucha brewing when a voice interrupts my musings.

"Don't be fooled. They give those types of awards to everyone who works for their organization," says a tall, long-haired man wearing a lab coat and stethoscope. He is leaning against the doorframe, his eyes twinkling with amusement.

My heart speeds up, and I blush at his comment. I may have a thing for guys in uniform.

"Dr. Peters," I say with a grin as I swallow my nerves. "Nice to see you again. However, I have to say that I preferred our last meeting. Less sterile stress, more downward dog fun."

He chuckles, the sound rich and warm. "Believe me, I'd much rather be doing sun salutations with you than skin checks. But apparently, your father declared your mole situation a national emergency."

I roll my eyes dramatically. "Oh yes, haven't you heard? My rebellious mole is the talk of the town. I'm pretty sure it's going to get its own reality TV show soon."

"Well, then," he says, gesturing towards the exam room, "shall we go meet the star of the show?"

Following him down the hallway, photographs from his humanitarian missions continue lining the walls. He must have done hundreds of trips. There's one with him smiling while surrounded by children in an impoverished village, another with doctors and nurses in surgical scrubs, and a third where he's solemnly listening to an elderly woman's story.

"Quite the clinic decor you have," I comment, trying to sound casual and not at all like I'm impressed by his global do-gooding. His office and practice are nothing like the pimple-popping, superficial skin clinic I imagined. I look down, embarrassed that I made that assumption.

He glances at me in front of the picture, his expression softening. "It's more than background decor. I wanted to share the efforts and my time in other less fortunate places. These experiences shaped me and my practice. They're reminders of why I became a doctor in the first place."

I'm still studying the one with the elderly woman, her eyes heavy with the history of trauma. "What's the story behind this one?" I ask, pointing.

His eyes meet mine, and for an instant, I see a deep compassion that takes my breath away. I'm slightly dizzy and have to remember to breathe again.

"That's Mrs. Rodriguez. She lived through a civil uprising and lost her family. We met in a makeshift clinic, and she shared her memories. I didn't just treat her wounds. I offered her comfort, sat with her, and acknowledged her pain. I think that's what helped her recover the most."

I nod, a lump forming in my throat. "You must have made a significant impact on her life."

"And she, on mine," he says softly. "It's about creating connections, Meaghan. Healing goes beyond the physical and surgical interventions. Working as a doctor is really about understanding and empathy."

Continuing to his examination room, I have much more warmth flooding me from his words than from his comfortably curated space. He has genuine empathy and confidence.

"So," I say, trying to lighten the mood, "Do you treat animals too? I noticed dogs in those pictures. Or are you secretly part of a dog rescue organization? I mean, you kinda seem too good to be true, Alex."

"But you've seen me do yoga. I can hardly touch my toes." He laughs, his eyes crinkling at the corners. "Canine therapy is a passion project of mine. Dogs have an incredible ability to comfort. Plus, they never complain about my bad jokes."

"Unlike your human patients?" I tease.

"Exactly," he grins. "Now, shall we take a look at this mole?"

Settling into the exam chair, I have a nervous flutter in my stomach. "I'm sorry my father has you doing this when I'm sure it's nothing. Also, don't think of me less, if my mole is totally unattractive."

"I've got my doctor hat on. I'll only see it as an unusual clump of cells," he chuckles as he closely examines my shoulder. "Well, it's certainly an odd clump of cells. But let's not jump to conclusions. I'll take a small sample to be sure it is completely fine, and I know your father would also recommend this."

My heart rate picks up. "A sample? As in, you're going to cut a piece of me out? I don't know if I'm ready for that level of intimacy on our second date."

"Remember, today I'm your doctor, not your date or yoga student," he says. His eyes meet mine, amusement tainted by concern shows in their depths. "It's tiny, Meaghan. I promise it won't hurt.More-then-likely it'll be nothing, but I want to have it tested. And if it makes you feel better, I'll let you see the mole before I send it off to the lab."

I nod and laugh, even though a twinge of fear ripples through me. "Oh, in that case, sign me up. I'll say a farewell to my ugly mole."

He prepares for the biopsy while I try to keep my breathing steady. "So, Dr. Peters, distract me. Tell me something about yourself that's not on those impressive plaques out there."

He pauses, considering. "I once tried to learn how to juggle to entertain kids in the pediatric ward. Let's just say it didn't go well, and I'm no longer allowed near the children's hospital's supply of rubber balls."

I snort with laughter, forgetting my nerves. "I would pay good money to see that. Please tell me, did anyone get it on video?"

"If such evidence exists, it was destroyed for the sake of my professional reputation," he says solemnly with laughter in his eyes.

He gently proceeds, and there's a slight pinch but nothing more. It's over before I can even say ouch.

"What made you decide to settle down and start a clinic here in Lakewood?" I ask, partly out of curiosity and partly to keep my mind off what he's doing.

"Would you believe me if I said it was for the excellent yoga classes?" he quips.

I roll my eyes and giggle. "Flattery will get you everywhere, Doctor. But seriously, why here?"

He's quiet for a beat, concentrating on labeling the biopsy. "Honestly? Your father had a lot to do with it. He was my mentor when in medical school, and we met on an overseas medical mission. He'd show me pictures of Lakewood, talk about the hikes he'd take with you. He always said a doctor needs balance, that you can't pour your life into helping others without building a life for yourself too."

"He's relaxed a lot later in his career. I promise he was a workaholic when I was young," I explain. A warmth spreads through me at the thought of my dad's importance and influence on Alex. "My dad is pretty great," I say softly.

"He is," Alex agrees. "I was looking to settle down, make roots and connect. When a job opened here, I called him. He put in a good word for me. And here we are."

"Here we are," I murmur, suddenly very aware of how close he is, of the gentle way his hands move and the soft glowing energy radiating from his touch. In this oddly intimate situation, I feel a heady electric energy sizzling between us. His hand seems to linger longer than necessary, holding the bandage and slowly applying pressure on the edges. A fiery spark ignites from my fingertips to my core, making me blush furiously.

"All done," he announces, finishing applying a small bandage to my shoulder. "Your mole is liberated, and the national emergency is averted. Any last words before we send the mole off to the lab?"

I pretend to wipe away a tear. "Goodbye, little mole. I never got a chance to know you, but maybe you'll help scientists learn more about moles. Make the world a better place and know you were seen." I blow a kiss to the tiny sample jar.

Alex shakes his head, laughing. "I think that's the most heart-felt farewell any mole has ever heard."

"I'm a mindful person, even of little odd moles," I grin with relief that the procedure is over. Despite his calm energy, I have a lingering nervousness about the testing.

He sees the flicker of worry in my eyes because his expression softens, and he sits to meet me at my level. "Try not to worry, Meaghan. More often than not, these turn out to be nothing. And even if it is something, we are catching it early. We'll look at the results together, okay?"

I nod, touched by his kindness. "Thanks, Alex. I appreciate it. Maybe we can celebrate my liberated mole with another yoga class? I promise not to judge your downward dog this time."

He grins, his eyes lighting up. "I'd like that. And maybe af-terward, you can tell me more about this Spreading Harmony business of yours. I have a feeling our philosophies on healing align more than you might think."

His phone vibrates, and he looks down. "My receptionist says the next patient is here. Let's get together later, not as a doctor-pa-tient."

"Okay," I hop up and smile as he stays to finish charting.

Leaving the office, my energy is muddled with a strange mixture of emotions—relief, lingering nervousness, and an unmistakable flutter of excitement at the prospect of seeing Alex again.

Who knew a doctor's appointment could be the start of something so intriguing?

I pull out my phone, unable to resist sharing my journey and unexpected turn of events with my followers:

Spreading Harmony Alert!

Hey, beautiful souls! Unexpected encounters are the spice of life! Who knew a doctor's office could be so warm and cozy?

I met this incredible human, Dr. Peters, a true humanitarian, and invited him to a yoga class!

After giving my rebellious mole a one-way ticket to the lab (goodbye, little friend!), we chatted about meditation, and guess what? He's keen on trying it!

Stay tuned, Harmony seekers! Breath exercises, positive vibes, and healing energy are coming your way! Inhale the future bliss, exhale the past stress.

Let's spread joy!

I hit the post, watching the notification counter tick up almost immediately. With a sprinkle of honesty and positive vibes added to their lives, I'm happy to have my social media post done, and it didn't even feel like a chore today.

My unexpected deep spiritual connection with Dr. Peters – Alex – sparks a warm glowing energy inside me.

Outside the sterile building, I hum a light-hearted tune, with a warmth washed over me, and my skin prickles. The earth's vibrations are telling me the universe is surprising and rewarding. Sure, there's a bit of uncertainty with the mole situation, but Alex's touch ignited new feelings. He made me feel safe, confident, and calm despite the scariness.

Who knows?

This may be the start of a beautiful relationship.

But what kind of relationship . . .

A doctor-patient relationship?

Yoga partnership?

Dating relationship?

Whatever it is, I'm excited about the journey, and it's giving me positive vibes. One thing I've learned from yoga is that the journey is often more important than the destination.

I'm ready to enjoy the journey.

With a spring in my step and a glow in my heart, I head home, ready to face whatever comes next. I shrug and shimmy with my good vibes. After all, with a mug of chai tea, doing some relaxing yoga meditation, and an upcoming date with a handsome, humanitarian doctor—who can't juggle—the journey is looking pretty darn good.

Chapter 7

Goat Yoga

The morning rush at Joy's Cafe is in full swing, and I'm in my element. My ponytail swings as I pirouette between the espresso machine and the pastry case, doling out caffeinated nirvana and vegan treats to the bleary-eyed masses. It's like a choreographed dance, and I'm the prima ballerina with the cafe as my stage.

"One oat milk lavender latte for Sarah!" I call out, sliding the purple-hued concoction across the counter with a flourish.

Turning back to the register, I catch sight of my phone lighting up with a notification. I look hoping it's Alex, but it's just my socials. My latest Instagram post about "Finding Your Inner Goat" just hit 10,000 likes. I do a little victory dance behind the counter, nearly knocking over a tower of eco-friendly cups in the process.

"Careful there, Twinkle Toes," Tara teases. "Save your nature-loving interpretive dance for your classes."

She tosses her hair and slicks on another coat of shiny lip gloss. I smile and wonder how she can always look so effortlessly beautiful under her layers of makeup and extensions. My publicist would love it if I looked as stylish and in fashion as her.

"Hey, are you going to give me a makeup tutorial sometime?"

"Hey, are you going to keep ignoring the line of customers at the drive-thru?" she quips back with a tilt of her head, flipping her thick, ombre hair.

I stick my tongue out at her. "You're just jealous of my mad barista skills and my soon-to-be viral goat yoga class."

"Goat yoga? Really?"

The deep voice behind me sends a jolt of hot recognition through me. I spin around, coming face to face with none other than Officer Conner, *aka Officer Hottie,* who I'm avoiding—except in my dreams.

Of course, his masculine energy pulses over me, and I can't look him in the eyes without a blush. He has a magnetic effect on me. He's in full uniform, looking every inch the stern protector of the law. But there's a hint of amusement in those piercing blue eyes that makes my heart do a disloyal little somersault.

"Officer Conner!" I squeak, my voice an octave higher than usual.

Tara obviously saw him, and she didn't even warn me!

I glare at her, and she winks back at me.

"What brings you to our humble caffeine dispensary?"

He raises an unamused eyebrow. "Coffee, generally. Though, I'm intrigued by your goat yoga. I thought you were going to do a canine yoga class next?"

"If you promise Rex will come," I say before I can stop myself. I laugh nervously, trying to ignore the way my pulse quickens under his gaze.

"He's got a busier social calendar than me. Maybe, because, I've been leaving my nights open, hoping for an elusive date with a fast girl I met on the freeway," he lifts his chin, and his eyes grin at me.

I have to look away before my legs get any weaker.

"Oh, about goats," I say to change the subject. "You know, it's the latest trend. Yoga but with goats. They climb on you while you do poses. It's very grounding."

"Is that even legal? Sounds messy," he comments, a smile tugging at the corners of his mouth.

"What are you, a cop?" I tease.

He taps his badge in response and lifts a brow.

"It's legal! And the class messiness is part of the charm!" I insist, warming to the subject despite my better judgment. "It's about embracing imperfection, finding joy in the unexpected. Plus, goats are excellent yoga partners. They never judge your wobbly poses."

Officer Conner breaks his serious demeanor, chuckling a warm, rich sound that does funny things to my insides. "I'll take your word for it. Now, about that coffee."

"Right! Yes, of course. What can I get for you?" I ask, suddenly remembering that I'm supposed to be working.

"Large black coffee, please. And one of those vegan blueberry muffins."

I raise my eyebrows in surprise. "Vegan muffin? Are you changing your ways? I didn't peg you for the plant-based type, Officer."

He shrugs with a hint of sheepishness in his expression. "My sister–*you know Bliss*–she's been on my case about eating healthier. Figured I'd give it a shot."

"Well, prepare to have your mind blown," I declare, grabbing the most oversized muffin from the case. "These babies are so good. They'll make you forget all about those artery-clogging donuts covered with bacon sprinkles that you cops are so fond of."

"Wait. Do you have bacon sprinkles? I'd like some of those on top of the muffin and in the coffee," he jokes.

Seeing his smiling dimples rather than the serious scowl, is making my heart melt a little. As I ring up his order, inspiration strikes. "Hey, you should totally come to my goat yoga class. It's this Saturday at Happy Haven Farm. You can bring Rex–he'd love it!"

The words tumble out of my mouth before I can think about them. I freeze, realizing what I've just done. I'm supposed to be avoiding Officer Hottie and not inviting him to yoga with me and farm animals.

Officer Conner looks equally surprised, shaking his head. "Me? Do you think I should do more yoga? With goats?"

I backpedal frantically. "Of course. I mean, only if you want to. It's probably not your thing. Forget I mentioned it. Here's your coffee!" I thrust the cup at him, nearly spilling it in my haste.

He catches it deftly, his hand brushing mine in the process. I try to ignore the spark of electricity that shoots up my arm at the contact and the blush coloring my cheeks, and my legs suddenly become weak.

"Actually," he says with a mischievous glint in his eye, "it sounds interesting. Rex could use goat socialization practice. And who knows?" His blue eyes meet mine, and they smile, even if his lips don't move. "Maybe I'll discover my inner yoga master only needed goats to unleash itself."

I stare into his serious eyes, trying to determine if this is a joke. "Oh, you're serious? Do you really want to come?"

He nods, taking a sip of his coffee. "Why not? It'll be good for Rex, and I'm curious to see how anyone can do yoga with goats."

"Oh, well, great, then," I say, trying to sound enthusiastic while inwardly panicking.

What have I done?

"It starts at nine in the morning. Don't forget your yoga mat!"

"Wouldn't dream of it," he responds, raising his coffee cup in a mock salute as he leaves.

As soon as he's out the door, I slump against the counter, groaning. "Mars in retrograde is seriously killing me!"

"Smooth moves, Yoga Boss," Tara giggles, shaking her head. "I thought you were trying to *avoid* Officer Hottie?"

I glare at her. "I was. *I am!* Inviting him just slipped out."

"Uh-huh. And I'm sure it has nothing to do with how he hot he looks in that uniform. Right?" She laughs, continuing, "After you're done teaching him animal poses, send him my way with the handcuffs." She grins and reapplies gloss, watching him swagger to his cruiser.

I swat at her with a dish towel. "Oh, hush. It's not like that. I'm exploring things with Alex, remember? Alex is perfect for me. He's sweet, kind, and a humanitarian doctor who doesn't ooze cockiness."

"But does the good doctor make your palms sweat? Does he have handcuffs?"

My heart skips a beat, and I glance at Officer Conner driving away.

My hands don't sweat when I think of Alex.

Oh, my chakra! What am I going to do?

Tara pats my shoulder sympathetically. "Embrace the chaos, my friend. Who knows? Maybe a goat will eat Officer Hottie's shirt and you'll both explode in lust and have a barnyard moment. It'll get him out of your system, solving all your problems."

"How would that solve any problems?" I can't help but laugh at the mental image.

She bites back a laugh and pouts her shiny red glossed lips at me.

"You're terrible. But thanks. I guess I'll just have to make the best of it. How hard can it be to avoid him with a class of people. I mean I'll be teaching yoga to a bunch of people, to goats, and one very attractive-" I pause to clear my throat. "I mean, one very professional police officer, customer?"

As the day progresses, I find myself alternating between excitement and panic at the thought of Saturday's class. I'm crafting the perfect Instagram post to promote the event when my phone buzzes with a text from Alex.

"Hey, Meaghan! Just wanted to let you know we are still waiting on your test results. But no need to worry. I'm really checking in because I want to see you. I noticed online that you have a unique yoga class this weekend. Is it for beginners? Hope you're having a great day! "

I smile at his thoughtfulness, feeling a warm glow of affection. Sweet, caring Alex with a warm, soft energy. So different from the intense, brooding Officer Conner's pulsating vibrations. I should focus on exploring the potential relationship with Alex, not getting flustered over a flirting police officer.

And yet...

Returning to my Instagram post, I find myself adding, "Beginners & Special Guests Welcome! " before I can think better of it.

·♥·♥·♥·♥·♥·

Saturday morning is bright and clear–not too hot, not too cold–perfect weather for yoga and connecting with the beautiful Pacific Northwest outdoors. I arrive at Happy Haven Farm an hour early, nervously checking and rechecking my setup. The goats are corralled nearby, bleating excitedly as if they know they're about to become yoga stars.

As my students arrive, I greet them with my best "zen master" smile, trying to project an aura of calm I definitely don't feel. Each time I hear a car pull up, my heart does a little flip, wondering if it's Alex and hoping it's Officer Conner. But, it looks like I'm off the hook since it's only my regular yoga followers.

Finally, as I'm about to start the class, I hear a familiar bark. I see Officer Conner striding across the field, Rex trotting ahead, and Bliss happily skipping along, holding two pink yoga mats. He's traded his uniform for workout clothes, and I must admit, the sight of him in form-fitting athletic wear is distracting, especially the black thick swirls peeking from under his t-shirt, just tempting me to trace them.

"Hey, Bliss! Hi, Officer Conner!" I call out, waving perhaps a bit too enthusiastically. "You made it!"

He nods, surveying the scene as he approaches. "Wouldn't miss it. Though I admit, I'm a little out of my depth here."

"He's been leading a more healthy lifestyle and taking my suggestions lately," Bliss says. "I can't imagine what motivated this change in him." She giggles and nudges me.

"Hey, I go to the gym daily and take supplements," he defends himself.

Bliss winks at me as she clips Rex to a shady tree and unrolls their mats at the front of the class.

Officer Conner picks up his mat to move it away from the front row.

I gesture to an open space near the back of the group. "Don't worry, just follow along as best you can. And remember, the goats are here to help and inspire!"

On cue, one of the cutest miniature goats trots over and headbutts Conner's leg gently. He pushes it away, causing me to giggle.

Rex is less entertained and lets out a bark in my direction.

"Rex, calm. Sit." Officer Conner says, and the dog immediately obeys.

"He is always well-behaved with people and animals," he says. "I'm not sure what's got into him. Sorry."

I smile and wave off the explanation. It's a very stimulating environment. I hear the pup let out a curious whine, but he stays obediently, sitting and waiting for Conner's command.

"He's just feeling the goat vibes," I laugh. "I think the goats like you, and you already look more relaxed!"

As I begin the class, I try to focus on my other students, but my eyes keep drifting back to the muscle-bound, towering Conner. He's clearly struggling with some of the poses, his muscles inhibiting his movements. Worse, the more he pushes away the goats, the more they crowd him. As he attempts to balance, a goat climbs onto his back.

Halfway through the class, during a particularly challenging pose, I hear a yelp followed by a thud. I look over to see Conner flat on his back, a triumphant-looking goat standing on his chest. The class erupts in giggles, and even Rex stands and cocks his head to watch, obediently waiting for a command.

"You okay there, Conner?" I call out, trying not to laugh.

He raises a hand, giving me a thumbs up. "All good. Just making friends with my inner goat yogi."

As the class winds down, I lead everyone through a final meditation. "Close your eyes," I instruct, "and picture yourself as strong and steady as a mountain goat, able to navigate any rocky path life throws your way."

I open one eye, sneaking a peek at Conner. To my surprise, he seems fully engaged. His face is peaceful as he follows the meditation. Even Rex is lying calmly, apparently soothed by the goat yoga energy.

Conner approaches me as the students pack up and say their goodbyes. He flashes a quick grin, looking slightly sheepish.

"So," he says, rubbing the back of his neck. "I was the best in class, right?"

I smile up at him. "Well, you didn't run screaming when the goats started climbing on you, so that's a win. You get an A plus for effort."

He chuckles. "The class was different. But kind of fun, actually. Rex enjoyed it, too."

I nod, unsure what to say, and start gathering my stuff and herding the goats.

Conner watches me interact with the goats, a soft expression on his serious face that gives a different, more at-peace-with-the-world energy, making my heart flutter. "You're good with animals," he comments. "And I'm sorry Rex barked earlier. He usually is on his best behavior. He was distracted by all the goat activity, or maybe there are magic mushrooms in this field."

I giggle and shrug, playing it cool. "Goats have been known to distract people. Even I can get distracted, like if a new hot student catches my eye." I clap my hand over my mouth, wishing those words would have stayed in my head.

"You? Distracted?" he says softly, his eyes meeting mine.

We stand there for a moment, the air between us charged with something I'm not quite ready to examine and label. Then, a goat bleats loudly, breaking the spell.

I laugh, shaking my head. "Well, duty calls. Gotta herd these little guys back to their pen."

"Need a hand?" Conner offers.

I'm about to refuse, to maintain some semblance of professional yoga teacher distance for him, but something stops me.

"Sure," I say with a shrug. "Why not?"

My energy is so giddy and high that I giggle and skip as we corral the goats together. Conner is on the goat high, too, chatting and laughing with me. It's easy talking with Conner in a way I hadn't expected, and I didn't need alcohol to fuel it. Our hands brush as we guide a particularly stubborn goat, and I feel that same electric spark from before.

"You know," Conner says, his voice low and warm, "I'm glad I came today. I love spending time with my sister. And, I haven't laughed this much in a long time."

I look up at him, struck by the sincerity in his eyes. "Hum. Laughter is good for the soul. And the abs. It's practically a workout in itself."

He grins, and I swear my heart skips a beat. "In that case, I might need to come to more of your classes. Purely for the health benefits, of course."

"Of course," I echo, my voice breathier than I'd like. "Can't have our local law enforcement not getting positive goat vibes."

Finishing up with the goats, Rex trots over, eyeing me curiously. He sniffs at my leg, then lets out a soft whine and a tentative bark.

"What's up with him?" I ask, a bit nervous. Animals usually love me, but Rex is acting strange, like I'm a drug suspect, and he's ready to take me down on Conner's command.

Conner frowns slightly. "Not sure. He's specially trained. Sometimes he picks up on things we can't. We have been partners for a long time. Maybe he's jealous of you. He could be sensing my feelings toward you and getting protective."

Did he just admit he likes me?

I open my mouth, but nothing comes out as I'm too surprised to form a remark.

Before I can ask more, Bliss bounces over. "That was amazing!" she gushes. "Meaghan, you have to let me know when your next class is. Oh, and are you still doing that sunrise yoga tomorrow? Can I come?"

I blink, momentarily thrown by her cheerfulness and the change of subject. "Oh, um, yes! Tomorrow at six AM, at the park. You're more than welcome to join."

"Great!" Bliss beams. "We'll be there, right?"

Conner looks surprised. "We will?"

Bliss elbows him. "Yes, we will. It'll be good for you. Plus, Rex loved it today. Didn't you, boy?"

Rex wags his tail, looking between Conner and me and accepting the neck massage from Bliss.

"Well," I say, trying to ignore the flutter in my stomach at the thought of seeing Conner again, "the more the merrier. I'll miss our cute goats though."

"Me too," Bliss cries, patting a nearby immature goat as Rex barks.

"Not me," Conner says under his breath. "Rex! We have to go," Conner calls out.

I wave, watching them walk to the parking lot and then load Rex. He's happier away from the farm. Maybe dogs and goats don't mix. Rex's head hangs happily out the window, and I wave again as they drive away.

Bliss puts her hand out to wave back, and Conner bumps his horn.

I'm left with a swirl of conflicting emotions, which is becoming my norm. On the one hand, there's Alex—a kind, thoughtful doctor who sends sweet texts and cares about my health. But he did stand me up for our first date, and he isn't here today despite the class announcement I put on my social media pages.

Conversely, there's Conner—an intense, masculine, surprisingly funny Conner who threw himself into goat yoga for me and his sister.

I'm lost in thought as I clean up the last yoga mats when my phone buzzes.

As if he heard my thoughts, it's a text from Alex. "Hey Meaghan, hope the goat yoga went well! Sorry, I missed it. I was wondering if you'd mind if I joined your sunrise class tomorrow? I've been meaning to practice those yoga moves you showed me. No pressure, I don't want to distract you or upset the energy of the class!"

I send a thumbs up before I think about it.

I gasp and stare at the message, my mind reeling. Alex and Conner at the same yoga class tomorrow morning! Just when I thought my good karma had returned, I've got upcoming yoga class drama.

"For the love of kale, karma gods, please, don't cause chaos," I pray.

With slightly shaky fingers, because maybe it's meant to be, I add, "Of course you can come! The more the merrier. See you at six!"

As I hit send, I pull up my Instagram to post about the success of yoga at the farm class. But instead of my usual upbeat message, I type: "Sometimes life is like goat yoga—messy, unpredictable, and full of surprises. But maybe that's not such a bad thing. #EmbraceTheChaos"

I hit post, then tuck my phone away, smiling to myself. Whatever happens next, I have a feeling the universe will work it all out for me. And hey, if all else fails, I can always blame it on the goats this time.

Driving home, I ponder Rex's strange behavior. There was something in Conner's eyes when he mentioned Rex's special training and commanded him to calm down.

Was it a concern for Rex? The goats? Me? Is Rex's keen canine sense telling him that I'm not right for him?

My stomach tightens and my indigestion returns as I ponder it.

Maybe Conner is right, and it's just some magic mushrooms at the farm.

I absently rub at the small bandage where Dr. Peters took the biopsy. A tiny seed of worry plants itself in my mind. My gut feeling is that something is wrong, and it's not simply Conner and Alex in tomorrow's class.

A dark, foreboding energy presses into my bones, and I pull my jacket tighter against my chest.

Chapter 8

MEDITATIVE SUNRISE DATE

The familiar forest is alive with the muted sounds of nature awakening. I'm wearing my leafy-print yoga pants and a comfortable tank top because there's no way I'm wearing the push-up ballet and yoga skirt Brad gave me for a class with Alex and Conner. I didn't even take time to put on lip gloss or makeup because I was so sleepy from tossing and turning, thinking about the possible disaster that may occur, having Officer Conner and Alex in the same class.

I take a deep breath and smile at my calm sunrise yoga class that started my whole yoga influencer journey. Being connected to the forest, sunrise, and class energy are the best vibes. I set up my yoga mats at the edge of the serene woods. The sun is rising, casting a soft glow on the dew-covered grass and soft mossy-shrouded trees.

The scent of pine and the gentle rustling of leaves set the stage for my serene, meditative class as my followers trickle in. Their faces are glowing with anticipation, absorbing nature's energy.

"Good morning, everyone!" I greet the class, setting up my camera as I begin. Neither Alex nor Conner are here, so I breathe a sigh of relief. All that stress, and I don't even have to worry.

Just as I'm about to start, I hear an all-too-familiar voice. "Meaghan, darling! Don't forget to smile, big, for the camera!"

I turn to see Brad, my publicist, wielding a professional camera like a weapon of mass destruction for my peaceful zen. He's decked out in what I can only assume is his idea of "forest chic"—a safari hat, cargo vest, and boots that look like they've never seen a speck of dirt.

"Brad," I hissed through a forced smile. "What are you doing here?"

He beams, handing me a red lipstick and waiting for me to slick it on. He starts snapping photos rapid-fire. "Capturing the magic, of course! Your followers will eat this up. Now, can you look more glamorous and chic yogi?"

He pulls the lipstick from my hand and waves jaunty at the class. "Good morning Spreading Harmony Followers. Isn't Meaghan the best?"

I stare at it, dumbfounded, as he takes over and hands me another tube.

"Lip gloss for extra sparkle. Just apply and try to look perky," he tells me.

I resist the urge to show him a very un-yoga-like hand gesture and instead turn back to my class, trying to ignore the constant click of the camera.

I guide my students through poses, encouraging them to breathe, be in the present, and connect with nature. Positive energy flows from my intentions, and the rhythmic flow of yoga brings unity to the group and energizes me. Or at least, the energy would flow if Brad wasn't constantly stage-whispering: "Smile with pouty lips." "Look soulful. "Now, look at the sunrise."

"Meaghan, honey, can you adjust your ponytail? It's blocking your face in this shot. Oh, and maybe we could get some more light here? Can someone hold up their phone's light?"

I grit my teeth. "Brad, this is a sunrise class to enjoy natural light. And please, for the love of all that is zen, stop talking."

Suddenly, a figure emerges from the trees, and I gasp in surprise. The pause in my rhythmic instructions makes everyone turn to greet Dr. Alex Peters.

"Good morning, everyone! Sorry for my tardiness," Alex warmly greets the class, his smile genuine and infectious. "Mind if I join in on the zen today?"

His lean, tall body is relaxed in loose-fitting yoga attire and a broad smile. The surfer-godlike confident stride instantly captivates the classes and Brad's attention.

"Who is that?" he hisses and snaps a pic.

People move over, offering their spots to him, but he stays in the back, nodding to me and mouthing an apology for his interruption.

My mouth drops open, and nothing comes out as my heart rate increases, feeling his energy overtake mine. Positive vibes. Relax. I compose myself and force my mouth into a grin at the surprise of seeing him. He looks even hotter than when I last saw him in his lab coat. Maybe it's not uniform, but hotties that are throwing me off my game.

"We have a special guest today. Please warmly welcome my friend, Alex Peters back to class this week. Looks like I got him addicted to sunrise yoga."

The class bursts with enthusiastic smiles and waves as Dr. Peters acknowledges the warm reception with a humble smile. I'm grinning, too, and his infectious, easy-going energy makes me blush as Brad snaps pictures.

Just as I'm about to resume the class, another familiar voice cuts through the clearing.

"Room for one more?"

My head snaps up to see Conner, looking too hot to handle in fitted workout gear, with Rex trotting obediently at his side.

"Officer Conner!" I squeak, my voice cracking. "I... of course! Welcome! This is my friend, Police Officer Conner, from yesterday's goat's yoga class. Looks like we are gaining more followers," I giggle with nerves as my students say hello to him.

As he makes his way to an open spot, I notice Alex's face light up with recognition. "Hey Stranger! I didn't know you were into yoga," Alex calls out, grinning.

Officer Conner chuckles, setting up his mat next to Alex. "I could say the same about you, Doc. Are you hiding a secret life from me?"

"Doctor by day, yoga master at daybreak," he quips, and they bump fists.

I blink, looking between the two of them. "Wait, you two know each other?"

They exchange a too-friendly glance that can only be described as bromance at first sight. "Yeah," Conner explains, "Alex patched me up after a little work-related incident. When he met Rex, let's just say it was love at first sight. I can't keep those two apart. We've been friends ever since."

Rex lays between them, his eyes glued to his bestie, Alex.

"Small world," Alex adds with a wink and rubs Rex's ears—the ears he hasn't let me touch yet.

Great. Not only do I have both of my potential love interests in the same yoga class, but they're already best buds. *What in the name of all the kale goddesses is happening? Bad squirrel karma?*

Brad, ever the opportunist, is practically vibrating at this turn of events: *two hot guys with a dog in my yoga class. It's the perfect photo opportunity for my socials and brand.*

"Meaghan!" he stage-whispers, again—"This is gold! Can we get a shot of you between these two hunks? Maybe in a tree pose?"

I shoot him a glare that would wilt flowers. "Brad, you're *too much*. You can take pictures but STOP killing the vibe." I hiss at him.

"Namaste, everyone!" I say through gritted teeth, plastering on my best yoga instructor smile. "Let's begin again with some deep breaths. Inhale peace, exhale frustration." I scan the class and make eye contact with Brad when I say the word 'frustration.'

The class proceeds, and I do my best to maintain my composure and lead everyone through the poses. But it's proving to be quite the challenge with Brad's constant "helpful" suggestions and the distracting laughs and murmurs between Alex and Officer Conner. So much for being worried about what to wear, their eyes are on each other more than me, and *I'm the instructor!*

"Psst, Meaghan!" Brad hisses as I'm demonstrating a warrior pose. "Can you hold that pose for just a second? The lighting is perfect!"

I wobble, nearly face-planting into the dewy grass. "Brad," I mutter, "I swear I will downward dog you right off this hill if you don't stop."

Meanwhile, my two potential love interests are chatting in not-so-hushed tones as they attempt to follow along.

"So, Doc," Officer Conner grunts, struggling to hold a plank, "you never mentioned you knew our famous yoga influencer? Should I refer to you as Dr. Yoga now?"

Alex chuckles, effortlessly moving into Chaturanga. "Could say the same about you, Officer Tight Ass, and tighter muscles. Maybe you should stretch before yoga. It's a small town, huh?"

I clear my throat pointedly. "Gentlemen, less chatting, more focusing on your breath, please."

They both flash me identical sheepish grins that do funny things to my insides. *Focus, Meaghan. You're the professional.*

As I wander the class, encouraging and helping students move comfortably into the poses, I notice how gracefully Alex moves through each position. He must have practiced the yoga from last week. His flexibility and balance are impressive for a beginner. When I come to help him adjust his triangle pose, my hands itch to touch him, but I recall his reaction to the last time I tried to adjust his position so I just verbally tell him to straighten his arm and move his weight to his left leg. My fingers twitch to touch him and my cheeks burn with treacherous thoughts.

"Thanks for inviting me," he whispers, his breath warm against my ear.

I swallow hard. "Absolutely, Alex. I'm honored to have you here."

Moving on to Officer Conner, I find him struggling with a particularly challenging balance pose, his large frame too tense to get into the proper position. As I approach to offer guidance, my hand is helping to loosen his tight muscles and ignite a fire inside me. Rex, lounging peacefully nearby, suddenly perks up and trots over to me.

"Whoa there, Rex. Relax," he says, losing his balance and toppling over. I reach out instinctively to steady him, and suddenly, we're face to face, his strong hands gripping my arms.

"Nice catch," he murmurs, his blue eyes twinkling.

I step back quickly, my heart racing. "Right, well, um. Maybe try widening your stance a bit."

Brad, of course, chooses this moment to start rapid-fire clicking his camera. "Perfect! Now that's what I call yoga chic and hot!"

I shoot him a look that could curdle milk. "Brad, I swear to all that is zen and holy-"

"Meaghan, darling," he cuts me off, oblivious to my murderous glare, "Can you maybe do that again? But this time, look more spiritual and glam in the morning light?"

I take a deep breath, channeling all my yoga training to maintain calm. "Everyone, let's move into savasana. That's a corpse pose, Brad. Very spiritual."

I center myself as the class settles into the final relaxation pose. But my mind is a whirlwind of confusion. Why is there no sensual vibe or energy from Alex at all? I itched to touch him, only to see how he'd react this time, but I held back.

And why does my skin still tingle where Officer Conner touched me?

As the class winds down, the atmosphere is light, and my students stand quickly, ready to use the positive vibes they absorb. Other students approach Alex and Officer Conner, chatting animatedly about the class.

Demi sidles up to me, a knowing grin on her face. "So, two hot guys in your class, huh? Talk about a yoga teacher, student love triangle. You might be the third wheel in this though. They seem pretty close."

The guys are standing next to each other, joking around and chatting.

I roll my eyes. "It's not like that, Demi. We're all friends. *It is a small town.*"

She winks conspiratorially. "Sure, sure. And I'm the Queen of Sheba. I sense the sparks flying and the energy!"

I bite my slick lips, shaking my head at Demi's teasing. And Alex approaches me with a warm smile, Officer Conner not far behind.

"Thank you for having us, Meaghan. Your class is truly invigorating," Alex says.

"Anytime, guys! I'm glad you enjoyed it. Who wouldn't with this fantastic group of people and this beautiful forest?" I say, packing up my mat and clicking my camera video streaming off.

Alex takes a step closer, his deep brown eyes sincere. "I wanted to ask you something."

"Sure, what's up?" I ask, trying to ignore the way I catch Officer Conner watching our interaction with a tight jawline.

"I was wondering if you'd like to join me for a charity fundraiser gala this weekend. It's for Physicians Global Initiatives. I'd love to have you there as my guest and your father is attending." His boyish smile and the twinkle in his eye make the invite seem more friendly than romantic.

Caught off guard, I have mixed emotions. On one hand, I'm thrilled by the invitation, and I love the charitable organization. But on the other hand, the lack of physical chemistry between us is unsettling compared to my pulsing energy with Conner nearby, which is having its usual effect on me.

The forest holds its breath as Alex waits, looking at me earnestly. Alex is a sweet gentleman who gives so much of himself to others, and he came to this class to support me. Of course, I should go with him.

"That sounds amazing, Alex." I smile, attempting to navigate the situation gracefully.

"Super. I enjoyed this morning immensely and I will enjoy having you on my arm tomorrow night even more," Alex says, his voice carrying a warmth that resonates with the sunlight filtering through the trees.

As Alex turns to leave, Officer Conner steps forward. "Hey, Meaghan. Great class. I was wondering if maybe you'd like to grab coffee sometime? You know, to discuss yoga stuff, driving safety and all."

I blink, looking between the two men. "I, uh…"

Brad chooses this moment to reappear with the camera ready. "Ooh, yoga drama! Meaghan, can you look more torn with the guys flirting? Maybe bite your lip and puff out your chest?"

I glare at him. Then, closing my eyes, I took a deep breath. "Brad, I appreciate the help, but if you don't put that camera down right now-"

"Okay, okay!" He backs away, hands raised in surrender. "I'm going. But remember, sex and glamor sell!"

As Brad finally retreats, I turn back to both men, who are watching me with amused expressions.

"Sorry about that," I say, feeling my cheeks burn. "Um, Alex, I'd love to go to the fundraiser with you. And Officer, maybe raincheck on that coffee?"

They nod in unison, seemingly satisfied with this arrangement. As they walk away, chatting and laughing like old friends, the surprise of feeling like I've just narrowly avoided a disaster lingers—or is the bad squirrel karma finally catching up to me. I bite my lip and take a deep breath, which puffs my chest out. Here I am, looking sexy and glamorous, and Brad's not even coaching me.

Ugh! Positive vibes. *Positive vibes.*

I pull out my phone, unable to resist sharing my emotions and this chaotic morning with my followers:

Spreading Harmony Alert!

What a morning, beautiful souls! Today's class was full of surprises, bromances, and yes, a very persistent publicist (love you, Brad!).

Remember, the path to inner peace is sometimes paved with both giggles and stumbles. Embrace the chaos, find your balance, and always, always hide the cameras from your overzealous publicist.

Stay tuned for more adventures in zen! Namaste, and may your day be drama-free (unless you're into that).

#YogaLife #EmbraceTheChaos #HideYourPublicist

I hit post, then tucked my phone away, smiling to myself. Now, back home to my comfy clothes and chai tea.

Chapter 9

ZENFUL GALA

The Lakewood fundraiser is in full swing as Alex and I make our grand entrance on the red carpet for the glitzy, Hollywood-themed gala. Cameras flash, capturing my exit from his Black Model X Plaid Tesla as he holds the door at the entrance of the opulent Sapphire Heights Hotel—the posh location hosting the Physicians Global Initiatives Fundraising Event.

I smile at Alex with the flashes in the background. The camera people mistake him for a celebrity with his lean frame, lush brown wavy hair, perfect white teeth, and sophisticated demeanor. He is more Hollywood chic than a kindhearted healer tonight, and I melt with a wave of admiration being next to the refined man.

My dapper, black tuxedo-clad date, Alex, puts his arm around my waist, posing. He whispers, "You look gorgeous, by the way." He swallows and looks at me sideways as the photographers snap pictures, calling, "Dr. Peters, look over here."

"Thank you," I replied, smoothing the red velvet dress over my thighs. The dress is a sweetheart cut, long velvet with a slit up my thigh, and my black strappy stilettos showcase my toned legs. "But the cameras seem much more attracted to you."

He smiles with his eyes and shrugs nonchalantly, not wanting the attention. "My name is printed on the event as a speaker. They haven't learned your name yet, but you're a rising social media star, so they will."

I blush at his confidence, navigating through the sea of flashes and glamorous people, following him into the grand hotel and the ballroom.

"We have celebrity icons sponsoring the fundraiser and attending, bringing publicity. It's great for our organization's fundraising," he explains, "But it makes the gala a little hectic for the rest of us mere mortals attending it."

I nod, grateful I accepted my mother's invitation for a day of shopping and a fresh hairstyle instead of our usual brunch. When she heard I'd be going to the gala with Alex, her excitement hit new levels. Honestly, if I hadn't agreed to shop for a new dress with her, she might've exploded on the spot. She was so excited to do the girly stuff of shopping and getting ready for an event with me.

Now, standing among posh donors and famous sponsors, the over-the-top gown and glittering jewelry feel right at home. I adjusted the waterfall diamond necklace she insisted I borrow. I would not let her splurge on new jewelry for me. It's for one night only, and I couldn't justify buying the gaudy stuff. Plus, where would I even keep a necklace like this in my tiny loft?

I am not the glitzy, diamond-type, but for a good cause—and this is a good cause—I'll play along with my mother's fantasies of me wearing chic attire and being a socialite. Between my mother and Brad, I'm definitely getting outvoted on my usual relaxed style and becoming a glam girl, which is totally not my style.

The red-carpeted venue is tastefully and expensively decorated. We find our way to a white linen-covered table adorned with an array of forks, knives, and wine glasses—his name card is at the front table. The elaborate setup suggests a meal with carefully paired courses. I take in the scene, realizing this high-profile event is unlike anything I've attended, and a far cry from the fun community charity events and community dances I've attended before.

I might look like a glamorous socialite, but I don't feel like it. This life is my mom's dream for me, not mine.

"Darling," my mom's voice interrupts as if reading my thoughts and appearing.

"Mom," I say with a smile, and I lean in to greet her by air kissing her cheeks and avoiding red lipstick stains.

"I wanted to surprise you. We asked to be seated by you and the famous Doctor Peters," she explains, nodding to Alex with a raised brow. She's wearing diamonds, stilettos, and a silvery shift dress that looks casual, but the price tag is more than my rent.

Alex steps forward, greeting her, "It's an honor to see you, Mrs. Mitchell." He takes her hand and kisses it formally.

Her eyes light up in delight at the gesture.

"And please, as I've asked you before, call me Alex."

"Of course," she nods with a blush and waves across the room. "My husband is chatting about some new procedure. He will be back here soon."

The ballroom lights flicker, signaling people to find their tables for the beginning of the gala's dinner and award presentations.

"Hello, my Darlings," my father greets us. He nods to Alex, "Dr. Peters."

"A pleasure to see you, Dr. Mitchell," Alex says to my father, pulling the chair out for me, then for my mother, sitting on his left side.

I should've guessed she'd crash our date with her excitement that I'm finally dating her choice—a country-club-ready man. I can read her thoughts, and she's planning our wedding colors, I'm sure of it.

The other couple, an elderly set with the look of old money, introduce themselves as Mr. Walter Walters and Mrs. Madeline Walters.

"Walter Walters?" I ask, and he nods.

"Your mother must have had a sense of humor," Alex comments with a smile.

With the table formalities complete and wine uncorked, I spread the white linen napkin over my lap as the waiter served bread with small seashell-shaped butter. I grab the white roll, and the pat of butter melts into it as I listen to the speaker, ignoring my mother's frown at my roll. She didn't let me eat lunch, as we were getting our nails and hair done. She told me she wanted me to look "my best" in the sleek gown. I gave up arguing and decided a little afternoon fasting wasn't such a bad idea.

"Welcome, friends and patrons to the Physicians Global Initiatives Hollywood Gala Fundraising Event. And a special welcome to our own Hollywood stars." The announcer gestures to the table with the high-profile guests.

The songwriter/artist Tea Candez rapper is engrossed in his phone. There's a Bollywood star with two girls seated around him that I don't recognize. Next to them is the recognizable and always-glamorous Natalie Portman, flanked by our Seattle philanthropists, Bill and Melinda Gates. Untouched food covers their table. I imagine they are leaving shortly, as soon as they've posed for the cameras and made their required appearance to support the cause.

The announcer continues, "We are delighted to be serving Chef Bosch's curated courses and the award-winning Pacific Crest Cellars wine pairing with each course. And, of course, the reason we are all here is to celebrate the amazing work of our humanitarians. As the evening continues, we are presenting awards to some astounding individuals. Please open your wallets to support them and enjoy this wonderful Hollywood themed evening."

The sultry saxophone melodies and the laid-back vibe of the Emerald Groove Ensemble fill the room. I enjoy jazz and relax in the unique and festive atmosphere. My hand itches for my phone, but I left it in the car. I didn't want to be tempted to use it during this event. Enough photographers are scattered about to catch a glamorous picture of me that I can tag and repost for my platform—or rather Brad—later.

I want to be present and enjoy the evening—and aside from that, this dress has no pockets and my tiny matching purse only fits lipstick.

The first round of appetizers appears: individual escargot trays with snails in a buttery herb sauce. My mother lifts her small escargot fork, and I look away, not wanting to imagine the snail once a beautiful soul and now a tiny bite most won't even eat.

"Dr. Peters, how are you involved with the organization?" Mr. Walter asks.

"I've traveled abroad with the organization, most recently when I performed skin grafting and other surgeries in the Haiti Clinic. I saw about two hundred patients in the three weeks I was over there. It's difficult but extremely rewarding work," Alex explains. "And how are you involved, Sir?"

He pours me wine and gives me a wink, making me forget about the tiny purse and the snails. I give him a small smile back with my lips pressed together in a teasing pout.

Let's see if I can spark some chemistry with Alex tonight.

"I'm not a medical professional. I financially support the efforts," he responds to Alex.

My father announces, "I used to volunteer overseas, and I help organize these fundraisers." My mother pats his hand and glows beside him like she's the surgeon.

The waiter places a different vegetable appetizer in front of me—one that appears vegan.

Alex leans to me and says, "I called ahead and requested the chef's eggplant hummus appetizers for us. I wanted to assure you had a vegan option."

"How thoughtful," my mother utters with an obvious wink to me.

"I prefer eating clean, too," he adds.

I had mentally prepared to make a meal of the bread basket and the steamed vegetables that inevitably accompany the meat. Instead, I'm pleasantly surprised to actually enjoy eating the pricey dinner. The rest of the table stares at our better-looking appetizer, and a fluttering in my stomach that's from more than hunger begins.

Alex's thoughtfulness and attentiveness are super-attractive. He's very dapper-looking, and he does have my mom's beaming approval.

A delicious chilled gazpacho comes out when the next course of a seafood bisque comes out for the rest of the table.

"How are you involved in this charity?" Mrs. Walters asks me between courses.

"I accompanied my father to India on one of his medical trips," I explained. "It's a wonderful organization, and I loved learning about the people and the culture there. I teach yoga now. I fell in love with yoga when I was overseas. Then, when Alex asked me to be his date tonight, I couldn't say no."

She nods, and the waiter pours us more wine. The night progresses with occasional announcements, awards, and speeches as I enjoy a layered vegetable noodle creation. The table was served a gross veal and duck main course.

I shake my head. This humanitarian gala is killing on the land, sea, and sky! What horrid plate is next, *Narwhal sushi?*

Luckily, the dessert course came, and no animals were maimed for this course. The waiter presents a triple truffle chocolate mousse with a macaroon as the background speaker drones on, talking about skin grafts. Suddenly, I hear "Doctor Peters" from the announcer.

"I guess I'm up," Alex says, nodding to excuse himself, then striding to the podium for what must be an award since the announcer is holding a glass trophy.

My mother nudges me and winks, clearly pleased by the announcement and my date.

The ballroom sparkles with a galaxy of chandeliers, their light dancing off the sequins and jewels of the well-heeled crowd. As Alex approaches the podium, I'm perched at a table near the front, my heart thrumming with pride and nervousness. He looks devastatingly handsome in his tuxedo, but it's the quiet confidence in his eyes that truly takes my breath away.

"I am honored to receive this humanitarian award tonight. Thank you for highlighting my work in Haiti," Alex begins, his soft voice filling every corner of the vast room. He pauses, his gaze sweeping across the audience, making eye contact with individuals as if he's speaking to each of them personally. The crowd leans in, captivated.

I sip my coffee, marveling at how Alex can command attention without raising his voice. Women at nearby tables are literally on the edges of their seats, and even the usually stoic business people look intrigued.

"They asked me to speak tonight about the work I've done over the years," Alex continues, a slight smile playing on his lips. "About the huge changes that I've seen the Global Initiative make worldwide. But instead, I want to share something a little different. Something smaller, but no less miraculous."

He pauses again, and I swear you could hear a pin drop. Even the waitstaff have stopped in their tracks, trays of dessert forgotten in their hands.

"I want to tell you about a local charity I've been collaborating with this year—the Canines in Cancer Treatment group." His voice takes on a note of wonder. "When we were in Haiti, we encountered something extraordinary—dogs with the ability to detect cancer through scent alone. It wasn't an expensive piece of machinery or painstaking genetic testing, unlike in the US."

A murmur ripples through the crowd. Alex's eyes light up with enthusiasm, and I have a surge of affection for this man who can get as excited about dogs and local charities as most guys would talk about sports.

"One patient," he leans in, his voice dropping conspiratorially, "was marked by a dog as having cancer, despite negative test results. Two months later, that same patient tested positive. These dogs aren't just amazing—they are lifesaving."

I glance around the room. Every eye is locked on Alex, every ear straining to catch his words. Even the ever-present clicking of phone cameras has ceased.

"Now, I don't want your desserts to get cold," Alex says with a chuckle, breaking the tension. A wave of appreciative laughter ripples through the room. "So I'll just tell you a bit about the incredible work this group is doing right here in Lakewood."

He leans forward, his voice taking on an almost conspiratorial tone. "Did you know that skin cancer can be incredibly hard to detect in its early stages? This group and the research from abroad is making medical testing easy, pain free and affordable for all. Retired military bomb-sniffing dogs, who are already well-trained, are learning a new skill—how to smell cancer."

"These canine heroes," Alex continues, his voice filled with admiration, "are getting a second chance to save lives. They're going from detecting bombs to detecting cancer cells that are invisible to our most advanced medical equipment."

A picture of a group of dogs in a rural hospital flashes on the screen. I see Alex hugging a dog, and my legs get weak. My heart melts at the sight of his caring work. But then, something catches my eye. *Rex,* Conner's dog, is in the background.

The next slide pops up, and there's Rex, looking like the goodest boy ever, sitting attentively next to a patient. His ears are perked up so high, I swear he could pick up satellite signals. It's adorable and impressive all at once, reminding me of how he acts around Officer Conner—all business with his police work and the occasional belly rubs from Conner.

This four-legged wonder is the reason Conner and Alex are friends in the first place. Talk about an unlikely duo—the stern cop and the compassionate doctor, brought together by a dog with a nose for crime and cancer. It sounds like some sort of weird true crime and medical docu-series.

Who knew that the key to bringing guys together in a bromance was a wagging tail and puppy dog eyes?

I smile at the thought as Rex's cute picture flashes on screen.

Alex continues, "One of our star canines, Rex, has already helped detect early-stage skin cancer in three patients during our pilot program. His handler, a local police officer, is instrumental in his training and success."

I have a mix of emotions—pride for Rex and Officer Conner, admiration for Alex's work, and a strange tightening in my stomach. As Alex continues to speak, painting a vivid picture of these remarkable dogs and their even more remarkable abilities, his passionate storytelling captivates me. He is a man who sees the extraordinary in the ordinary and who believes in the power of his compassion and convictions to change the world.

I glance around the room, noticing the impact of his words. People are nodding, whispering to each other, clearly moved and inspired. I even spot a few people discreetly wiping away tears when he talks about the patients who can be saved by early detection.

"Thank you again for your support," Alex concludes, and the room erupts in applause.

It is deafening. I watch Alex making his way back to our table, accepting handshakes and congratulations. His eyes find mine. I beam with pride that I get to be his date for this special moment, to see the accomplished humanitarian and compassionate doctor getting recognized.

I stand and clap at my table, my mother nudging me again. "He's quite the date. Maybe he can come to brunch next week?" she murmurs as Alex returns to our table.

She's working fast.

"That was a great speech," I congratulated him, trying to push the lingering thoughts of Officer Conner out of my mind.

Does Conner see Alex often?

What would Alex think—or Conner—that I'm kind of flirting with both of them and undecided on who I should start a dating relationship with?

"I hope it helps garner donations. The foundation asked me to speak on this topic because one of the dogs in the program detected cancer in the Director's mom and saved her life. Tonight, they will split all donations between the two charities," he responds, placing the crystal award on the table.

"You have my donation, Doctor. I survived thyroid cancer last year," Mr. Walters says, writing out a check and handing it to Alex.

I see the amount—*five million dollars.*

Well, I guess, at least, the veal and snails died for a good cause.

"Great work, Alex," my father praises, and the announcer encourages people to move to the next room to view the silent auction and enjoy the live jazz music with curated cocktails.

The Walters offer their congratulations as they depart with a wave.

"Why didn't you tell me you were getting an award and doing a speech?" I ask Alex as he moves the check into his coat pocket.

"I get them all the time. And I didn't want to discourage you from coming if you thought this was a huge event," he explains, waving at the massive event surrounding us.

My parents are about to head to the adjacent ballroom, but my father pauses, turning to Alex. "Alex, I have a favor to ask. I'm supposed to speak at a conference in Hawaii next month, but something's come up. Would you be willing to take my place and give this speech there? I think it's an important, innovative topic. All expenses paid, of course."

Alex looks surprised but pleased. "Send me the dates and details. I'd be honored, Dr. Mitchell. Thank you for thinking of me."

My father beams. "Excellent! And Meaghan, you don't mind the change of plans, do you?" He looks towards Alex and explains, "Meaghan is going to vacation in Hawaii during the conference. The condo has two bedrooms, so completely proper. And it would be a shame to waste the opportunity."

I blink, caught off guard. "Dad, I—"

"That's a wonderful idea!" my mother chimes in. "You two could make a little trip out of it. Meaghan can show you around the island. What do you say, Alex?"

Alex turns to me, his eyes warm. "I'd love that if you're interested, Meaghan. No pressure, of course."

A flutter in my stomach moves up to form a lump in my throat. My mother's stare is definitely not following the "no pressure" vibe. In fact, I have a feeling my mother orchestrated this entire situation, even Alex inviting me tonight.

A trip to Hawaii with Alex is moving fast, but I do need a vacation after all my hard work doing the yoga influencer stuff, plus my usual cafe work. Now with my recent stress on getting the skin check and the weird push and pull between Conner and Alex, I want to run away to Hawaii more than ever.

But with Alex?

I do *like* Alex. And with separate living areas, and my early yoga schedule and his late conference schedule, we might hardly see each other.

"Sure," I hear myself say. "Why not? It sounds like fun. I can share my favorite beaches with you, and we could do sunrise yoga together if you can sneak in time for it around your conference schedule."

My parents exchange a look that's far too pleased for my liking. Before they can say anything else, I grab Alex's hand. "Let's go check out that silent auction, shall we?"

As we walk away, my mother's voice floats after us. "Don't forget to bring your swimsuits. And I'm sure Alex will help you apply sunscreen."

There's an uncomfortable beat as we enter the auction room, and I laugh, "My mother doesn't hide her intentions very well." I hope Alex will take it as a joke or too much wine. "So, more wine?" I suggest trying to distract him.

He chuckles and quickly replies, "I'd love that." He takes two glasses from a tray and leads me to a quieter corner.

Sipping our wine, I find myself relaxing. Something about Alex puts me at ease, even in this glitzy, over-the-top environment.

"When did you know you wanted to become a doctor?" I ask, genuinely curious.

His eyes light up. "I've always known, since I was a little boy, that I wanted to help people. And in medical school, I saw the disparities between the rich upper class and poor who couldn't afford basic medical care, which is why I work with this organization."

"That's amazing," I say, his gentle energy and vibe adding to the wine flush on my cheeks. He's a gentle soul with a soft aura, making me warm and happy next to him. "You're making a difference in the world."

He smiles a hint of shyness in his expression. "I try my best." He pauses, uncomfortable with the attention, and asks, "But what about you? Why did you choose yoga?"

"When we traveled to India, I fell in love with the people, the Buddhist temple, and yoga," I explained. "I wanted to bring that joy and peaceful meditation to America. I figured the easiest way is by teaching it, and my furthest reach is through social media. So Spreading Harmony, my social media platform, was born."

"You've certainly enlightened me with your instruction," Alex says softly. "And, if it doesn't bother you, I'd love to share your meditation practices at the medical conference in Hawaii. Low cost, effective treatments is a passion of mine, and yoga is a time-tested one that isn't used enough here in the US."

I nod, feeling the connection growing between us, not a physical connection, but a profound, spiritual energy. "I'd love that. Let me know how I can help, and I'll do it," I say, meaning it. "Maybe we can brainstorm ideas on the beach in Hawaii."

Alex laughs. "Sounds perfect. I only do working vacations, and I could use some beach time."

With the night winding down, we find ourselves swaying to a slow jazz number on the dance floor. I rest my head on Alex's shoulder, feeling content. And he's relaxed, too, with my head on his shoulder.

"Thank you for coming with me tonight," he murmurs.

I lift my head to look at him. "Thank you for inviting me. It's actually a better night than I expected."

He cocks a brow.

Blushing, I quickly explain, "Not because of you. I didn't think it'd be a terrible date, but usually there's nothing for me to eat. And I thought I'd be bored out of my mind."

He chuckles, "I'm happy to feed and entertain you. You look stunning, too."

"Don't get your hopes up. I'm only wearing shorts and summer dresses in Hawaii," I tease.

"Me, too," he teases back.

As we continue to dance, I realize that while there might not be fireworks or passionate sparks igniting between us, there's something else—a connection, an understanding, and a shared desire to make the world a better place.

Twirling under the glittering lights, I'm light on my feet and begin to think that this could be the beautiful energy the world—and I—needs. The soft feeling of caring compassion, not thundering passionate love, but a warm and comfortable love. I adore that Alex helps so many people, and his adventurous, caring spirit is something I'm attracted to.

My parents envision him as my future husband, because he is stable and educated. But there's something sweet and genuine about Alex—beyond my parent's desire—a safe energy that makes becoming friends more important than trying to date him. And making a meaningful connection with him is vital to me, after learning more about his amazing life. He's saving lives and changing the world every day, and that's my exact goal.

I'm willing to explore and build our relationship, and who knows what will happen in Hawaii.

Chapter 10

BREATH OF UNCERTAINTY

I'm sprawling on my yoga mat, stretching after an afternoon workout, when my phone buzzes. A grin spreads across my face as I see it's another text from Officer Conner. We have been texting back and forth since sunrise yoga class, as friends—after all he is Alex's friend, and we live in a small town so avoidance is an impossible strategy.

"Just finished my morning run. How's your day going, Yoga Queen?"

I giggle and text, "Just wrapped up a core-crushing session. My abs are crying."

"Sounds intense. Need me to arrest your yoga mat for cruel and unusual punishment?"

I snort-laugh, then quickly look around my empty apartment as if someone might have heard my decidedly un-ladylike noise. "Ha! I think you should let it off with a warning this time. How about you?

Still working on that six-pack?" I bite my lip, and try not to hope he'll send me a pic.

"You know it. Rome wasn't built in a day, and neither are these rock-hard abs."

"Pics or it didn't happen, Officer ." I hit send, then immediately clap a hand over my mouth, giggling.

Did I really ask a hot cop to send me shirtless photos? What happened to my zen, my balance, my...

Oh, who am I kidding?

I'm only human, and Conner is a beautiful human.

My phone buzzes again, and I nearly drop it in my haste to check the message. There it is—a photo of the Police Officer, shirtless and glistening with sweat, clearly fresh from a workout with the gym weight bench in the background.

I groan, unable to hide my appreciation for his abs. His body is impressive, but it's the playful smirk on his face that really gets me. It looks like he's not so serious in the gym.

"Your turn, Yoga Queen. Show me some of your wicked power poses."

I bite my lip, considering as I look at my branded skimpy workout bra and shorts. Sending a shirtless photo is a bit forward, but it is what I'm wearing. I did just put myself through a long yoga session, and I'm feeling pretty cut and confident. Plus, it's fitness motivation for an instructor to post pics to a student, right?

Before I can overthink it, I prop my phone up on a nearby shelf and set the timer. I strike a pose, channeling my inner fitness goddess, and snap the photo. I check it quickly—*not bad, if I do say so myself.*

My sports bra shows off my toned arms and abs. Also, I've managed to capture that post-workout glow rather than looking like a sweaty mess, which is a difficult feat. Without overthinking it, I quickly hit send.

"Your move ." I wait for a response, my heart racing in a way that has nothing to do with my recent workout. Minutes tick by, and there's no reply.

Did I go too far? Was the photo too much? Or not enough?

Just as I'm about to throw my phone across the room and dunk my head in a bucket of ice water, it buzzes.

But the name that pops up on my screen isn't Officer Conner.

It's Alex.

Oh, my kale iced mocha!

My stomach drops as I realize my colossal mistake. In my hurry to reply, I clicked on the wrong conversation. I sent my sultry, sweaty, half-naked yoga photo to my sweet, gentle Dr. Alex Peters.

"? I think there might have been some confusion with your last message. While I appreciate your dedication to fitness and see you're healing nicely, I'm not sure I'm ready for this jump into sexting in our relationship."

I groan, burying my face in my hands. This is it. *This is how I die of embarrassment.*

They'll write it on my tombstone: "Here lies Meaghan, who couldn't take a second to check her text before sending it."

With shaking fingers, I type out a response. "Oh my god, Alex! I am SO sorry. That was meant for someone else. I'm absolutely mortified." After I release the send button, I realize that my message may sound like I send half-naked pictures to people regularly.

I add, "It was a fitness-selfie for workout partner inspo. I don't normally send racy pictures to people."

Interrupting me, Conner's text appears, "I didn't scare my favorite yoga teacher, did I? It's post workout testosterone—I'll do better."

I quickly respond with a laughing/crying emoji before Alex's text appears.

"No need to be mortified. These things happen. However, this might be an excellent opportunity to discuss our relationship and expectations. We've both been too busy to talk lately."

I blink at my phone. This doesn't sound like a breakup text but it isn't exactly cheerful. *Is he gay?*, pops in my mind, and I shake the thought out. He would have told me and I don't get gay vibes from him. I don't get *any* sexual vibes from him.

I flip back to the picture I sent him to see how sexy-inappropriate it looks. Blushing, while studying it, I can see the details of my nipples and no detail is left to the imagination, despite me wearing a yoga outfit.

It's bad—he's just too nice to outright break up with me. I type back, "Of course. I'm all ears. Or eyes, I guess, since it's texting." I hold my breath waiting to see what Alex says.

"I appreciate your honesty, Meaghan. The truth is, I've been meaning to talk to you about this. I'll be frank, I'm asexual. Physical attraction and sexual relationships aren't something I desire or have any experience with. I consider shared emotional experiences, and open communication to be how I enjoy and experience intimacy. I value our relationship and growing connection but want to be clear about my boundaries. What do you need to feel connected in a relationship?"

I stare at my phone, processing this information.

Asexual?!

It explains so much about our interactions and the lack of 'spark' I'd been feeling despite how much I enjoy Alex and his company. However, it also raises a lot of questions. "Alex, thank you for trusting me, being open and sharing that with me. I really appreciate your honesty. I value our friendship, and I also feel a strong connection with you. And I'm so glad we can be open like this. Can I ask, though...what does this mean for us? For our relationship? Do you want to keep it in the friendzone?"

"That's a great question. We can discuss more in person but sometimes it's easier to explain over text to be able to take time to consider the questions, answers, no social pressure, and emotions and reactions aren't playing a big factor. Being Ace looks different for each person but for me, it doesn't mean I don't want a relationship or a life partner. It just means that physical intimacy isn't a priority. I care about you deeply, and I enjoy our connection. I'm open to hugging, some touching, but I'm more interested in exploring you as a person and sharing the hidden parts of our lives with each other. I'm open to exploring more forms and types of intimacy but I don't think I will ever have or enjoy conventional sex."

After Alex sends this long explanation, I see the three dots like he is adding more, then he stops. Nothing is added to the message.

I take a deep breath, trying to sort through my feelings. On one hand, Alex is amazing—kind and thoughtful, and we share so many values.

On the other hand, can I be in a relationship without physical intimacy—without sex?

And what about the way my heart races and my body reacts to Conner? Will I never be able to experience that again if I chose a relationship with an asexual person?

I have more questions than answers, but I type the one thing I know for sure. "I care about you too, Alex. And I'm definitely open to talking more about this. Maybe we could meet up for coffee and chat in person?"

He responds quickly, "I'd like that. How about tomorrow afternoon at Joy's Coffeehouse?"

I'm working at the cafe with Tara and Hailey, and I'm not sure I want to have a serious relationship conversation with two of my co-workers nearby. However, it may be the reverse, as it's the perfect opportunity for me to consult them.

They are non-judgmental about relationships and despite traveling and teaching yoga, my relationships have been mostly vanilla. I could get their advice to help me weigh my options and open my mind to different views. Most of all, they will give me their honest opinions between Dr Peters and Officer Conner.

My stomach tightens, and a boulder rests in it. I trust the knot in my gut and type back, "Actually, tomorrow afternoon doesn't work. How about the day after?" That will buy me time to decide if I should friendzone Alex, ask others opinions, research more, or move forward into a serious relationship with him.

"Sounds perfect. Looking forward to it."

As I set my phone down, I have my angry stomach and heart pounding like it's a warning bell. I am relieved at Alex's honesty and confused about what this means for our relationship. I wrap my arms around myself in an embrace to center my emotions. Guilt washes over me about my lack of honesty with Alex regarding my desire for his friend, Conner.

Speaking of which, I switch back to my conversation with Officer Conner. His shirtless photo awaits me, making my lip quiver and my hand shake while typing. It's a stark difference than my conversation with Alex. All sex appeal and no shared emotional experiences. I laugh and lean into it, because I haven't decided yet. I might as well enjoy the moment.

"You are looking fit! I am so sorry for the delay in responding! Had a bit of a phone mishap. You might say I really over stretched and hurt myself texting. "

Impulsively, I sent him the pic I took. Let's see what reaction Conner takes to it—a relationship boundaries talk like with Alex? I don't have to wait long.

"Wow! Yoga really is a good workout, huh? Good job on your dedication & results, Yoga Queen. Everything okay with the mistake/texting strain?"

I smile. I'm glad I sent the pic. "Let's say I had a lesson in double-checking who I'm sending photos to. At least I know my yoga instructor insurance is up to date. You never know when you might need coverage for 'accidental flexing.'"

" NO! This sounds like quite the story. Care to share it over coffee tomorrow?"

My heart does a little flip. Despite turning down Alex, my heart and energy are shouting, *Yes!*

"I'd love to. Fair warning, though: I sent you the only picture you get. Can't risk any more potential lawsuits with my tech incompetence. "

"Deal. I'll even delete this pic if you want. You know, for security purposes—after I print it out to poster size and hang it above my bed, that is."

My cheeks flush as I read his message. This man is going to be the death of me. "Careful, Officer. I might just do a citizen's arrest. Question- Can I borrow your handcuffs?"

"No way, I don't trust you with handcuffs! See you at Joy's tomorrow at two-ish. Cool?"

I text back, "It's a date!"

Then, I groan and quickly amend that text, "I mean, not a date-date. Unless you want it to be. Or not. You know what? I'm going to stop typing now." I laugh at my poor communication skills tonight. I think I should eat something and rest. I should definitely stop texting for the night.

He sends a .

I set my phone down, excitement and nerves buzzing after flirting with him.

With a date setup with Officer Conner and a deep conversation with Alex after his surprising revelation, my emotions got a better workout than my body today. After everything that's happened, it feels like the universe is throwing me into the deep end of the dating pool, and I'm a poor swimmer. I take one last look at my pic—I do look stunning and if Alex didn't get a physical reaction from that pic, I don't know what else I could do.

Putting my phone away for good, it buzzes with a notification from Instagram. Brad posted pictures from the other morning's sunrise yoga class, and my stomach drops faster than a yoga student attempting their first headstand.

There I am, looking serene and put-together next to Alex, our poses perfectly aligned, the sunrise casting a golden glow over us. We look like the picture-perfect couple, cut straight from a wellness magazine. Or maybe a stock photo for "Couples Who Drink Green Juice Together, Stay Together."

And then there's the next photo. Me and Officer Conner, both a little sweaty, him looking slightly confused in warrior pose while I'm blushing, mid-adjustment, my hands on his hips. I'm red-red, like a tomato. It's a natural photo with fun vibes, but compared to the one with Alex, it's decidedly less polished—more like a "Before" in a "Before and After" yoga ad.

Brad's caption reads: "Sunrise yoga with @SpreadingHarmony! Featuring special guests Dr. Alex Peters and Officer Levi Conner. Which duo has better alignment with our Spreading Harmony's Meaghan? #ChooseYourTeam #YogaGoals #CoupleGoals?"

I groan, flopping back onto my yoga mat. Leave it to Brad to turn my confusing love life into a social media poll. The comments are already rolling in, people picking sides and debating which "couple" looks better together.

Great. My love life has officially become a reality show. "The Lakewood Bachelorette: Downward Dog Edition."

My phone buzzes again. It's Bliss.

"Girl, have you seen Brad's post? You and my brother are looking ! Though I gotta say, you and the doc make a pretty picture, too. I'm not taking sides, but my brother is pretty awesome, just FYI. He'll get better at yoga with practice, and I know just the teacher to help him."

I groan, flopping back onto my yoga mat. The universe giveth, and the universe taketh away. I sigh, and then I smile. My life may be chaotic, but at least it's never dull. I'm starring in my personal rom-com, except instead of a meet-cute, I've got a meet-confused.

I compare the pics, and I vote for Conner and me, liking the more natural and real pic.

As I scroll through the comments, I notice my follower count. 999,876. Holy kale chips! I'm almost at a million!

A tiny part of me—*okay, a big part*—does a mental happy scream.

I should trust Brad and the process, even if my dating life is completely public and up for public discussion. He obviously knows what he is doing, and he is getting paid to grow my brand.

Speaking of the devil, my phone pings with a message from Brad.

"Meaghan, darling! Don't forget-RuRuRamons pants and sweatband for tomorrow's live stream. We're THIS close to landing that sponsorship. Think of all the chakra-aligning, swag possibilities!"

I groan. I appreciate Brad's enthusiasm, but encouraging my followers to buy 250 dollar yoga pants feels about as aligned with my core values as eating bacon-wrapped veal on camera.

Yoga is about the calming vibes, and it should be accessible to everyone, not a fashion show for the rich. The last thing I want is for people to think they need designer gear to find inner peace.

You should be able to meditate in any clothing, even if it's just your rattiest old college t-shirt and the leggings you—maybe or definitely—wore yesterday. No judgments here!

With a sigh, I pick up my phone one last time and open Instagram. If I'm going to embrace this chaos, I might as well share it with my followers. After all, nothing says 'authentic,' like airing your romantic confusion to a million strangers, right?

Spreading Harmony Alert!

Life lesson of the day, beautiful souls: Sometimes the path to inner peace involves a few detours through Confusion City. But hey, that's where all the good stories come from, right?

Remember, true harmony isn't about perfection–it's about finding balance in the beautiful mess of life. Sometimes, that mess includes accidental gym selfies, well-meaning friends, and social media managers who think your love life is the next big reality show.

Stay tuned for more adventures in zen, love, and the occasional public yoga mishap. Namaste, and may your journey be as entertaining as it is enlightening!

P.S. You don't need fancy pants to find your zen. Your favorite comfy clothes work just fine. Promise.

#YogaLife #LoveAndOtherMishaps #EmbraceTheChaos #ZenInAnyOutfit

I hit the post, then tossed my phone aside. Brad is going to kill me for that post.

I roll out my yoga mat once more and settle into a child's pose. I breathe deeply, centering myself. Life may be unpredictable, but I always have my passion, yoga.

Positive vibes.

Chapter 11

COSMIC CONVERGENCE POSE

The afternoon lull at Joy's Cafe is prime time for girl talk. I'm perched on a stool behind the counter, watching Tara meticulously arrange muffins in the display case while Hailey, our newest barista, attempts to create latte art that is more like an amoeba blob or dinosaur profile, than the heart she's aiming for.

"It's looking better," I say with a smile.

"Do it again," Tara commands, and looks at me shaking her head.

"Okay, ladies," I say, leaning in conspiratorially. "I need your wisdom. My followers are split. Should I choose Dr. Alex or Officer Hottie?"

Tara straightens up, brushing imaginary crumbs from her impeccable apron. "Is this even a question? Dr. Alex, hands down. He's a doctor, Meaghan. *A doctor.*"

"But, his asexual thing kinda throws a wrench in the decision. It's all new to me. I'm used to having a guy who is all about my body and being physical. I'm not sure how to be in an asexual relationship," I explain, scrunching my nose at how shallow and narrow-minded I sound, saying it aloud.

Tara laughs. "But, honestly, that's a bonus. You get his paycheck and fancy gala dates without the strings. Plus, he will never stray and cheat on you with a younger girl with bigger boobs. He won't be demanding in bed! Also, your mother loves him. And he's a doctor." She gives me her wide eyes to indicate that I'd be crazy not to choose Alex over Conner.

Hailey, her fiery red hair escaping from her ponytail in a rebellious and very sexy-looking way, rolls her eyes. "Oh please, financial stability isn't everything. What about passion? Chemistry? The ability to make your toes curl with a ravenous look at you?"

My cheeks flush, remembering the way Officer Conner's eyes seem to eat me up. "Well, there is that."

"See?" Hailey exclaims, waving her piping hot milk dangerously close to my face. "I'm voting for Officer Hottie, all the way. You need some excitement in your life, not a man who probably color-codes his sock drawer."

Tara snorts. "And what's wrong with an organized sock drawer? Besides, think about your online brand, Meaghan. Dr. Alex fits perfectly with your image. Wellness, healing, all that zen stuff you're always going on about."

I'm about to retort when the cafe door swings open with dramatic flair, announcing the arrival of Brad. He's clutching a tiny pink shopping bag like it contains the Holy Grail of Instagram likes.

"Ladies, prepare yourselves," he announces, striding towards us without even saying hello. "I have procured the key to hitting one million followers."

With a flourish that would make a magician jealous, he pulls out what appears to be a bright, lemony-colored sports bra and yoga pants set. At least, I think that's what it is. It looks more like something a six-year-old would wear to gymnastics class.

"Ta-da!" Brad exclaims, holding up the microscopic outfit. "RuRuRamon's latest and greatest. This, my dear Meaghan, is your ticket to sponsorship heaven."

I eye the tiny garments skeptically. "Brad, that wouldn't fit a Barbie doll, let alone a grown woman, and how much does this cost a regular person?."

He waves off my concern. "It's special stretchy athletic fabric, and it's supposed to be form-fitting to show off all your assets." He winks, and I resist the urge to dump the mug with the deformed dinosaur over his head.

"And how much does this dental floss masquerading as workout gear cost?" I ask, already dreading the answer.

Brad beams. "Only $350 for the whole set! A small price to pay for beauty and Instagram domination, don't you think?"

I nearly choke on my green tea. "$350? Brad, I can't promote that. Most of my followers can barely afford a $20 yoga mat, let alone a $350 outfit they can't wear outside without risking being arrested for indecent exposure."

"But think of the follower engagement," Brad insists. "You in this outfit, doing beach yoga at sunset in Hawaii, it'll break the internet!"

I shake my head firmly. "No way. I'm not asking my followers to spend that kind of money on clothes that aren't even made of natural fibers. What happened to yoga being accessible to everyone? I want people to connect with nature, not get distracted by overpriced spandex wedgies while doing yoga?"

Brad looks like I've told him I'm quitting yoga to become a professional eater, a mukbanger for likes. "You agreed to trust my judgment, and follow my advice when you hired me. This is what you need to do, *wear this,* for a sponsorship."

My phone rings, saving me from Brad's impending meltdown and lecture. I excuse myself, stepping away from the counter to take the call.

"Hello, Meaghan? This is Sheila from Dr. Peters' office," a voice says, all business and no warmth.

"Hi Sheila, what can I do for you?"

There's a pause, and I feel a bad vibe as my stomach drops. "I'm calling about your test results, Meaghan. I'm afraid we need you to come in as soon as possible. The biopsy showed cancer, a melanoma. You need to talk to Doctor Peters and do a minor procedure to remove more tissue."

The world tilts on its axis.

Melanoma. Cancer. The words echo in my head, drowning out everything else.

"Meaghan? Are you there?" Sheila's voice sounds far away.

"Y-yes," I manage to stammer. "I'm here. When... when do you need me to come in?"

"We have an opening tomorrow at two pm. Can you make it?"

I nod, then remembering she can't see me, I say, "Yes, I'll be there."

I hang up with my hands shaking. *Cancer.* Alex said everything would be fine. *How is this possible?* I do everything right - I eat clean, exercise, and meditate. There's no cancer in my family. *This cannot be happening to me.*

Turning back to the counter, I'm face to face with Tara, Hailey, and Brad, all watching me with concerned expressions.

"Meaghan? What's wrong? What happened?" Tara asks, her usual snark replaced with genuine worry.

I open my mouth to respond, but all that comes out is a choked sob. And then, like a dam bursting, the tears start flowing uncontrollably. I'm vaguely aware of Hailey rushing around the counter to hug me and Tara shooing away curious customers.

"I... I have cancer," I finally manage to get out between sobs.

Brad gasps, and the cafe goes silent, save for my sniffles and the gentle hum of the espresso machine. The rest of the customers excuse themselves so it's just us.

"Oh, honey," Hailey murmurs, hugging me tighter.

Tara's face is a mask of shock. "But... you're so healthy. How...?"

"Remember the mole from last week," I explain, wiping my eyes. "I guess it's bad. They need to remove more tissue."

Brad, for once, is speechless. He's staring at the tiny RuRuRamons outfit in his hands as if it's turned into a venomous snake, dropping it to the ground.

Just then, the cafe door chimes. I look up through tear-blurred vision to see Officer Conner walking in, Rex at his heels. He takes one look at my tear-stained face and is by my side in an instant.

"Meaghan? What's wrong?" he asks, his voice soft and concerned. "What happened?"

Before I can answer, Rex starts barking, pulling at his leash. To everyone's surprise, he heads straight for me, sitting on a nearby chair to stare rigidly at me.

"Rex, heel!" Conner commands, but the dog is insistent, whining and pawing at the ground.

"What's he doing?" I ask, momentarily distracted from my grief by his disturbing display.

The cop's brow furrows. "He's... he's indicating. It's what he does when he detects something. It's from his training."

"Training?" Hailey asks.

"Rex is trained as a police dog but is also part of a program that trains dogs to detect medical conditions, too," he explains, his eyes never leaving mine. "Meaghan, is everything okay with you, really"

The weight of Rex and the feeling that this is real crashes over me, and fresh tears spring to my eyes. "I... I just found out I have melanoma. Skin cancer."

Conner's face cracks and softens with understanding and compassion. Without a word, he pulls me into his arms. I melt into his embrace, letting out all the fear and confusion I've been holding in. Sobbing, limp in his arms.

"I've got you," he murmurs, rubbing soothing circles on my back. "You're not alone in this, okay?"

I nod against his chest, feeling the steady beat of his heart. I have a glimmer of hope in his arms. I continue taking calmer breaths, and my tears slow, along with my racing heart, for the first time since I hung up the phone.

Brad says, "We are all here for you." Tara and Hailey nod.

"But... my followers," I hiccup, pulling back slightly to look at Brad. "How can I do beach yoga with my skin all cut up and being unhealthy? I can't be a health influencer with cancer. I'll lose everything I've worked for."

Conner cups my face in his hands, his blue eyes intense. "Hey, listen to me. You are so much more than your follower count or your perfect yoga persona. Your followers love you for your spirit, kindness, and ability to find joy in the little things. Your Meaghan, Spreading Hrmony. This diagnosis? It doesn't change who you are."

I blink up at him, touched by his words. "But... my sponsorships..."

"The sponsor doesn't need to know, you can wear a shirt instead of the sports bra," Brad pipes up. "We'll figure something out. After we get the sponsorship, you will run a campaign about body positivity and healing. How you used yoga to become a cancer survivor."

I look around at the faces of my friends–Tara's determined nod, Hailey's encouraging smile, Brad's newfound support, and Officer Conner's unwavering compassion with his muscular arms holding me together. And Rex is faithfully sitting and watching me, no like I'm a criminal, as I had thought earlier. He's watching me, as if he's standing guard over me.

"You're right," I say, straightening up and wiping away the last of my tears. "This isn't me. I'm okay. I'm going to be okay. I can bend, I'm flexible. I don't need to freak out."

"You haven't even talked to the doctor yet. It could really be something else. People get false positives and wrong test results all the time," Tara chirps.

Hailey adds, "They told me I was ADHD when I am obviously the most normal person here."

Tara stifles a noise, and Brad frowns, looking at her mismatched socks. "They're right. No need to worry before you see Dr. Peters."

"Worrying has never been my jam anyway," I say, lifting my chin and wiping my eye on my sleeve. "I'm sure it'll be fine. I've got too much good karma built up for any bad juju."

Officer Conner softly smiles at me, his hidden-dimpled smile that never fails to make my heart skip a beat. "That's my girl."

My entire body heats up to a thousand degrees when he says "my girl." I look down so he doesn't see how his words affected me.

"How about we get you some tea and talk about your next steps? I happen to know a thing or two about dealing with scary stuff," Conner says. He reaches out, his thumb gently brushing away a stray tear from my cheek. The tenderness of the gesture catches me off guard, and I feel a warmth spread through my chest that has nothing to do with the steaming mug of chamomile. Tara discreetly slides in front of me.

"I'm going to give you some time and don't worry about anything for Spreading Harmony. I have plenty of things to post," Brad says, taking the opportunity to slip out. I nod at him and say, "Thank you."

"Thank you, all," I murmur.

"No problem. Just chill out. We will do the cafe closing stuff." Tara says.

"I'll bring you more tea," Hailey volunteers.

With only Conner left holding me, I look up at him. "Thank you," I murmur, my voice barely above a whisper. "For being here, for understanding... For everything."

His deep blue eyes lock with mine, and suddenly, the cafe fades away. It's just us, in this moment, connected by something unexpected and more profound than I ever expected. He moves his hand to his pocket and places something in my hand.

I look down and see my favorite meditation stone, smooth, cool and blue in my palm. I wrap my fist around it and smile at him, tears in my eyes, that he has been carrying this the whole time.

"Always," he says softly, his hand still cupping my cheek. "You don't have to face this alone, Meaghan."

The sincerity in his voice, the strength in his presence—it hits me all at once how safe I feel with him. How right he feels, despite all the reasons I've been telling myself I shouldn't pick him.

"Would you," I start, then hesitate, suddenly feeling vulnerable. But the encouragement in his eyes gives me courage. "Would you come with me to my appointment tomorrow? I know it's a lot to ask, but–"

"Yes," he interrupts, with no hesitation in his voice. "Of course, I'll be there. Rex and I are at the hospital all the time. You don't even have to ask."

Relief washes over me, and I find myself leaning into his touch. "Thank you, Conner."

He chuckles softly, shaking his head. "I think we're a bit past 'Conner' now, don't you? I'm not on duty. Call me Levi."

"Levi," I repeat, testing the name on my lips. It feels intimate like I'm crossing a line I can't uncross. But I realize I don't want to step back. "I like that. Thank you, Levi."

"Thank you, Meaghan," he says, and a new heat in his gaze makes me forget to breathe. "Because I like you.. A lot more than I probably should."

Before I can process what's happening, he's leaning in. His lips meet mine, soft and sure, and the world around us fades away. It's not a passionate, movie-style kiss – it's gentle, comforting, full of promise, and positive intentions. It's exactly what I need now: a lifeline in the stormy seas of uncertainty.

When we part, I'm breathless, my heart racing. Levi's eyes are bright, his smile warm and a little triumph in them. Tara and Hailey are discussing clothes, and the cafe is the same but different.

"Wow," I manage to say, earning a low chuckle from him.

"Wow, indeed," he agrees, taking my hand in his. "Now, about that tea."

We settled into a booth with no complaints from my coworkers about clocking out early. There's no way I could work. Rex curls up at our feet, and I feel a brief calm over me. But it's fleeting, quickly replaced by a tidal wave of conflicting emotions.

I try to keep my smile in place, but my mind is in turmoil, grappling with the bizarre twists life has thrown me. Cancer, maybe, and my decision about which guy to pick is only getting tougher.

Both men adore me, each representing a different path, a different future. Alex, with his stability and shared values, and Levi, with his passion and unexpected tenderness. I know I must make a choice, risking losing one of them from my life forever. This new life stressor only makes me want to choose someone to hold and share my worries with.

This is one more reason I should pick Alex, a doctor who can take care of me, but I need more than my physical well-being taken care of.

Then there's my brand, my life's work, thriving but veering into a commercial direction I never anticipated. The pressure to conform, to sell out my principles for the sake of sponsorships and follower counts, weighs heavily on me. Cancer might end my dreams and yoga influencer career.

And my mind wheels in a negative loop back to – *cancer.* The word alone sends a chill down my spine, even as Levi's big, positive energy envelops me. The uncertainties loom large– *Will I survive if it is cancer? Will I still be me after treatment? Can I continue to inspire others when I'm struggling to find hope myself? How do I tell everyone?*

As I sip my tea, I feel like I'm standing on the edge of a precipice. Everything I've known, everything I've worked for, is crumbling beneath my feet. The future I envisioned now feels ridiculous, like the crumpled yellow outfit left on the floor. My dream future is a distant, forgotten, replaced by a sharp, terrifying unknown future.

Looking up at Levi's eyes, I see a strength that bolsters my own. I've got people around me, family, friends, coworkers, community, and my followers. I know I can't give up.

Not now, not ever.

My eyes swell with tears, and I'm completely overwhelmed. I swallow and breathe—the only way forward is to accept and stretch to meet the negative energy with my positive resolve.

Chapter 12

ROMANTIC TENSION TRIANGLE POSE

Sitting in Dr. Alex Peters' office, I swing my legs nervously from the exam table, the crinkly paper beneath me making an oddly harmonious chorus with each fidget. Levi stands beside me, his hand a comforting weight on my shoulder.

I have both my potential boyfriends in the same room, and weirdly, there are no negative vibes at all, just a unified caring vibe to support me. The irony of the underwhelming reaction of having my love interests in the same room for my cancer treatment isn't lost on me. Where's the jealousy and testosterone-fueled fighting?

I'm scared but also confused about why I'm even here. If this were one of my yoga classes, I'd call it the "Triangle Pose of Romantic Ease." Apparently, doctors and cops are very good at compartmentalizing and managing emotions, which means I'm the only one ill at ease, as they project calm and supportive energy.

"Alright, Meaghan," Alex says, his voice calm and professional as he enters the room. "Are you ready to go over the results and treatment plan?"

I nod, trying to channel my inner zen master. "Hit me with it, Doc. And remember, if it involves kombucha or wheatgrass shots, I'm totally on board."

Alex chuckles, his eyes crinkling at the corners. "You can do both of those, but I'm afraid it's a bit more involved than that. The sample we took is malignant melanoma, but we could have removed it all with the mole, in which case, you're cured. Or it might be deeper. We're going to remove the surrounding skin to measure the depth and make a treatment plan. I'll minimize the scarring, and you should heal quickly."

I feel Levi's hand tighten on my shoulder, and I grip my mediation stone.

"How extensive is the removal procedure?" he asks, his authoritative cop voice coming out to define and control the situation.

Alex pulls up some images on his computer screen. "We'll need to remove this area here," he points to an area around the mole area, on my back. "It's not huge, but it's not insignificant either."

I swallow hard. "So, what you're saying is, I won't be doing any yoga poses on my back for a while or wearing backless gowns to gala events?"

"Meaghan," Alex says gently, "this is serious. We need to focus on your health first."

I nod, feeling properly chastised. "You're right. I'm sorry. It's just... easier to joke about it, you know?"

Levi squeezes my shoulder. "It's okay to be scared, Meaghan. And joke if it helps. We're here for you."

His words warm me, and I reach to place my hand over his. "Thanks, Levi. I don't know what I'd do without you guys."

Alex clears his throat, a flicker of something—*jealousy?*—crossing his face before he continues. "Also, that conference in Hawaii is coming up. It may be a good time to let your body recover and heal. I know you had a big yoga photo thing Brad planned, but do a little less and focus on rest and recovery. You can do light yoga. However, no strenuous movements or weight bearing activities that stress or stretch your back skin as you're recovering."

"I almost forgot about that trip," I say, brightening a little. "It's okay to go then. I was looking forward to beach yoga and enjoying the lush natural environment. Hawaii is such a special place that renews my energy well and resets my vibes."

"It's fine. And I will be there to make sure you get plenty of rest and recovery and that you don't overdo your activity," Alex says lightly.

I see a flash of anger in Levi's eyes, this time, but he says nothing. I realize this is the first he has heard of our Hawaii trip. I just hadn't had time to tell him, and if I picked Alex, I wouldn't have had to tell him about it anyway.

"It was a pre-planned vacation," I explained quickly. "Alex is helping my father with the medical conference so no big deal. It's not a romantic vacation or anything."

Alex cocks his head and lifts a brow at my explanation but stays silent. The vibe is so much more tense with my explanation, so much for my calmness in pacifying the situation and compartmentalizing their emotions.

I clear my throat and change the subject. "So, what's the plan to minimize scarring? I hate to be vain, but..."

"But your career depends on your appearance," Alex finishes for me. "I understand. That's why I've developed a specialized treatment plan for you."

He pulls out a jar of what looks like golden ointment. "This is Manuka honey. It's known for its healing properties, especially for skin. We'll use this with skin treatments to promote healing and minimize scarring."

I eye the jar suspiciously. "Are you sure that's honey and not some genetic-chemical experiment you know I'd refuse? If this is really organic honey, I'm going to be seriously impressed."

Alex laughs, and even Levi cracks a smile. "No experiment, I'm afraid. It is good old-fashioned science that is a bit of nature's magic."

"Speaking of magic," Levi chimes in, "is there anything I can do to help with her recovery?"

Alex turns to him, his expression softening. "Actually, yes. Having a support system is crucial. Your presence and support will make a significant difference."

I feel a rush of affection for both of them. The energy is calming and positive again. "You guys are going to make me cry. And not in the 'I just did hot yoga for two hours' dehydrated kind of way."

As Alex goes over the rest of the treatment plan, I find my mind wandering. Here I am, stuck between two remarkable men—one who makes my heart melt but can't offer me the physical intimacy I crave, and another who seems to set my soul on fire but comes with a whole set of complications. And now, I'm throwing cancer into the mix."

"Meaghan? Did you hear what I said?" Alex's voice breaks through my reverie.

"Sorry, what?" I blink, focusing back on him.

"Do you want your parents here?"

"I decided not to tell them until we see how bad or not bad it is," I say weakly, and he nods.

"I was saying that I can do the removal today as I cleared the rest of my afternoon for you. The sooner we do this, the better."

I nod, trying to ignore the knot forming in my stomach. "Right. Of course. Let's do it."

Levi turns to me as Alex leaves to get the procedure room sorted. "Hey, you okay?"

I look up at him, his blue eyes full of concern, and suddenly feel overwhelmed. "I... I don't know. This is all happening so fast. And I haven't even figured out how to tell my followers. I'll lose my sponsorships if I have visible scars. How am I supposed to be a yoga influencer if I can't show my back?"

Levi kneels in front of me, taking my hands in his. "Meaghan, listen to me. You are so much more than your appearance. Your followers love you for your spirit, your kindness, your ability to find joy in the little things. This doesn't change who you are."

I feel tears welling up in my eyes. "But what if it does? What if I can't be the person they expect me to be anymore?"

"Then you'll be someone even better," Levi says firmly. "Someone who's faced a challenge and comes out stronger. That's the kind of influencer people need."

Before I can respond, Alex walks back in. He pauses, taking in the scene before him. "Should I step out? Is everything alright?"

I wipe my eyes, managing a shaky smile. "Just having a minor existential crisis. You know, the usual."

Alex's expression softens. "Meaghan, I know this is scary. But I promise you, we're going to get through this together." He looks at Levi, including him in his statement. "All of us."

And suddenly, looking at these two men—one holding my hands, the other promising to heal me—I feel a surge of hope and, weirdly... desire. This is the strangest love triangle in the history of love triangles—a barista, a cop, and a doctor coming together to fight cancer.

"Ready?" Alex asks, all sterile and doctor-like.

"Okay," I say, taking a deep breath. "Let's do this. But fair warning, if you try to take away my yoga mat during my recovery, we're going to have words."

Levi chuckles. "Don't worry, I'll sneak it in if I have to. Can't have you losing your zen, can we?"

Alex rolls his eyes, but there's a hint of a smile on his lips. "Don't tell me about all the activities you are doing that you shouldn't be doing during recovery."

The next hour passes in a blur of minor discomfort and my rambling thoughts. When it's over, I'm bandaged up and wheeled into recovery, where Conner is pacing very impatiently, waiting with Rex at his heels.

Rex moves and sniffs me without barking or his usual frantic energy. I move my hand to stroke his head.

"Hey, you," he says softly as I blink awake. "How are you feeling?"

"Like I just did a thousand backbends with some dizzy head-stands added in," I groan. "But otherwise, peachy."

Alex joins us, looking pleased. "The procedure went well. We got all of the affected areas, the lab confirmed. And it was only along the mole's borders, a very superficial melanoma, not even enough to be stageable. Malignant melanoma, in situ, which is positive, no more surgery or aggressive treatments. I'm very optimistic about your prognosis and the healing process."

I manage a thumbs up. "Great. So when can I get back to my goat yoga classes?"

"Never," Levi answers for him.

Both men give me identical looks of exasperation mixed with fondness. It's a weird moment of synchronicity that makes me wonder if the universe is playing a cosmic joke on me.

"Let's focus on healing first," Alex says. "We'll start with the Manuka honey treatments tomorrow."

"I'm glad you are here to drive her home," Alex turns and says to Levi. "Can you stay with her tonight to make sure the site stays clean and covered? Sometimes, patients accidentally rub the bandages off in the night. The tape feels irritating."

Levi nods, his eyes never leaving mine. "Of course. I'll be there as long as she needs me."

The fierce intensity in his blue eyes as they meet my gaze makes my heart skip a beat, and I feel a blush creeping up my cheeks.

Alex's voice fades into a distant hum, detailing post-op care to an intensely focused Levi. But I'm sure it's all in the handout, so I zone out.

The reality of my situation crashes over me like a tidal wave of cosmic irony. Here I am, sprawled on this sterile bed, a yoga influencer whose body has betrayed her with the very thing I've spent years teaching others to prevent through wellness and mindfulness. Is the goddess testing me, or did I commit a terrible crime in my past lives?

I look at the caring guys who are teamed up and discussing my recovery. On one side stands Alex, the epitome of the perfect partner on paper. He is compassionate and brilliant, with a passion for healing that mirrors my dedication to wellness. He's the green juice to my yoga mat, the logical choice that would make my followers swoon and my mother breathe a sigh of relief. Yet, my traitorous heart barely flutters in his presence.

Levi, the walking, talking antithesis of everything I thought I wanted, but sets my heart aflame. He's the double cheeseburger to my kale salad, the chaotic yang to my carefully cultivated yin. Every fiber of my being screams that he's wrong for me, that he'll throw my carefully balanced life into disarray. But oh, how my soul sings when he's near like every cell in my body is waking up from a long, peaceful slumber into a wild, exhilarating dance.

As I lie here, caught between these two men, I wonder about who I thought I was and who I might become. I realize my cancer scare might break me before any other decision. If this emotional tangle were a yoga pose, I would name it the "Warrior of Complicated Emotions."

"You guys," I say, interrupting their discussion about dressing changes. They both turn to look at me. "I just... thank you."

Levi takes my hand, his thumb rubbing soothing circles on my skin. Alex places a gentle hand on my shoulder. And in that moment,

I feel it—a connection between the three of us that transcends the weirdness of our situation.

"We're here for you, Meaghan," Alex says softly. "Whatever you need, whenever you need it."

"Always," Levi says with his unwavering confidence.

Tears well up, but they're tears of gratitude this time. "You guys are going to ruin my chill yoga instructor image, you know that?"

They chuckle, and the tension in the room eases a bit.

"Can you bring her back tomorrow at four pm for her post-surgical follow-up appointment?" Alex asks Levi.

"Yes, I will, Doctor," Levi affirms. "I've already cleared my schedule."

"If she has a fever or bleeding tonight, call me right away," Alex says while handing him my discharge paperwork.

"Of course. I have your number, and I know where you live. I won't hesitate," Levi answers with a threat that makes Alex smile..

Shutting my eyes and relaxing, I listen while Levi asks Alex more questions about my care. I make a mental note to devise a name for this new pose I've found myself in. "Threesome of Healing?" No, it's too risqué for my family-friendly brand. "Triangle of Support?" Getting warmer—

I'll work on it and post it for my socials.

For now, I'm content to enjoy the present by resting in this strange, wonderful pose, supported by two incredible men, facing whatever comes next with as much grace and positive vibes as I can muster.

"Hey," Levi's soft voice breaks through my thoughts. "Are you still with us?"

I open my eyes to find them looking at me with matching expressions of concern.

"Just thinking about how lucky I am," I say, my voice slightly hoarse. "And also trying to come up with a yoga pose to express this entire situation?"

Alex laughs, shaking his head. "Only you would be thinking about yoga poses right now, Meaghan."

"How about the three musketeers?" Levi suggests.

I laugh, "A little dated in the reference but there are three of us."

"Threefold Harmonious Asana?" Levi suggests, and Alex chuckles.

I smile and feel a warmth spread through my chest. "Levi Conner, are you secretly practicing yoga? That pose sounds believable."

He shrugs, a slight blush coloring his cheeks. "Maybe I've been paying attention to your classes more than you realized."

The look that passes between us is charged with something I'm not quite ready to name. When I glance at Alex, he averts his eyes.

"Triangle Support Warrior," I muse. "What do you think?

"I like it," Levi says.

"You better write that down. She's a little loopy and might not remember this conversation," Alex says, and I laugh, making them laugh.

My face relaxes, and my spirit hums, surrounded by their care and support. A calm washes over me while realizing that maybe, just maybe, this whole mess might lead to something beautiful. Finding balance and harmony, even in the most challenging poses, is my passion.

Triangle Support Warrior Pose, namaste.

Chapter 13

Dazed Spoon Meditation

I'm barely conscious as Levi guides me into my apartment, his strong arm around my waist keeping me steady. The medication Alex prescribed is doing its job a little too well, making the world fuzzy around the edges and my legs about as stable as a palm tree during a hurricane.

"Easy there, Zen Master," Levi murmurs, his breath warm against my ear. "Let's get you to bed before you lose your balance and do an unintentional headstand."

I giggle, the sound coming out more like a snort. "Headstands are for amateurs. I could totally do a full lotus right now."

"Sure you could," he humors me, steering me towards my bedroom. "And I could sprout wings and fly. Let's not test either theory, okay?"

As Levi helps me onto my bed, I hear him fumbling with his phone. I hug the pillow, and he must think I'm asleep because his voice drops to a low murmur.

"Hey, Alex? Yeah, we made it to her apartment. I'm just putting her to bed now."

There's a pause, and I can almost hear Alex's concerned voice on the other end.

"No, no fever. She's a bit loopy from the meds, but otherwise seems okay. Yeah, I'll keep an eye on her through the night. I'll sleep on the floor if I need to. Don't worry, I've got this."

Another pause. "Thanks, man. I appreciate you watching Rex while I watch our patient. I'll pick up Rex from you in the morning."

"Tell him he's the bestest of doggies from me," I chime in.

Levi jumps slightly, clearly not expecting me to be awake. "I thought you were asleep," he says, a hint of embarrassment coloring his voice.

"Nope," I pop the 'p' sound and giggle at the feeling and sound of it. "Just resting my eyes and eavesdropping. It's a vital skill for any good influencer, you know." As Levi ends the call, I crack open one eye. "Aww, you guys are doting over little old me?"

"Your dad called Alex and gave him an earful after he found out you were fine. He got strict orders to watch you. And we already dote over Rex, so why not add our favorite yoga teacher into the dogsitting mix?" he explains to my sleepy eyes.

"Either way, I hope I get belly rubs and you guys are totally adorable," I murmur, trying to stay awake but failing.

He shakes his head, but I can see his serious face fading as a smile tugs at the corners of his mouth. "Alex watches Rex while I do regular shifts. I met him when Rex was doing hospital training. Alex and Rex hit off. I think it's the perfect arrangement, he travels and works too much for dog ownership. I let him borrow Rex whenever he wants, and when I'm scheduled for any police shifts I can't take him on."

I wrinkle my brow as I have never considered how lonely the life of a busy doctor is. Alex gives so much to his patients and then to his humanitarian efforts that he can't even own a dog. It must be hard to enjoy life without an adoring family to relax with after a stressful day, like my family.

"That's kind of you, to dog-share. You aren't the mean, stern cop I thought you were when we first met," I say, then I giggle with the bluntness of my words. "Sorry, you aren't mean—I really am a bad driver."

Levi chuckles, his eyes softening. "I know. But I'm glad I've managed to change your mind about me. There's more to me than the badge and rock hard abs, you know."

"Oh really?" I tease, propping myself up on my elbows and suddenly awake enough to flirt with this very masculine guy who is close enough that I smell his musk of sweat and shaving soap. My heart speeds up, and my mind is suddenly clear. "Do tell, Officer Hottie. What hidden depths are under that tough exterior?"

He pretends to consider for a moment. "Well, for one, I make a mean chocolate chip cookie. And I've been known to tear up at PETA commercials."

I gasp in mock shock. "A cop with a soft spot for animals and baked goods? Be still my heart!"

"Hey, you are supposed to be sleeping, not discussing cookies. You're something else, you know that?" Levi says, shaking his head with a grin.

"Yep. *Yeppp*," I say, popping the 'p' and giggling. "I'm one of a kind—an open-minded yoga teacher who makes lattes and spreads joy. I'm a unique snowflake. A rare *poppppppy* pop. A..."

"A handful?" Levi suggests, his eyes twinkling with amusement.

I gasped in mock offense, giggling with the tickling p, still feeling on my lips.

Why don't I use the word pop more often?

"Officer Conner, are you sassing me? I'll let you know I'm a *popular* person. Just ask my followers."

He runs a hand over his face and shakes his head. "Yes, they all love you," he says, sitting down on the edge of the bed. "But they aren't here to make sure you don't fall out of bed when you underestimate your current state."

"Oh, *poop*. You're no fun," I stick my tongue out at him, an incredibly mature response that proves I'm fine. "I'll have you know, sir, that I am the picture of grace and elegance, even under the influence of doctor-prescribed happy juice."

As if to prove my point, I attempt to sit up and immediately get tangled in my hair.

Levi reaches out to steady me, his hand warm on my shoulder.

"Whoa there, graceful one. How about we save the acrobatics for when you're not freshly post-op, hm?"

"*Post-op*," I giggle. Then, I huff, blowing a strand of hair out of my face. "Fine. But only because you asked so nicely."

He chuckles, the sound low and warm. "Alright, Miss Yoga Master. Let's get you changed and comfortable for the night."

Only then do I realize I'm still in my hospital clothes, complete with the super stylish open-back hospital gown. "Oh god," I groan. "Please tell me I didn't flash the entire parking lot on our way out."

"Don't worry," Levi assures me, his eyes crinkling with amusement. "Your dignity is intact. Alex said you could wear it home. Though you did refer to me as *Officer Hottie* and Alex as *Doctor Hottie* since you woke up."

I bury my face in my hands. "Please tell me you're joking."

"I guess you'll never know, Yoga Hottie," he teases. "Now, where do you keep your pajamas?"

I point vaguely toward my dresser. "Top drawer. But fair warning, they're not Victoria Secrets."

Levi rummages through the drawer and pulls out my favorite pair of soft, well-worn flannel pants covered in little cartoon sloths and an oversized t-shirt that reads "Namaste in Bed."

"Ah," he says, holding them up. "I see you've prepared for this exact scenario. Very thoughtful of you."

I snatch the pajamas from him, sticking out my tongue again. "Hey, don't knock the sloths. They're very zen animals. We could all learn a thing or two from them."

"I'm sure," Levi agrees solemnly. "Like how to sleep for twenty hours a day and look adorable?"

He really does love animals—*how cute.*

I flush and hide my face under the blankets. "Exactly," I say, sticking my head out of the covers and nodding, then immediately regretting it as the room starts to spin. "Oof. Okay, maybe I'll hold off on the vigorous head movements for a while."

Levi's expression softens. "Here, let me help you. Can you sit up?"

With his assistance, I got into a somewhat upright position. "Okay, now for the tricky part," I say, eyeing the hospital gown. "I don't suppose you'd be willing to let me go to the bathroom to change. *Please.*" I end with giggles at the hard P sound.

Levi shakes his head and raises an eyebrow. "As much as I'd love to see you twirl and crawl to the bathroom, I think we'd better play it safe. How about I close my eyes and turn around while you stay in bed? I'll help you if you need it, and I promise to be a perfect gentleman."

I consider for a moment, then nod. "*Perfect,* but if you cop a feel, I'm reporting you," I giggle. "Do cops have an HR department? Wait, are Cops allowed to cop a feel? I'll report you to the *Police People,*" I giggle at the playful words.

He laughs, shaking his head. "I'll be on my best behavior, scout's honor. Now, arms up."

With careful movements, Levi keeps his eyes averted, helping me out of the hospital gown, and into my oversized t-shirt. His touch is gentle, clinical almost, except there's a hot, electric shiver that runs through me as his fingers brush against my skin.

"Cold?" he asks, misinterpreting my reaction.

"A little," I lie, grateful for the excuse.

Once I'm safely in my shirt, Levi turns around as promised, allowing me to awkwardly shimmy into my sloth pants. It's a process that involves far more grunting and muttered curses than I'd like to admit.

"You know," I pant, flopping back onto the bed once I've finally conquered the pants, "I don't think I've worked this hard since that hot yoga class in Death Valley."

Levi turns back around, his eyebrows raised. "Do I want to know?"

"Probably not," I admit. "Let's just say it involved a cactus, a lost yoga mat, and a very confused park ranger."

He shakes his head, a smile playing on his lips. "You really are something else, Meaghan."

"That's what they tell me," I yawn, suddenly the day's heavy energy pressing down on me. "Though usually it's followed by 'please don't post anymore without checking with me' by Brad."

Levi laughs softly. "I, for one, am enjoying the Meaghan Mitchell After Dark show. Though, I think it might be time for the star to get some rest."

I nod sleepily, allowing him to help me under the covers. As he tucks me in, a thought occurs to me. "Wait, where are you going to sleep? I don't have a guest room."

"Don't worry about me," he says, patting my hand. "I'll camp out on the couch. I've slept in worse places during stakeouts."

The thought of him uncomfortably scrunched up on my tiny couch makes me frown. "Don't be silly. This bed is plenty big enough for both of us. I promise not to snore too much."

He hesitates, and I can see the internal debate playing out on his too-serious face. "I don't know, Meaghan. It might be too tempting for you, and I don't want to accidentally seduce a drugged woman."

I roll my eyes. "Oh, please. I'm fresh out of surgery and high as a kite on painkillers. I'll be out like a light. I promise not to make a move—your virtue is safe for one night, *Polite Police Person*."

He raises a brow, shaking his head. "It's not my virtue I'm worried about."

"Well, it should be," I mumble, sleep tugging at me. "I'm a very virtuoushish. The virtuest. Is that a word?"

"Alright, alright," Levi concedes, kicking off his shoes. "But if you try any funny business, I'm giving you a stern warning and then writing you a ticket."

"Deal," I murmured, my eyes already drifting closed.

I feel the bed dip as Levi settles beside me, careful to keep a respectful distance—but I feel a hot wave of energy that makes me giggle. I try not to scare him from the bed, but in my painkiller-induced haze, all I can think about is how warm he is, and how safe I feel with him here.

Without thinking, I scoot myself in closer, nestling into his side. I feel him hold his breath, his muscles tense, then slowly relax as I lay still against him. His arm comes around to gently wrap around me, keeping me from the edge of the bed.

"This okay?" I mumble into his chest. "Is your virtue okay?" I feel rather than hear his deep chuckle.

"Yeah, it's okay. Get some rest, Meaghan."

As I drift off to sleep, I'm struck by how right his vibrating masculine energy feels next to me. His vibe is not the deep, soulful energy I have with Alex—our minds and spirits are so similar we vibe easily. Levi's big, electric vibe is so different, almost primal. With Levi, his opposing rough and tough energy balances mine. Next to him, I'm more grounded—anchored. Like no matter what storms may come, he'll keep me steady.

My last coherent thought before sleep claims me is that maybe, *just maybe, there's enough room in my life for both types of energy and connections.*

After all, isn't my brand, Spreading Harmony, all about finding balance in all things and spreading joy as wide as possible?

Melting into Levi's masculine body, my mind drifts off into a soft haze of warmth. Before completely succumbing, Levi's hot whisper caresses my soul, "Sweet dreams, Yoga Hottie. I've got you."

And in this moment, despite the pain and hazy uncertainty, I'm utterly and completely where I'm meant to be.

Chapter 14

CAFE CALM

The morning rush at Joy's Cafe is in full swing. I'm behind the counter, carefully maneuvering around my coworkers with all the grace of a newborn giraffe. It's been a week since my surgery. While I'm feeling better, I'm still not entirely up to my usual yoga instructor-barista-extraordinaire standards.

"One oat milk chai latte for Demi!" I call out, sliding the drink across the counter with what I hope is a winning smile and not a grimace of pain.

"Thanks, Meaghan!" Demi chirps. "How are you feeling? We've really missed your sunrise yoga sessions."

I manage a genuine smile this time. "Getting better every day, thanks to some seriously miraculous honey and two very attentive caretakers."

As if on cue, the bell above the door chimes, and in walks Officer Levi Conner, looking too tasty in his uniform. He's followed closely by Alex, sporting his impeccable suit and easy confidence.

"Speaking of caretakers," I mutter under my breath.

"Well, well, well," Tara sidles up next to me, her eyes twinkling with mischief. "If it isn't the dynamic duo. Your personal knight in shining armor and your very own doctor. What's their new nicknames, *Officer Hottie* and *Doctor Hottie*?"

I elbow her gently. "Shh! They'll hear you!"

"Good morning, ladies," Levi greets us with a nod and that crooked, dimpled smile that is reserved for me and never fails to make my heart do a little flip.

"How's our favorite patient doing today?" Alex asks.

"Oh, you know," I say airily, waving a hand. "Just living my best life, one careful movement at a time. I haven't tried to do a headstand in at least twenty-four hours, so I'd say I'm making progress."

Alex chuckles, shaking his head. "I'm glad to hear it. Though I hope you're still taking it easy. No heavy lifting, remember?"

I roll my eyes good-naturedly. "Yes, Doctor. You sound like my dad! He calls me daily and has even stopped by to check on me. With all of you, there's no way I can hide my new weight lifting hobby. I promise I haven't been overdoing it."

"Good," Alex nods approvingly.

"I'd hate to have to put you on home arrest for not following Doctor Hottie's orders," Levi says with a wink.

"You wouldn't dare, Officer Hottie," I laugh, unable to believe my dazed nickname stuck. Guess those names are here to stay since we use them like it's second nature.

"Try me," he smiles wide and flashes his handcuffs.

I swear the temperature in the cafe rises by at least ten degrees, and my face automatically flushes despite never using, or having any intention of using his handcuffs.

"Alright, alright," Tara interrupts, fanning herself dramatically. "Before you two set off the sprinkler system with all that heat, can I get you gentlemen some coffee? Does Rex need his usual pup cup?" She gives Rex a smile, he found his way to the cafe dog bed and is napping.

Demi shoos me out into the cafe for a break. "I'll bring you guys some coffee. Sit and relax for your fifteen-minute break." She winks at me, and I roll my eyes.

I notice Bliss walking in, carrying what looks suspiciously like a yoga mat.

"Uh oh," I laugh. "I sense an impromptu yoga session coming on."

Sure enough, Bliss makes a beeline for me, her face lit up with excitement. "Meaghan! Guess what time it is?"

"Time for me to conveniently develop temporary amnesia about how to do yoga?" I suggest, hopefully.

"Nope!" Bliss grins, popping the 'p' in a way that reminds me of drug-induced giggling. "It's time for a quick meditation session! Brad has been blowing up my phone since you aren't answering. He asked if I would get some brand pics when I visit you today. Can we do a little gentle yoga sesh for some content?"

I glance at Alex, and he shrugs. "If you feel up to it, the stitches look fine."

I smile, "I have been getting a lot of messages asking for posts. Do you think you can keep doing a daily post for me? I'm undecided if I want to share my recovery drama with everyone. Can we do a child's pose and call it good?"

Levi frowns, "Are you sure she's ready for yoga stretches, Alex?"

"She's ready. Meaghan, follow what your body is telling you. Stop if there's any discomfort, okay?"

I nod. "Just no pics of my bandage or groaning," I tell Bliss as she squeals and jumps.

"Spreading Harmony is back!"

"As your doctor, I can't condone headstands," Alex adds, his eyes twinkling. "But as someone who's seen Brad's crazy requests, I fully support doing a child's pose to appease him."

"Doctor's orders - child's pose it is," Bliss announces.

"Super," Demi calls out. "I've missed my yoga time. There's no one here. Let's all do a quick sesh in the cafe."

I look around and she's right. "Okay, and while I have you and Bliss, we can squeeze in a quick yoga relaxation session. I want to focus on connections and friends. We'll even rope these two yoga hotties in," I gesture to Levi and Alex.

Bliss laughs, "I'm sure your followers and Brad would love to see your, ahem, 'choices' in action."

I look between Levi and Alex, who shrug in a 'why not?' kind of way.

I give Tara my puppy dog eyes and slowly untie my apron.

"Fine," she sighs dramatically. "I'll watch the counter and the drive-thru for both of you. But you guys are switching shifts with me the next time I ask."

"Of course," Demi says, already moving tables and spreading our yoga mats.

I move to a quiet corner of the cafe, where I have extra mats that Bliss sets up. As we settle into comfortable positions—or as comfortable as I can get with my still-healing shoulder—I notice Levi and Alex flank me protectively. This healing process is providing me with some absurdly attractive bodyguards, and my yoga followers are engaging even more with less content.

"Alright, everyone," I say, slipping into my yoga instructor's voice. "Let's start by closing our eyes and taking a deep breath in."

As we sink into the gentle meditation, I steal glances at my mismatched group of companions. It's like the setup for a joke—a yoga instructor, a cop, a doctor, and two baristas walk into a meditation session...

Bliss is the picture of serenity, as if she finds her personal nirvana stretching.

Demi, bless her heart, is attempting to sneak bites of her muffin with all the stealth of a toddler raiding a cookie jar. Each time she thinks no one's looking, another chunk of muffin disappears. By the end of this session, she'll have achieved inner peace with a sugar high.

But it's Levi who surprises me the most. Gone is the alert, ready-for-action cop. In his place sits a man who looks like he's discovered the secret to life itself. His usually furrowed brow has smoothed out, and there's an almost childlike wonder to his expression.

Who knew Officer Grumpy had an inner zen master?

And then there's Alex. Alex is so in sync with my instructions, it's like we're performing a perfectly choreographed dance. He could probably teach this class himself. I make a mental note to tease him later about moonlighting as a secret yogi.

Bliss, ever the social media pro, occasionally breaks her zen to snap photos for Brad and my growing online empire. I can almost hear the 'likes' rolling in already. I am so glad she's helping me with my platform.

After fifteen minutes that feels like an eternity and no time at all, we wrap up the mini-session. The energy around us has shifted, a calm settling over our little group like a warm, cozy blanket.

"Well," I say, stretching carefully and feeling every muscle sing with the movement, "that was actually pretty nice. Thanks, every-one, for indulging me in a little impromptu om-ing."

As I look around at my friends, I'm hit with a wave of gratitude so strong it nearly knocks me off my feet.

This.

This right here is why I fell in love with yoga in the first place. Not for the fancy poses or the cute outfits, but for moments like these. Moments of connection, of peace, of finding your tribe in the most unexpected places.

I smile, feeling a surge of confidence course through me. My body still moves the way it should, my mind feels clearer, and my heart? Well, it's so full it might just burst.

Bring it on, world. This yoga girl is ready for whatever you've got next.

"Anytime," Bliss grins. "Oh, by the way, I meant to ask—are you excited about Hawaii? It's coming up soon, right?"

I nod, a mix of excitement and nervousness bubbling up in my stomach. "Yeah, next week. I'm looking forward to it, but also a little nervous about traveling after surgery."

"Don't worry," Alex pipes up. "I'll be there to keep an eye on you. And the beach vibes will be great for your recovery. The salt water air has natural healing properties."

"Plus," Bliss adds, "you'll have plenty of time to perfect your 'lounging on the beach' yoga pose while drinking fresh coconut milk. You need the recharge, and Brad will stop needling you for pictures when you send him your beach yoga shots."

I stick my tongue out at her. "Laugh all you want, but I'll have you know that 'Sloth on a Sunbed' is a very advanced pose."

"Speaking of lounging," Bliss chimes in, "I'm going to recreate our goat yoga with Rex. Levi, are you ready to do yoga with me? I'm going to totally rock dog yoga and post pics."

Bliss grins mischievously. "I figure if I can get Rex to do a downward dog, I'll break the internet."

"Oh god," I groan. "My brand is doomed. How can I compete with that?

"I'll name it 'Pups and Poses'." Bliss and Demi giggle.

"Hey," Levi calls out. "I bet dog yoga would be a hit!"

As we all laugh, I'm struck by how normal this feels. A week ago, I was freaking out about cancer and scars and losing my career. Now, here I am, surrounded by friends—*and whatever Levi and Alex are*—planning beach yoga and joking about dog poses.

"You know," I say, looking around at everyone. "I just want to say thank you to all of you. I haven't been all positive vibes this past week, but the week has not been as terrible as it could have been. And it's all thanks to you guys."

"Aww, look at you getting all sappy on us," Tara teases, but I can see the caring in her eyes.

"It's the least we could do," Alex says softly, placing a hand on my shoulder.

Levi nods in agreement. "Yeah, what he said. Though I have to say, watching you try to make chai lattes while hopped up on painkillers was pretty entertaining."

I gasp in mock outrage. "I'll have you know I was a paragon of grace and professionalism!"

"Sure you were," Levi grins. "That's why we had to stop you from trying to blend a yoga mat into a smoothie."

As everyone dissolves into laughter again, I feel a warmth spreading through my core that has nothing to do with my healing incision. This, right here, is what it's all about—*finding joy and harmony even amid chaos.*

"Alright, alright," I say, trying to sound stern but failing miserably. "Enough making fun of the invalid. Don't you people have jobs to do?"

"Yes, I do, yoga boss," Levi salutes playfully.

"Back to the grind we go." Tara playfully calls out, grinding.

As everyone starts to disperse, Bliss pulls me aside. "Hey, I almost forgot to mention that Manuka honey Alex recommended is working for my chapped hands, too. Your incision healed so fast, I thought I'd try it. It's like magic. You should totally share it with your followers."

I nod enthusiastically. "I know, I'm half convinced Alex is secretly using experimental drugs in it. Don't tell him I said that, though. It might go to his head. I'll check with Brad on using it in a post."

Bliss laughs. "Try not to worry too much about Brad and his approval of everything, okay? I'm one of your followers and I like the real, unfiltered stuff you post. Focus on healing and enjoying Hawaii, not posting tight outfits and wearing full makeup."

I give her a grateful smile. "Thanks, Bliss. I needed to hear that. Also, thanks for lending your brother to me."

"He needed someone to look after besides his little sister. You bring out his playful nature. So does Alex." She smiles, looking across the cafe at her brother, laughing with Alex.

As Bliss leaves and I head back behind the counter, I catch Levi and Alex in what looks like a serious conversation. They both glance my way, and I raise an eyebrow questioningly. They quickly smile and wave, but I can't shake the feeling that something's up.

Before I can dwell on it too much, the afternoon rush hits, and I'm swept up in a whirlwind of coffee orders and pastry recommendations. Working, I find myself humming contentedly. Despite everything—the cancer scare, the surgery, the uncertainty about my career—I'm feeling good. My aura is back to my usual soft blue. The energy with my hotties and followers is all harmonizing in a positive way.

I sneak glances at Levi and Alex, who have settled into a booth with their coffees, still deep in conversation, probably about Rex.

Chapter 15

HAWAIIAN VIBRATIONS

The Hawaiian sun is beating down on me as I stand outside the Aloha Medical Conference Center, feeling about as out of place as mango on pizza. I'm surrounded by a sea of crisp white coats and serious expressions, clutching my yoga mat to protect me from the seriousness.

"Deep breaths, Meaghan," I mutter to myself. "You've got this. It's just a room of doctors. No big deal. Just pretend they're all future Spreading Harmony Followers and wearing neon colored RuRuRamons wedgie-tight yoga pants doing a cow pose."

The mental image of a hundred doctors in white coats attempting yoga with wedgies is enough to make me snort-laugh, earning me a few curious glances from nearby attendees.

"There you are!" Alex's voice cuts through my yoga-induced giggles. I see him striding towards me, looking unfairly comfortable and handsome in his business suit. "I was starting to worry you'd decided to ditch us for a solo beach meditation session."

I wave and laugh. "Dr. Peters, I would never! Well, okay, maybe I considered it for like, a millisecond. But I'm here, reporting for duty or a yoga pep talk, whichever is more appropriate in this setting." I cock an eyebrow at him, I'm only half joking.

Do these doctors really want to learn yoga?

They don't look as open-minded as Alex.

Alex chuckles, shaking his head. "Come on, let me introduce you to some colleagues. They're excited to meet the yoga guru who's going to teach about alternative medical treatments."

As we walk into the conference center, I'm overwhelmed by this super-professional environment. It's nothing like the relaxing forest or beach that is my usual workplace. "Alex," I whisper, tugging on his sleeve. "Are you sure about this? I usually teach yoga to people whose idea of stress is running out of avocados for their toast. These are doctors who deal with life-and-death situations."

Alex turns to me, his expression softening. "Meaghan, you've got this. Your perspective is exactly what they need. Yoga has helped me with my high stress practice. It'll help them, too. Trust me."

"Also, your dad talked you up. He's a proud father and everyone wants to get into Dr. Mitchell's good graces," he whispers into my ear, tickling my neck with his warm breath, which is too reminiscent of Levi's whispers. My heart flutters, and I flush.

Positive Vibes.

I stand taller with his support and having him next to me.

A group of doctors approach, and he hooks my arm and brings me over to them. "Ah, Dr. Ramirez, Dr. Chen," Alex greets them warmly.

"I'd like you to meet Meaghan Mitchell, my girlfriend and our guest speaker for today's alternative treatment session."

I nearly choke on the air.

Girlfriend?

When did that happen? But seeing the nods of approval and respect from the doctors, I clam up. I quickly paste on my best 'namaste' smile and extend my hand.

"It's a pleasure to meet you all," I say, silently thanking the universe for all those improv classes I took in high school. "I'm excited to share some positive meditation ideas with you today."

Chatting, I sneak glances at Alex, trying to communicate that I want to get out of this conversation and talk with him alone, *stat*. He catches my eye and winks, which does nothing to clarify the situation or end the conversation, leaving me more confused.

"Meaghan's an amazing yoga and meditation instructor who can help us find better treatments for trauma patients, and post-surgical patients," he explains.

What?

I'm not teaching the doctors to empathize and meditate with their traumatized patients. I aim to guide them in coping with their trauma from working in a high-stress field. The constant need to make split-second decisions, the immense responsibility, and the weight of playing God all take a toll that needs addressing. I guess I didn't quite convey my plan to Dad or Alex, and it's too late to change my speech now.

We take our seats before I can talk with Alex. Alex goes up to give his talk, and then I hear my name and see Alex motioning me to the podium. Standing at the front of the room, facing their sea of expectant faces, I take a deep breath and channel my inner yoga goddess.

"Thank you, Doctor Peters, for the introduction. And thank you, doctors, for having me here today." A sense of discomfort lingers as I'm not teaching the trauma patient care he introduced. I'm here for them, not their patients, to spread healing and peace in their lives. I decided to dive in with no PowerPoint or corrections.

"Relax, be comfortable, and focus on being present with me. If you need a bathroom break, now's the time. Grab some water," I explain, moving off the podium, to their level and meeting their gazes with my warm smile. "We are doing a guided meditation together, a practice you can incorporate in your own lives to ground yourselves between patients or before transitioning home from work."

Alex dims the lights at my wave as I encourage them to embrace relaxation. "We're going to feel our bodies through guided meditation. Close your eyes if you're comfortable. Remember, you're in control."

Some set down their notes, and others look up from their phones. Alex takes the chair on stage and opens his palms on his thighs, taking a deep breath and closing his eyes to demonstrate.

"Alright, doctors," I say, smiling at their more relaxed position. "There's no test or memorization needed. We are going to get our om on."

A few chuckles ripple through the room, and I relax a bit.

"Now, I know you were probably expecting me to talk about patient meditation techniques," I continue. "But today, we're doing something a little different. We're going to focus on you, and how to keep your energy calm and steady."

I see a few raised eyebrows and curious glances, but there are some nods and smiles.

"As healers, you're constantly giving of yourselves. You deal with trauma, and stress daily. But who heals the healers? Today, we're going to explore some trauma meditation techniques that you can use for yourselves. You can't fill another's cup with an empty well."

As I guide them through various breathing exercises and meditation techniques, I'm struck by how much tension I can see melting away and the energy shift in the room. These brilliant minds, usually so focused on others, are finally taking a moment to focus their energy on themselves.

"Sometimes we focus so much on helping others that we forget that our bodies and our spirits require our attention." I take a shaky breath and realize that I need this as much as they do. I feel tears well up in my eyes, and the stress I was holding on to about my cancer and recovery dissolves as I continue demonstrating deep centered breathing.

As I look out at the room full of doctors, they follow my lead and trust me to guide them. Most have their eyes closed but I lock eyes with Alex who gives me a supportive nod. I find my own energy being restored and I am centered. This is what I'm meant to do: bring joy and love into the world and be an example for others.

"Remember," I say, my voice stronger, fueled by my positive intentions and confidence, "healing isn't just physical. It's mental, emotional, spiritual. You can't pour from an empty cup, so let's work on filling yours first."

"Namaste, doctors," I say. After the quiet meditation, tears glisten on some faces, and the room feels as if everyone has released their breath at once. I take my recording phone off the tripod in the back. I'm happy that the class went better than expected, wiping my own eyes at the emotional release found in the room.

Alex announces the end of the day and adjusts the lights. As I smile at the relaxed faces and my new followers. The doctors are more relaxed and more open. As they file out, many stop to thank me, their words full of gratitude and newfound respect.

I shake hands and thank them for participating. I'm still riding the high of a successful presentation when Alex approaches, his eyes shining with pride.

"That was unexpected," a female doctor with the name tag, Dr. Ramirez says, shaking my hand firmly. "And exactly what we needed. Thank you, Ms. Mitchell."

As the room clears, Alex beams with pride. "See? I told you you'd be great." He tilts his head with his easy grin. "Meaghan, that was," he pauses, searching for words. "Incredible. The whole energy shifted, even I noticed."

A blush creeps up my cheeks. "Really? I was so nervous."

Alex laughs, a warm sound that sends a little shiver down my spine. "Trust me, you are the highlight of the conference."

"I must admit I had a tough time with that meditation today. I felt more tense and like I was about to have a good cry in front of everyone. I was not as completely present as usual," I confess. I bite my lip and wonder if I should ask about the "girlfriend label" or wait until we are at the condo.

"Why do you think that is?" Alex furrows his brow and gives me his compassionate, doctorly eyes.

I shrug and chicken out. "I actually think it's just my remaining stress from the cancer scare. There's a lot of what-ifs. What if I wouldn't have caught it in time? What if it comes back?" I reveal, being totally honest.

He smiles warmly and takes my hand. "I think that's totally normal, and it's good you're processing it. It was a big deal and I'm glad it was only superficial. We found it early and removed everything."

"Thanks for your support, as my doctor and my friend," I punch his arm lightly, changing the heavy vibe to something more playful. "Now, care to explain the whole 'girlfriend' thing, Doctor Hottie?"

Alex looks a bit sheepish. "Ah, about that. I may have told a few colleagues we were dating to fend off my persistent admirers. I hope you don't mind playing along. I promise to make it up to you with as many piña coladas as you can drink."

I pretend to consider it, relieved he doesn't actually think I'm his girlfriend. With our busy lives, we haven't discussed where we are in our relationship, and I'm not about to bring up the topic in a hotel lobby. "Throw in a sunset yoga session on the beach, and you've got yourself a deal, 'boyfriend.'"

"I like the sound of that," his eyes twinkle and his smile is contagious.

My phone buzzes, interrupting our laughter. It's Brad, of course.

"Oh kale smoothies!" I exclaim suddenly, remembering that I promised him a video clip. I look through my phone, sending him the amazing video clip showcasing the beautiful conference center and my positive vibes while teaching.

I text, "Conference pics. You edit & post. Make the magic happen!"

"Send a selfie, too."

I sigh, feeling the weight of his expectations crushing my good mood. Dutifully, I snap a quick selfie by the conference sign and send a few shots that Alex took during the yoga session. Despite my irritation with Brad, I can't help but feel a flicker of pride as I look at the photos. I look good, confident, and at peace, like someone who actually knows what they're doing.

But Brad, ever the buzzkill, has other ideas. "No makeup? Seriously? How many times do I have to tell you—STAGE MAKEUP for everything. These are a disaster. I'll have to work overtime to edit them to make them usable."

I roll my eyes so hard I'm surprised they don't get stuck.

Why did I hire him again?

Oh right, because he promised to build my platform and make me a household name to spread my joy.

But at what cost?

It feels like every day, he's trying to change another part of me.

"I'll send some beach yoga shots later," I text back, hoping to placate him. "More on brand."

As we mingle with other conference attendees, I can't shake the nagging feeling that I'm losing myself in all of this. The Meaghan who started this journey would never have cared about "stage makeup" or being "on brand."

Just as I hit send to post a conference picture myself, another notification from the Manuka Honey company pops up—they must have noticed my last week's post promoting their healing benefits.

"Ms. Mitchell, we'd love to invite you to our corporate retreat to teach a class on wellness and natural healing. Interested?"

I squeal so loudly that Alex jumps. "Everything okay?" he asks, looking concerned.

"Okay? It's amazing! The Manuka Honey people want me to teach at their corporate retreat! Alex, do you know what this means? I can finally get an organic earth friendly sponsor or at least get free merch from them."

Alex laughs, shaking his head fondly. "You need it. Did you rub that honey on your sore muscles yesterday?"

"I did. And it worked," I proclaim. As I'm doing a little victory dance, my phone buzzes again.

"You are a popular lady. Schedule in some time for me, will you?" Alex teases.

This time, the alert is a comment from Bliss. "OMG, Meaghan! Congrats on hitting 1 million followers! You're officially Insta-famous!"

I freeze, then frantically open my profile. Sure enough, there it is, *1,000,000 followers.*

"Alex!" I screech, shoving my phone in his face. "Look! A million! That's like a million people who want to watch me do yoga! And a million people I can help to spread joy and positivity to." This is a real career now.

Alex gently pushes my phone away from his nose and gives me a sparkling smile. "Congratulations, Meaghan. You deserve it. I'm one of those million people."

My phone buzzes again—this time, it's an email from a name I recognize, the one Brad has been hoping for, RuRuRamon. Secretly the ultra-luxe yoga wear brand I've hated, I'm starting to love the snug fit and bright colors despite the expensive price tag.

Holding my breath, I open the email.

"Dear Ms. Mitchell, We at RuRuRamon have been following your journey and are impressed by your dedication to wellness, and your growing influence in the yoga community. We would be honored if you would consider becoming the face of our new eco-friendly, all-natural fiber yoga line. Please get in touch with us at your earliest convenience to discuss this exciting opportunity. Namaste, RuRuRamon Team"

I read the email three times before I'm convinced I'm not hallucinating. Then, in a very un-zen-like manner, I scream, which scares half the lobby and even the tropical birds outside, fly from the trees.

"Meaghan!" Alex exclaims, looking up from his phone, alarmed. "What's wrong? Is it your incision?"

I shake my head, unable to form words. Instead, I thrust my phone back at him.

Alex reads the email, and his eyes widen. "Wow, Meaghan. This is wow. Congratulations! This is huge!"

I nod, still too stunned to speak. Then, as the reality of the situation sinks in, I start laughing. It bubbles up from my chest, slightly hysterical but full of joy.

"Alex," I finally manage to gasp out between giggles, my voice reaching a pitch that probably only dogs can hear. "Do you realize what this means? I hit my influencer goals: landing a major sponsorship, a million followers, and being invited to a honey retreat. And someone informed me that I'm dating a hot doctor." I laugh in delight and hug him, but he stiffens in surprise at my embrace, so I release him.

"Is this real life?"

Alex grins, his eyes crinkling at the corners in a way that makes my heart do a little salsa dance. "It's real, Meaghan. You've earned this. All of it."

"Alex, I—" I start, but a shrill voice cuts me off.

"Dr. Peters! There you are!"

Dr. Ramirez approaches, her heels clicking loudly against the floor. The smartly dressed woman swoops aggressively into the space between Alex and me, like a seagull stealing the last French fry. She barely spares me a glance before focusing on Alex.

"That was a wonderful idea to have a guest speaker at the conference," she gushes her hand landing on Alex's arm with the precision of a heat-seeking missile. Alex physically recoils from her touch and frowns.

"Join me at the bar to discuss some of my alternate treatment ideas," she purrs, looking at Alex, completely ignoring his signals, and my existence.

A flare of jealousy shoots through me, surprising me. I guess it's time for me to earn those pina coladas. I clear my throat.

Alex shifts uncomfortably, his eyes darting between Dr. Ramirez and me. He shoots me a look that screams 'help me.'

I spring into action, taking a step to put myself between them. "Thank you, I'm so happy you enjoyed it!" I chirp, flashing my best 'I'm-totally-not-jealous-and-definitely-a-real-girlfriend' smile.

The woman looks right through me like I'm a piece of furniture, her eyes fixed on Alex with laser-like intensity. I mean, who can blame her? Alex is more attractive than almost any other man with his Hollywood Keanu Reeves features and beach hair that begs you to run your hand through the soft waves.

Alex looks like he'd rather perform emergency surgery with a spork than spend one more second in this conversation. "This is my girlfriend, Meaghan," he explains, stepping back. "After that relaxing meditation, we're returning to our room."

"Right, honey?" he says, taking my hand firmly—the first time he's held my hand—looking at me with an intensity that makes my breath catch. Alex's soft, comforting energy flows through his touch despite her negative energy nearby.

I nod, keeping my cool. "Absolutely, Doctor Hottie."

The woman's face falls faster than my attempts at crow pose after a big meal. She mutters something that might be congratulations but sounds like a curse before clip-clopping away on her sky-high designer heels.

Once she's out of earshot, I turn to Alex, my eyes wide. "Oh my god, you can call me your girlfriend anytime. She's more persistent than Brad, and I pay him to nag me."

Alex's shoulders relax, and he lets out a breath that he's held since Miss Handsy aggressively approached. "I'm sorry about that. Dr. Ramirez is intense."

"Intense?" I snort. "Alex, honey, kale-cayenne smoothies are less intense than her. That woman was going to drug you and take you home."

He laughs, the sound warm and genuine. "Thank you for the rescue. I owe you a pina colada, you earned it, social media superstar."

"Oh, that?" I wave my hand dismissively, radiating happiness. "Just a typical Tuesday for me. Teaching yoga, revolutionizing medical mindfulness, and acquiring a million followers. No biggie." I bite my lips in an effort to suppress my enormous smile. Instead, my cheeks burn with pride, and I hiccup giggle, making Alex laugh too.

Alex shakes his head, amusement dancing in his eyes. Then, without warning, he pulls me into his stiff hug with positive vibes spiraling through me, making my toes curl in my eco-friendly sandals. "You're something special, Meaghan Mitchell," he murmurs into my hair when he releases me.

I feel the slight awkwardness of his initiating physical contact. Grinning, I appreciate his efforts to create a physical connection, and the energy. A hot tide rises from my belly to my chest. My mind flashes to the last time I was in Levi's arms and how easily my body melted into his.

The faint antiseptic smell from Alex's hug lingers, returning me to reality. The scent also reminds me of my dad, which immediately kills the budding sexual energy. I shrug and smile.

"Doctor, you are something special, too. Thank you," I say to him with a warm flush of pleasure.

Alex's eyes are soft as he looks at me and then scans the room for an easy exit. "Let's go back to the condo. I want to celebrate. I'll make pina coladas, and we can eat dessert for dinner."

"A man after my own heart," I say, fluttering my lashes at him. "But fair warning—if you have a coconut cream pie, I can't be held responsible for my actions."

Alex laughs, guiding me towards the exit with a hand extended for me to hold. "I'll take my chances. Though I should probably warn you—I'm a bit of a dessert fiend myself. We might have to establish ground rules, especially about the last piece."

I reach out and lightly hold his hand as we walk out into the warm Hawaiian evening, the sky a canvas of pinks and oranges. I'm floating high on all the positive vibes and good karma. If this is a dream, I never want to wake up.

But then, because the universe likes to remind me who is in charge, my phone pings with a message from Levi.

"Hey, Yoga Master. How's Hawaii treating you? Rex misses you and wants to talk. I miss you too. Call when you can."

I stare at the message, my stomach doing a complicated series of flips that would make an Olympic gymnast jealous. Because, of course, everything isn't perfect. If I pick Alex, then I will lose Conner.

"Everything okay?" Alex asks, noticing my sudden silence.

I paste on a smile, tucking my phone away. "Yep! All good. Just, uh, Brad reminding me to post about the conference. You know how he is." Guilt gnaws at me, but Alex is radiating positive vibes and joy I can't ignore. Here I am, living my best life in Hawaii with Alex while Levi is back home thinking of me.

Alex turns to me, his face lit up with a smile that rivals the Hawaiian sunset, and I push the guilt aside to enjoy Alex and the present moment. Alex is finally initiating physical contact, and we are vibing.

Officer Hottie is Future Meaghan's problem, not Hawaiian Meaghan's problem.

Chapter 16

DEEP DESSERT MEDITATIVE STATE

"Mmm," I murmur as Alex feeds me another spoonful of creamy coconut pie with a surprising chocolate layer between the pie and crust. The decadent dessert melts on my tongue, rivaling the sweetness of the moment we're sharing.

Wrapped in a cozy, thick blanket on my parents' condo couch, I'm nestled against Alex, my phone buzzing incessantly with notifications. The RuRuRamons announcement about me being the face of their new SoulCurve yoga line is skyrocketing my follower count.

A million followers and climbing—I can hardly believe it!

"You know," I say, turning to Alex with a grin, "I think I've discovered the secret to enlightenment. It's not meditation–it's coconut pie."

Alex chuckles, his warm brown eyes twinkling with amusement. "Is that so? Should I be worried about losing my star patient to the dark side of desserts?"

I pretend to consider this seriously. "Well, Doctor, I think we might need to conduct a thorough study. You know, for science. How many pieces do you think we'd need to reach a conclusive result?"

"At least one," he plays along, his face serious but his eyes dancing with glee. "Maybe two, just to be safe."

I laugh, the sound bubbling up from deep in my chest. It feels good to be silly, to let go of the pressure and excitement of the day, and just be.

Alex watches me with amusement and adoration as I frantically respond to messages, thank my followers, and plan upcoming photo shoots and marketing campaigns. "Slow down, Meaghan," he chuckles, offering another spoonful. "You'll get carpal tunnel syndrome from all that tapping. Plus, you're here to relax and heal. Remember the doctor's orders from your dad and the specialist, Doctor Hottie?"

I shoot him a grateful smile between texts. "Okay, Doctor Hottie, But, I can't help it. This is incredible! I never expected my platform to blow up like this. It's like... remember in yoga class when I tried to demonstrate a headstand and ended up doing an accidental awesome slow mo somersault into a backbend? This feels like that, but in a good way."

"I'm proud of you," he says sincerely, wiping a bit of chocolate from the corner of my mouth with his napkin. The gesture is so tender and intimate that it makes my heart skip a beat. "You worked hard for this well-deserved success."

His support warms me more than the delicious dessert, making me do a little happy-shimmy while I finish typing another response of thanks. As the adrenaline of my influencer dream becoming a reality starts fading, exhaustion sets in. I stop to rub my eyes and yawn, finally putting my phone down.

"Thank you," I say, my eyes meeting his and filling with tears. "I'm sorry for being a horrible date and fake girlfriend tonight. I promise I'm usually a much more fun fake girlfriend. You know, cartwheels, bad jokes, the occasional impromptu dance party."

He laughs, a warm sound that wraps around me like a hug. "You've been at this for hours," he says gently. "You need some rest. And for the record, you're an excellent fake girlfriend. Top-notch, really. You could add it to your list of talents."

I snort-laugh at that, nearly choking on my pie. "Oh yes. 'Meaghan Mitchell–Exceptional fake girlfriend. Proficient in yoga, green smoothies, and teaching doctors how to relax."

"Don't forget 'expert pie taster,'" Alex adds, feeding me another bite.

"Ooh, good point. A vital skill."

We lapse into a comfortable silence, the soft glow of the bedside lamp casting a warm ambiance in the room. If he weren't asexual, I'd think this was a romantic set-up. But somehow, this feels even more intimate than any date I've been on.

I lean into him, enjoying the relaxed vibes. There's a comfortable silence between us as we savor the vibes.

Alex watches me with a gentle smile. He scrapes the last spoonful of his chocolate mousse, offering the bite to me, his eyes reflecting a sweetness beyond the dessert.

I smile and open my mouth, indulging in the creamy sweetness. A magnetic energy transcends the exquisite taste lingering on my lips. I lick my lips as Alex pulls himself under the blanket with me and pulls me into his chest.

He leans in, his deep voice smooth and warm, caressing my neck. "You know, Meaghan," he begins, "I've been thinking about us, and what I want in a relationship."

I lean further into him, curiosity sparked. "What's on your mind?" I ask, trying to keep my voice light despite the sudden flutter in my stomach.

He shifts, locking his clear eyes onto mine, his expression turning serious. "Meaghan, I've never felt so connected to a woman before. I know we're very different—you being a sensual, ravishing free spirit, but I wanted to discuss more than you being my fake girlfriend and me being more than the placeholder for your boyfriend."

"First off," I reply, my heart racing, "I'd never use you as a placeholder. If you were my boyfriend, you'd be my boyfriend. Full stop. No placeholding, no fake anything. Just us."

He smiles a soft, vulnerable expression that makes my chest tight. "Thanks. My past relationships were more surface level and nothing that reaches the deep emotional connection that I have with you. I usually avoid getting close to women, especially women that have your sensual energy. I worry that you'd need more physical affection than I can provide. This wanting to hold someone is new for me."

"Honestly, Alex, this is new for me too. I've always lived such an open lifestyle that I haven't had an actual boyfriend before. I talk about relationships and connections, but really I haven't been in very many serious relationships. I'm more like a relationship taste-tester.

You know, like how they give out free samples at the grocery store? That's been my love life, a taste here or there, but never the whole pie."

He chuckles at my analogy, his eyes crinkling at the corners. "I hope I'm a flavor you might want more than just a sample of."

I feel my cheeks heat up at his words. "I think you might be," I admit softly. "I want the whole pie."

He nods and moves his hands to hold mine. We're facing each other, holding hands, and looking into each other's eyes. He hesitates for a moment. "I've never felt such strong feelings for a woman before. It's strange, but in a good way. Meaghan, would you be up for trying something?"

The question catches me off guard, and I'm unsure. "Yes," I responded intrigued. "What kind of something? Because if it involves kombucha, and downward dog, I might need a minute to prepare after eating all that coconut pie."

He laughs, shaking his head. "No, nothing like that."

Alex's laughter fills the room, and I find myself joining in. When the laughter dies down, he continues, his tone more serious. "I've never been one for the physical, sexual aspects of a relationship. It's not about you–it's the way I am. But that doesn't mean I'm not attracted to you or that I don't react to you."

"Alex, I am definitely attracted to you, too, and not just your intelligence, and spiritual side, I'm really shallow and like your fit body, Doctor Hottie," I say, giggling as I squeeze his lean, muscular thigh.

"Where's Doctor Ramirez to protect me *from* you," he teases.

"In all seriousness, I love that you are such a kindhearted person. You're like... the human equivalent of a really amazing hug. You know, the kind that makes you feel all warm and fuzzy inside."

He smiles at me, his eyes soft. "I could say the same to you. You're such an inspiration with your platform to spread kindness into the world. I mean, you're not so bad to look at either," he ribs me back and laughs.

I look into his warm brown eyes, searching for the depth of his feelings. "Can you tell me more about what you're proposing? Because I've got to say, you've got my curiosity more than that time I saw a guy doing yoga while juggling at Venice Beach."

"Well," he begins, a hint of nervousness in his voice, "I've never really slept with a woman. I mean, not in that way, because I don't want any insertion, fluid, or–" he pauses to shutter. "I enjoy the company of women and spending time with them. But in my past relationships, we've slept in separate beds when we shared a room."

"So, that isn't an issue because there are two rooms here, but are you suggesting something?" I ask, biting my lip and holding my breath at his answer. His touch is addictive, and I want more, even if it's not in the way I'm used to.

He laughs and moves his arms around me. "No. I want to try sleeping with you—together. No expectations, just an experiment," he explains, a vulnerability in his gaze that melts my heart.

"Sure," I say quickly, the warm energy between us boiling, and I'm almost unable to contain the sizzling energy. I smile, adding, "I'm up for that. Let's experiment. Though I should warn you, I've been known to sleep-yoga. So if you wake up and I'm in a mountain pose, just go with it."

He returns the smile, and his eyes sparkle at my response. "Thank you, Meaghan, for being so receptive and patient with me. And I promise, if I wake up to you doing sleep-yoga, I'll be sure to join in or at least take some pictures for you."

I laugh, feeling a warmth spread through me that has nothing to do with the blanket we're wrapped in. "Okay, but just so you know, I expect only flattering pictures."

Talking and laughing, I realize that this connection, this intimacy we're sharing, is unlike anything I've experienced before, too. It's not about physical attraction or sexual tension. It's about truly seeing each other and understanding each other on a deeper level.

When we finally decide to move to the bedroom, there's a shift in the atmosphere. In his gentlemanly way, Alex pecks my cheek goodnight as he tucks the sheets over me and settles into the other side of the bed.

For a while, we lay there, the room enveloped in a gentle silence. I close my eyes, wondering how this experiment will unfold, and am now too excited to sleep.

"Hey, Alex?" I whisper into the darkness.

"Hmm?" he responds, his voice soft and sleepy.

"Thank you for tonight. For everything. You make me feel... . seen. Like, *really seen*. Not just as 'Meaghan the yoga influencer' or 'Meaghan, Doctor Mitchell's daughter', but just Meaghan."

I feel him shift beside me, and his hand finds mine under the covers. "That's because you're pretty amazing, just as Meaghan," he says, his voice warm and sincere. "You don't need all the titles or followers or sponsorships. Those things are great, but they're not what make you special."

His words wash over me, and I feel a lump in my throat. "Even if I can't do a full split without a lot of warming up or I end up with a scar on my shoulder and no longer have perfect skin ?" I joke, trying to lighten the atmosphere before I turn into a complete emotional mess.

He chuckles softly. "Even then. Especially then."

We fall into a comfortable silence again, but this time, it feels different. The air is charged with an unspoken understanding and acceptance. I realize that this, right here, is intimacy. It's not about a physical or sexual relationship. It's about feeling completely comfortable and accepted by another person.

Drifting off to sleep, this is what I've been looking for all along. Not the passionate, fiery relationships I've chased, but this quiet, steady warmth—the feeling of being truly known and accepted.

And as Alex's breathing evens out beside me, I smile to myself.

Who knew that my greatest lesson in love would come from a man who doesn't even want to have sex with me?

The universe, it seems, has a wicked sense of humor. But for once, I think I might be in on the joke.

This feels right.

I close my eyes and sigh. Wrapped in his tender arms, I drift into a peaceful slumber. I'm grateful for the unexpected night bringing us closer and altogether redefining intimacy for me.

I like this. I like this a lot.

Chapter 17

Hawaiian Barbie Pose

Stretching out my tense muscles on the lanai, I try to center myself for the day ahead. I'm supposed to be in full zen mode, preparing for an online beach yoga session with the Manuka Honey company, but my mind is buzzing louder than a hive of caffeinated bees. They want to see a live session—nothing recorded before, so I graciously offered to do a class with their leadership team

"Breathe in peace, breathe out stress," I mutter to myself, attempting to channel my inner yoga guru. "Breathe in coconuts, breathe out... Oh, who am I kidding?"

I flop back on my yoga mat, staring at the impossibly blue sky. Alex left for the conference hours ago, leaving me with a quick peck on the cheek and a promise to call later. It was sweet, but part of me couldn't help but wonder what it would be like to have a more passionate send-off.

My phone buzzes as I contemplate the merits of trying to teach my yoga class while buried in the sand like a zen ostrich. It's Brad.

I smile, thinking I should use my celebrity status now and demand that he attend one of my forest meditation sessions. My overzealous publicist needs to understand how to relax, especially after we hit a million followers and secured a sponsorship.

"Please don't be bad news. Please don't be bad news," I chant as I answer. "Hey Brad, what's up?"

"Meaghan, darling!" Brad's voice is so chipper that I cringe and hold the phone away from my ear. "I hope you're ready for exciting changes to your schedule!"

I groan internally. In Brad-speak, "exciting changes" usually mean "things that will make you wish you didn't agree to me being in charge of your schedule."

"What kind of changes?" I ask cautiously.

"I have some fabulous news and a, let's call it, opportunity for growth. Which do you want first?"

"Hit me with the growth, Brad. I'm already in a child's pose, so I'm prepared for anything."

"Right, well, we're going to have to cancel the beach yoga session with the honey company."

I sit up so fast I nearly give myself whiplash. "What? Brad, no! That session means a lot to me. The Manuka Honey people are amazing, and their product literally helped save me, healing my scar!"

"I know, I know," Brad soothes, "but we can reschedule that for another time. Here's the fabulous news–RuRuRamons wants you to do a huge mall event! It's going to be massive, darling. We're talking to hundreds of people, all in their branded yoga clothing, hanging on your every exhale!" He pauses, asking, "you brought the clothes I gave you, right? Can you put makeup on to cover that scar and make sure to really brighten up your face with some bronzer. I want you to glow."

My stomach sinks, and I swallow. "But Brad, this was the only time all of the leadership was available at the honey company. And I actually believe in their product. I can't just bail on them to the highest bidder and for a bigger company."

"Meaghan, sweetie, this is business. RuRuRamons is your sponsor now. You can't be seen promoting other brands, even if they did help your little issue."

I bristle at his dismissive tone. "It wasn't a 'little issue,' Brad. It was cancer–like I could've died if we didn't catch it super-early."

"Of course, of course," he backtracks quickly. "But think of the exposure! Think of the followers! Think of the free yoga pants! And mostly, think of your contract, you have to follow my recommendations."

I sigh, knowing I'm fighting a losing battle. "Fine. But I'm not happy about this, Brad."

"You'll thank me later, darling. Now, go get your zen on!"

As I hang up, a wave of frustration washes over me. This isn't what I signed up for. I wanted to help people, to spread joy and harmony. Now I'm canceling on people who actually helped me to promote overpriced yoga pants?

What happened to my platform? What happened to my integrity?

Just as I'm contemplating throwing my phone into the ocean and becoming a hermit, there's a knock at the door. Confused, since Alex isn't due back from the conference for hours, I pad barefoot to answer.

And there at the door stands Levi with a lei around his neck and a dimpled grin on his broad face.

"Surprise, Hawaiian Yoga Hottie!" he says, spreading his beefy arms open wide.

I just stare at him for a moment, wondering if the Hawaiian sun has finally melted my brain. Then, without thinking, I launch myself at the masculine mirage, wrapping him in a hug that nearly knocks us over.

"Levi! What are you–How did you–When–" I sputter, unable to form a coherent sentence.

He laughs, the sound rumbling through his chest. "Whoa there, take a breath. I thought you yoga types were supposed to be all calm and centered."

I pull back, swatting his arm playfully. "I'll show you centered, Officer Hottie. What are you doing here?"

"Well," he says, scratching the back of his neck sheepishly, "Alex called me. He said you might need some company while he's tied up at the conference. Apparently, he was worried about leaving you alone after your emotional rollercoaster yesterday, and you are working in overdrive since hitting a million followers."

A blush creep up my cheeks as I remember my mini-meltdown at the meditation session, and then being completely glued to my phone. "Oh god, I'm okay and I promise I'll relax today. That's so embarrassing. He didn't need to do that."

Levi's expression softens. "Hey, no shame in having feelings and having cancer and recovering is a big deal, even more than a million people watching you. I'm going to make sure you recover and stay stress-free. Besides, I wasn't about to turn down a free trip to Hawaii."

Settling onto the lanai, Levi fills me in on all the gossip from back home–apparently, my absence has led to a heated debate at the cafe about whether oat milk or almond milk is the superior non-dairy option. I feel some of my earlier stress start to melt away.

"Oh, and get this," Levi continues, his eyes sparkling with mischief. "Rex is living his best life while I'm here. Bliss is with Rex and is the pet sitter who apparently believes in 'doggy spa days.' Last I heard, Rex was getting a blueberry facial and paw-pedicure."

I burst out laughing. The image of a police dog being pampered was too much to handle. "Oh my god, I hope she posts the photos of that!"

"Bold of you to assume I haven't already changed my lock screen to Rex with a mud mask," Levi grins, pulling out his phone to show me a picture of Rex looking simultaneously blissed out and mildly confused, cucumber slices over his eyes.

"So," Levi says, eyeing my yoga mat, "were you about to do some of your bendy stuff? Because I gotta say, I've been working on my downward cat."

I snort. "Oh really?"

He gives me a crooked smile. "Well, I missed you so I watched a few of your YouTube yoga sessions and it seemed creepy to watch and not follow along."

"I'm assuming you meant downward dog, but this I have to see." I wink at him and give him a flirty scan with my eyes, taking in his muscular frame that seems to defy the laws of physics. His biceps are practically bursting out of his shirt sleeves, and I swear I can see his pecs trying to escape through the fabric.

"Good lord, Levi," I exclaim, circling him like a bemused art critic. "Did you grow more muscles on the way here? You're like a walking anatomy chart!"

Levi flexes dramatically, his muscles rippling in a way that would make Hercules jealous. "What can I say? I'm cultivating mass for my police uniform. Gotta intimidate those criminals with my guns." He kisses each bicep with an exaggerated 'mwah.'

I laugh until tears form in the creases of my eyes. "Seriously, how do you even fit in the uniform or fit your ego in a squad car? Do they have to grease you up like a Thanksgiving turkey to shove you inside?"

He grins, striking another pose. "Hey, this is all a tactical advantage. You should see me chase down perps. I don't run after them, I flex and let fear do the work."

"I bet you don't even need a bulletproof vest," I tease, poking his rock-hard abs. "You probably flex and the bullets bounce right off."

Levi nods solemnly. "It's true. They call me The Deflector down at the precinct. Bad guys empty their clips and I just stand there, letting my abs do the work. It's exhausting being this heroic, let me tell you."

I shake my head, grinning. "Well, Officer Beefcake, I hope you're ready for some yoga. Although I'm not sure we have a mat that can support all your tactical advantage."

"Don't worry about me," Levi says with a wink. "I'll just flex my way through the poses. Downward Cat? More like Downward Hulk, am I right?"

I groan at the terrible pun but can't wipe the smile off my face.

"You want to do a yoga sesh on the beach?" he teases and picks up a yoga mat, leaning close to the door.

"I actually was just about to leave to do a surprise flash yoga mob-thing at the mall," I say, my earlier frustration creeping back in.

He shakes his head, "Meaghan, I didn't know you did mall appearances. I guess you've got a busy schedule now that you're a superstar. I can be your bodyguard for your yoga mall thing."

"Thanks. I'm a little nervous as I kinda expected to ease into more intimate classes at the beach or in nature, but this is what Brad booked for me. Now I need to cover up my scar and look the part of perfect-yoga-instructor in bougie pants and full makeup–" I'm trying to get comfortable in the wedgie pants when he pulls me in for a wet, deep kiss.

My hands are on his thick arms and the world along with my problems fade away as I melt into the passion of his hot kiss.

"You're certainly in island vacation mode," I tease as my swollen lips itch for more.

He smiles, and I feel a little dizzy with all his sudden passion and seeing his sweet dimples.

"Wow," I breathe. "That was unexpected."

"Good unexpected?" Levi asks, a hint of vulnerability in his eyes.

"Definitely good," I assured him, then paused. "But also complicated. You know, I'm here with Alex, and we are getting close."

Levi nods, understanding in his eyes. "I know. Alex is a good guy. But I can't live without a small kiss now and then. We'll figure it out, Meaghan. No pressure, okay?"

I nod, grateful for his understanding. "Okay. Let's all talk about this tonight. Now, grab your mat and water bottle."

"Yes, Yoga Hottie," he says. "I'm here to help you even if I'm doing shopping center yoga crowd control."

I nod, and we take a taxi to the mall. What follows is the most hilarious mall yoga session I've ever witnessed. The surprise yoga session starts without a hitch. About forty people join in as I corral the crowd in front of RuRuRamon's store.

I giggle as I side-eye notice that Levi's "downward dog" looks more like a confused giraffe trying to do the limbo, and his "warrior pose" is less "peaceful warrior" and more "drunken sailor on a tilting ship."

"Levi," I whisper-yell as he nearly topples into a restaurant sandwich board advertisement, "I thought you said you'd been practicing!"

"I have!" he insists, wobbling precariously. "But it turns out, doing yoga in your living room with a dog trying to lick your face is not quite the same as doing it in a crowded mall."

I stifle a giggle, trying to maintain my serene yoga instructor facade. "Okay, everyone, let's move into tree pose. Ground down through your left foot, and slowly lift your right foot to your calf or thigh. Remember, it's not a competition–if you fall, just come back to your breath and try again."

As I say this, Levi attempts to lift his foot and promptly hops around like he's playing an invisible game of hopscotch before crashing into a rack of RuRuRamons leggings.

"See?" I say, managing to keep a straight face. "Falling is just part of the journey. Great job, Levi, for demonstrating."

He gives me a thumbs up from his position on the floor, surrounded by overpriced athleisure wear. "Namaste, y'all," he says, and I lose it, dissolving into giggles.

The class is a hit despite the chaos–or perhaps because of it. People are laughing, falling, and getting back up again. It feels more real, more human than any perfectly polished Instagram post I've ever made.

Maybe a shopping mall class isn't so terrible.

I see an employee taking videos with the store as the backdrop, displaying all their fancy, expensive apparel. Brad is going to love this.

As we're winding down, a RuRuRamons rep approaches me, all smiles and clipboard efficiency. "Meaghan, darling, that was wonderful! So authentic. Now, we just need to get you into hair and makeup for the promo shots. We're thinking of glowy goddess vibes–lots of highlighter, maybe some body shimmer and we have a blonde wig for you to wear, better for our ideal customer base, you know."

I blink, caught off guard. "Oh, um, I thought we were done? I was just doing a drop in class."

The rep–whose name tag reads 'Cynthia'–laughs as if I've said something adorably naive. "Oh no, sweetie. The class was just the warm-up. Now we need to capture the essence of RuRuRamons yoga–you know, that effortless, just-woke-up-like-this perfection, wearing our clothing line."

I glance down at my sweaty, flushed face and the yoga pants that are still trying to become one with my buttcrack. "Right. Effortless perfection. Got it."

Before I can protest further, I'm whisked away to a pop-up makeup station, where a team descends on me like a flock of very chic, very hungry Hawaiian Honeycreepers chasing an unattended tourist's beach picnic. They powder me and tug to straighten my hair while Cynthia chatters about engagement metrics and brand synergy like these are ordinary, everyday words.

"Now remember," she says as a makeup artist aggressively applies something called 'unicorn glow' across my cheekbones, "we want you to be relatable, but, also, aspirational. Zen, but also energetic. Natural, but also flawless. Got it?"

"Sure," I say, feeling about as zen as a caffeinated feral island cat. "Relatable flawless natural energetic zen goddess. No problem."

As they work, I catch sight of Levi in the mirror. He's leaning against a pillar, watching the process with amusement and concern. When our eyes meet, he mouths, "You okay?"

I give him a slight nod, but I'm not sure I am okay. This doesn't feel like me. It doesn't look like me. And it definitely doesn't feel like what I want my yoga brand to be about.

Finally, after what feels like hours, I'm deemed camera-ready. Cynthia hands me a microphone. "We're going to have you do a few yoga poses while talking about how RuRuRamons has changed your life. Just be natural!" She enthusiastically says to the crowd.

I take the mic, my stomach churning, the wig practically sewn into my scalp so I don't even notice the super-uncomfortable clothing. "Thanks for inviting me here today. Let's cool down." As I move into the first pose, I drop the mic. Cynthia rushes to pick it up and clips a wireless mic to the front of my top.

When I finish, I'm exhausted, tense, and more than ready for a drink.

"Was that terrible?" I ask Levi, who's been watching from the sidelines.

"No, it just wasn't like the classes you usually do. Seems more like modeling poses than yoga. But I'm sure they loved it." He waves his hand at the mall-goers and the posh storefront.

I frown with the frustration I bottled up all day, finally bubbling to the surface. "You know what? Real yoga doesn't involve expensive clothing or fake yoga events," I find myself saying. "It's about embracing your body and doing yoga in your living room or yard, not an expensive studio with designer gear. These stupid pants are stuck in my cervix! I wish I didn't agree to be the spokesperson for RuRuRamons."

The words start to spill out of my mouth, and I move away from Cynthia and the store, not wanting to be overheard.

"I wish I would have done yoga for the Manuka honey company that I scheduled with a product I believe in. Instead I'm doing yoga for RuRuRamons, who makes people feel like they're not pretty enough or wearing the right clothing to do yoga!"

Levi listens, his eyes widening slightly at my outburst. Before he can respond, Cynthia rushes over. Her clipboard clutched to her chest like a shield. She frowns and stops me from trying to unclip the wig.

"Before you leave, can we do a group picture with the staff?" she asks, her smile a bit strained.

"Sure," I say, pushing down my conflicted feelings. The over-dressed store employees gather around for the smiling picture with their newest yoga influencer. This mess isn't their fault and the staff is working hard so I don't want to ruin this for them. It feels fake, and I force myself to keep the smile plastered on my face for the photos.

Afterward, Cynthia unhooks the wig, my mic setup, and allows me to have a wipe to get off the layers of makeup. "You can grab some free items from the store to wear during your videos," she adds.

I look around at the bougie, overpriced clothing, and nothing looks comfortable or wearable. "I'll get something next time," I tell her, and she hands me a check for more money than I expected. I'm dizzy even looking at the number. I put the check in my bra since my pants have no pockets.

Walking away from the store, Levi throws an arm around my shoulders. "Beach bar?" he suggests, sensing my need to decompress.

"God, yes," I nod fervently. "I need something fruity, strong, and preferably in a coconut."

Heading out of the mall, I can't shake the feeling that I've sold a piece of my soul. The weight of the check in my bra reminds me of the compromise I've made. But Levi's solid presence beside me anchors me, and I tell myself to shake off the bad vibe and look forward to unwinding at the beach bar.

"Thanks for letting me vent earlier and being here to support me."

"You know," Levi says as we step into the warm Hawaiian evening, "I think what you said to me back there about real yoga? That's the Meaghan I know and that my little sister looks up to. You care about helping people, not overpriced leggings."

I smile up at him, feeling a little of the tension leave my shoulders. "That's true, Levi."

He grins. "Now, let's go find you that tropical umbrella drink. I have a feeling this night is about to get interesting."

The bar is a perfect slice of Hawaiian paradise – all tiki torches, swaying palm trees, and ukulele music drifting on the breeze. We snag a couple of seats at the bar, and soon, we're sipping on drinks that are indeed fruity, strong, and – in Levi's case – actually on fire.

"To yoga and vegan drinks," Levi toasts, carefully maneuvering his flaming cocktail.

"To making terrible crotch-choking career decisions," I counter, clinking my glass against his.

The evening wears on and the drinks keep flowing. I find myself relaxing more and more. Levi's always been easy to talk to, but there's something about the combination of Hawaiian air, fruity alcohol, and the day's events that makes me feel remarkably uninhibited.

"You know," I say, gesturing with my third—*or fourth*—mai tai, "I've been thinking a lot about authenticity lately. Like, what does it even mean to be real in a world of filters and hashtags and 'all of this is for likes' posts?"

Levi nods sagely, nearly setting his Hawaiian shirt on fire with his latest flaming concoction. "Deep thoughts, Yoga Master. Very zen."

I snort. "About as zen as your downward cat, Officer Hottie."

He gasps in mock offense. "I'll have you know that was a very advanced variation. I call it 'Downward Facing Disaster,' and it was designed to make everyone feel comfortable."

I choke back a laugh.

"They did all laugh," he responds. Making me dissolve into giggles, leaning against him for support. As our laughter subsides, I study Levi's face – the crinkles around his eyes when he smiles, the strong line of his jaw, and the way the tiki torches cast a warm glow on his skin.

"What?" he asks, catching me staring.

"Nothing," I mumble, suddenly feeling very warm. "Just thinking about authenticity."

"*Riiiight,*" Levi drawls, his eyes twinkling. "And I'm just thinking about proper yoga alignment. Speaking of which, I think my 'Chair Pose' is about to become 'Floor Pose' if I don't get some water soon."

As if on cue, my phone starts buzzing. I fumble for it, nearly knocking over my latest tropical concoction.

"Hello?" I say, trying to sound soberer than I feel.

"Meaghan?" Alex's voice comes through, sounding concerned. "Are you okay? I've been trying to reach you for hours."

"Alex!" I exclaim a bit too loudly. "We're greatly! We're just being very authentic, not fake blonde *yoga-ee-like*. Right, Levi?"

Levi nods enthusiastically, then seems to realize Alex can't see him. "Right-o, Doc! We're authentically tipsy. Wait, I'm blonde and real. I'm *yoga-y*, too."

I can practically hear Alex's eyebrow raising through the phone. "I see. Where are you? Do you need me to come get you?"

"That," I say, attempting to stand and immediately sitting back down, "might be a good idea. We're at the... what's this place called, Levi?"

"The Tipsy Tiki," Levi supplies helpfully. "Home of the Flaming Flamingo and other fire hazards cocktails."

Ten minutes later, Alex pulls up in a rental car, looking concerned.

Stumbling towards the car, I hoot with a brilliant idea striking me.

"Guys," I say, grabbing Levi and Alex by the arm. "We should get tattoos!"

Levi's eyes light up. "Yes! Something to commemorate this beautiful, authentic moment of friendship! I haven't got a new tat since forever."

Alex looks skeptical. "I'm not sure that's the best idea."

But Levi and I are already dragging him towards a conveniently located tattoo parlor because it's the island, so there's one right next to a tourist bar. Luckily, they were giving free shots and Levi and I forced Alex to catch up with us. The plan went much smoother when we were all vibing.

We're all staring at our fresh ink in disbelief an hour later.

"The Three Mus-cat-eers?" Alex says, looking at the one small, cartoonish cats wearing a musketeer hat on his forearm. "With cat puns?"

"What should have gotten?" Levi asks, he grimaces and says slowly, "What, Doctor Hottie, did you think we should've gotten?"

"It's purr-fect!" I giggle, admiring my cat doing an impossible yoga pose.

"You don't even like cats, Alex," Levi complains.

"Neither do you, Officer Hottie," he shoots back.

"We couldn't agree on anything else, but we all agreed that none of us likes cats. So we got a tattoo of what we agreed we all didn't want. It seemed the most *fairestest*," I explained a little hazy on the details that made sense an hour ago.

"Yes. We equally hate it." Alex pipes up. "But mine is cute. I even think I'd let you pet it."

Levi flexes, making his cat–which is wearing a tiny police uniform–dance. "I think you mean it's claw-some!"

Alex sighs, shaking his head and holding back a laugh, the corners of his mouth twitching.

"Well, at least we're all in this together. Literally. I for all and all for MEOW," I howl. and we laugh together at our ridiculous tattoos.

"You know," I muse, leaning my head on Alex's shoulder while my feet rest in Levi's lap, "maybe this is what authenticity is. Just... being in the moment. With the people you care about. Even if the moment involves questionable decisions and bad cat puns."

"Here, here," Levi says solemnly, then ruins it by adding, "Or should I say, *meow, meow*?"

As Alex groans, I dissolve into giggles again, I can't help but think that for all the chaos and confusion in my life right now, there's nowhere else I'd rather be than right here, with my two *mus-cat-eers*.

Piling back into an Uber, I'm sandwiched between these wonderful, ridiculous men. Despite the alcohol-induced haze and the slight sting of fresh ink, I feel a warmth that has nothing to do with the Hawaiian night.

"Wait, wait!" I exclaim, fumbling for my phone. "We need to document this moment of... what did I call it? Authenticity?"

"Purrfection," hoots Levi.

"Oh no," Alex murmurs, but he's smiling.

I hold up my phone, trying to angle it to capture all three of our new tattoos in one shot. "Say 'meow'!" I giggle.

"Meow!" Levi obliges enthusiastically while Alex shakes his head, grinning.

I snap a few photos, squinting at the screen to ensure they're not too blurry. "Meow, these are going straight to Instagram."

"Meaghan, maybe we should wait until—" Alex starts, but I'm already typing furiously.

"Just got inked with my purr-fect partners, making us a cuddly throuple," I narrate as I type. "#TheThreeMusCateers #BestFriends-Forever #AdventuresTogetherForever #ThreesCompany." I hit post before anyone can stop me, then beam at both of them. "There! Now it's official."

Levi peers at the post and bursts out laughing. "Oh man, your followers are gonna have a field day with this one."

Alex pinches the bridge of his nose, but I can see he's trying not to laugh. "Our tattoos really made it official. I suppose your followers will enjoy the cat puns. Better turn off your phone before Brad sees it though."

I take his advice, not wanting to hear a lecture. As we go back to the condo, the warm Hawaiian night breezes through the open windows, carrying the scent of salt and plumeria. I find myself humming contentedly, my head on Alex's shoulder and my feet in Levi's lap.

We stumble into the condo, a tangle of limbs and laughter. The world is soft around the edges, and I have a surge of affection for these two men who have, in their unique ways, turned my life upside down and made it wonderfully complete.

"We should probably get some sleep," Alex suggests, always the voice of reason, even after shots.

"Mmm, sleep," I agree, already making my way to the bedroom. I flop onto the king-sized bed, not bothering to change out of my clothes. "C'mon, there's room for everyone. Where are my boys? *Meow*!"

There's a moment of hesitation, a silent communication between Alex and Levi that I'm too tired to decipher. Then, with a shrug, they join me. I end up in the middle, Alex's arm draped over my waist, Levi's hand resting nearby my arm.

As I drift off to sleep, I have a fleeting thought that this should feel weird or complicated—but it doesn't. It feels right. It feels authentic, with all our energy swirling in *pawsitive* purrfection. I giggle.

The last thing I hear before succumbing to sleep is Levi's drowsy voice: "Goodnight! I'm *furr-tunate* to have you, my fellow *mus-cat-eers*," and Alex meows at him as I snuggle closer.

Chapter 18

DISASTROUS POLY FLEX

Ugh.

My head feels like it's been used as a bongo drum by a very enthusiastic, untalented street performer. I crack open one eye, immediately regretting this life choice as the Hawaiian sun assaults my retinas with the fury of a thousand Instagram ring lights.

"Note to self," I groan, "never try to out-drink a cop and a doctor. You will lose, and you will lose spectacularly."

I roll over, expecting to find either Levi's muscular form or Alex's lean frame. Instead, empty sheets and the faint scent of my regret and tequila greet me.

Great.

I'm abandoned like last season's yoga skorts.

A sharp sting on my forearm catches my attention as I sit up. I look down and—

Oh. My. God.

There, in all its glory, is a tiny graphic cat doing what appears to be a drunken version of the Warrior yoga pose. It's wearing a little musketeer hat and silly grin.

"What in the name of Kale loving, Warrior One?" I mutter, squinting at the fresh ink. "Did I join some sort of feline fight club last night?"

Before I ponder this further, my hand hits my phone for the time and it erupts in a cacophony of buzzes and dings, threatening to shatter my fragile head. Every person I've ever met and their mother, has simultaneously decided to play a rousing game of "Let's See How Many Times We Can Message Meaghan's Today?"

I grab my phone, fumbling it as if it's a bar of soap in a prison shower–*I'd never make it in prison!* The screen lights up, and suddenly, I'm facing more notifications than I've ever seen. And trust me, that's saying something with my recent boyfriend polling.

"Okay, okay," I mutter, scrolling through the barrage of personal text messages. "Let's see what kind of chaos I've managed to create *this time*." Drunken Meaghan always leaves messes for hungover Meaghan to clean up!

First up, a series of texts from my parents make me wish I could crawl back into the womb and start over.

My mother messaged, "Meaghan Elizabeth! What is the meaning of this? A threesome? Matching tattoos? I raised you better than this. Call. me."

My dad followed with, "Your mother is hyperventilating. Please call ASAP. Also, nice tattoo. I like the vibrant colors."

I groan, burying my face in my hands. "Great. I've officially become the family disappointment. Move over, Cousin Eddy, with your pyramid schemes. There's a new black sheep in town."

Next, there's the flood of DMs from my followers:

@YogaLover23: "OMG Meaghan! I can't believe you said that about RuRuRamons! You're so brave!"

@FitnessFanatic99: "A threesome? With those hotties? GET IT GIRL!"

@ZenMasterFlex: "I'm confused. Are you promoting cat yoga now?"

@AKYoga: "I LOVE you. No one can afford those painted on pants! You are sooo right, yoga should be done in cozy clothes!"

"What the *actual downward dog*?" I mutter, giving up on scrolling through the hundreds of messages popping up every second. frantically through the messages. I've stepped into an alternate universe where I'm suddenly the star of a very odd, very public reality show.

Wait, is this Brad's universe?

I click on Brad's messages to see, the cherry on top, a series of increasingly panicked emails from Brad, indicating he is my soon-to-be ex-publicist.

"Meaghan, call me ASAP. We need to do damage control."

"Why aren't you answering? This is a PR nightmare!"

"Call me now, or consider this a breach of contract!!!!"

There's too many missed calls from him to count and my voicemail is full. The next message reads, "That's it. You're fired as a client. I've locked you out of all Spreading Harmony social media accounts. It's for your own good. And mine. Mostly mine. I won't be associated with you trashing the sponsor I worked so hard to get! This is my hard work, and income, too."

I stare at my phone, my jaw on the floor. "Fired? Locked out? What in the name of hot kale yoga did I do?"

With trembling fingers, I open my social media apps, only to be greeted by the dreaded "incorrect password" message. It's like being told I can't sit at the cool kids' table anymore, except the cool kids' table is my entire career and world.

"Okay, Meaghan," I say, taking a deep breath. "Let's retrace our steps. What's the last thing you remember?"

I close my eyes, trying to piece together the fragments of yesterday. There was the mall event, the uncomfortable yoga pants, and Levi's ridiculous attempts at yoga–

My phone vibrates. "Did you know the mic was on and that someone recorded this?" Bliss' message pops in my inbox with a clip of me at the mall, along with the audio of my RuRuRamons complaints that I thought were made in private to just Levi.

Oh no.

Oh no, no, no.

Like a horror movie playing in slow motion, it all comes back in violent flashes. The rude, entitled rant about RuRuRamons. The drunken tattoo session. The ill-planned Instagram post.

I scramble out of bed, nearly face-planting as I get tangled in the sheets. I rush to the mirror, holding up my phone to compare the tattoo on my arm to the one in the photo I posted last night.

"Just got inked with my purr-fect three-some," I read with disbelief and growing horror. "#TheThreeMusCateers #BestFriendsForever #AdventuresTogetherForever #ThreesCompany."

I stare at my reflection, taking in the smeared makeup, the bed-head that looks like I've been styled by a tornado, and the sheer panic in my eyes.

"Congratulations, Meaghan," I tell my reflection. "You've officially become canceled, a health-influencer's disaster."

Just then, my phone buzzes again. It's a text from Alex:

"Hey, YogaHottie. You might want to check your neighbor's security cameras. Apparently, we gave quite the performance last night.
"

With a sense of impending doom, I open the link he sent. And there we are, in all our drunken glory, attempting to recreate our new tattoos through a series of increasingly ridiculous yoga poses on the condo's front lawn. Alex is trying to maintain some semblance of dignity, Levi is flexing so hard I'm worried he'll sprain something, and I'm–oh, kale-loving goddess–giving an impassioned speech about the commercialization of yoga while failing at balancing on one foot.

"I'm not a sellout!" *Video-Me* declares, wobbling dangerously. "I'm a... a... yoga revolutionary! Down with overpriced leggings! Up with authentic... uh... stretchiness!"

I close the video that Alex must have found since I'm tagged in it. There's no way to untag myself.

My stomach drops, as my entire career goes up in flames while I dance around the lawn in a drunken haze.

"Well," I say to the empty room, "I guess this is what rock bottom looks like. Very zen. Much enlightenment. Wow." I flop back onto the bed, the weight of reality crashing down on me like a tsunami of regret. The ceiling blurs as tears fill my eyes. I've lost everything: my sponsorship, social media presence, my followers, my platform, and dignity. All because I couldn't keep my big mouth shut during a drunken night of "authenticity."

"Some influencer I turned out to be," I whisper, my voice cracking. "I've influenced myself right out of a career and probably ruined the lives of the people I care about most."

The magnitude of what I've done hits me in waves, each one more devastating than the last. My followers trusted me and looked up to me for positive encouragement and inspiration. And what did I do? I betrayed them, showing them that their yoga teacher was nothing more than a fraud in overpriced leggings.

What is my friend Demi and my other cafe coworkers going to say? Will I still have a job?

And my family—oh god, *my family!* The disappointment in my mom's text message echoes in my head. I've become the cautionary tale they'll whisper about at family gatherings. No wedding or baby shower invitations for me. They'll say, "Remember Meaghan? She had such potential before she threw it all away for a drunken threesome and a cat tattoo."

And Alex and Levi—my heart constricts painfully inside my chest. They didn't ask to be dragged into this mess. A respected doctor and a dedicated police officer—*what have I done to their reputations and careers?*

I curl up into a ball, hugging my knees to my chest as sobs wrack my body. This isn't who I wanted to be. This isn't the person I was even a month ago. How did I change so quickly? I've become a stranger to myself, a cautionary tale of what happens when you lose sight of who you are.

Tears blur my vision as I fumble for my phone. Staying here feels impossible. I can't face Alex and Levi—not after this. My influencer career is ruined, all because of one drunken mistake splashed across social media. We never even talked about a poly relationship or how we'd explain it to anyone. I'm destroying everything faster than I can fix it. The thought of seeing the regret in their eyes, realizing I'm just a selfish mess, is too much. My hands shake as I order an Uber to the airport

"I've got to get out of here," I mutter, stumbling off the bed and throwing items haphazardly into my suitcase. "I can't face them or anyone."

As I toss things into my bag, every item feels like a reminder of where I went wrong. The yoga mat I used to teach with passion? Now it feels like a prop in a life I no longer belong to. My affirmation journal? It's filled with words that once empowered me, but now seems empty and meaningless. Even the overpriced leggings—the ones that kicked off this whole mess—are sitting in the corner, silently judging me.

I catch my reflection in the mirror and freeze. Puffy eyes, makeup smeared like war paint, and the cat tattoo on my arm that is a badge of my failure more than a humorous story. This isn't the strong, confident instructor people look up to. This is someone who's burned down everything she's ever built.

"Who are you?" I murmur, resting my hand against the glass. "What have I become?"

The Uber app pings, notifying me that my ride is approaching. I look around the room, my eyes landing on the rumpled sheets where I felt so safe next to Alex and so drunkenly happy between the guys just hours ago. Now, that memory is tainted, just another mistake in a string of spectacular failures from yesterday.

I grabbed my suitcase, my hand on the doorknob, and heard a knock. My heart leaps into my throat. It's probably them coming to confront me about the mess I've caused and guilt and shame flood me. *I can't face them.* Not now. Maybe not ever.

Silently, I step back from the door, holding my breath as if they might hear me if I exhale—another knock, more insistent this time.

"Meaghan?" It's Alex's voice, concern evident even through the door. "Are you okay? We brought you breakfast."

Levi's voice joins in, "Come on, Yoga Hottie. We've got greasy hangover food and some ideas for damage control. Or we can double down and get hamster tattoos next?"

I bite my lip because somehow he almost made me laugh aloud. Their kindness and willingness to stand by me after everything is too much. A fresh wave of tears spills down my cheeks. I don't deserve their friendship, their support. I've ruined everything.

My phone buzzes—the Uber is here. It's now or never.

"I'm sorry," I whisper, too quietly for them to hear. "I'm so, so sorry."

With one last look at the door, imagining Alex and Levi on the other side, still believing in me despite everything, I turn and slip out onto the balcony. It's not an elegant escape, climbing down with a suitcase while nursing a hangover, but I manage it.

As the Uber pulls away from the hotel, I watch Alex and Levi's confused faces appear on the balcony. The distance between us grows, literally and figuratively. My heart shatters, and I wish I could take back everything. I close my eyes, wishing I could fade away too, disappear from the mess I've created.

Chapter 19

COUCH MEDITATION

"I'll be in next week. I promise. Thank you for checking in on me. Please, tell everyone I'm doing fine, and I appreciate all their nice messages," I quickly text, updating Demi at the cafe.

"Smile," my mom chirps, breaking my trance as she sets a room service tray of fruit and orange juice in front of me. I manage a weak smile and mumble, "Thanks."

I sigh, wondering how I ended up here – Meaghan, former yoga influencer extraordinaire, now professional disaster, slouching on my parents' couch in Lakewood, Washington. It's been a week since my great Hawaiian escape, and my life has been about as fun as doing a hot yoga class in a snowsuit in July.

I'm staring at my phone for the millionth time, willing Levi's name to appear on the screen. But nope, still nothing. Nada. Zilch. It's like he's fallen off the "People Who Want to Talk to Meaghan" list.

"John sent a strongly worded legal message to Brad and he basically told him to work with you, or release all your social accounts back to you, or he will have to pay you the lost profit. I know you'd think it is zero, but you have a lot of people sharing and liking your stuff, not that you've had the Hawaii debacle," she says, filling in the silence.

What? "John?" I ask.

"The Tax Attorney I was going to set you up with, before I saw your dashing police officer. He looks like Sean Connery, those brooding eyes and the jawline. I never told your dad, I dated a police chief once," she says this like she's talking about the weather and not this whole other person I've never met. *Who was my mother before she became a trophy wife?*

"Mother, I don't even know what to say. Thank you. I love you," I resort to the words that come easily and will always be true.

She smiles and winks.

I haven't heard from my Police Officer, however, Alex is blowing up my phone like it's his fulltime job. Not in the fun, flirty way, but in the concerned doctor way of: "Are you okay? Please talk to me. We're worried." Which, honestly, makes me feel even worse than if he ghosted me.

"Ugh," I groan, flopping dramatically onto my back. "Why couldn't they ghost me and let me die of shame alone?"

My mom eyes me like I've twisted myself into a perplexing yoga pose. "Sweetheart, who could let you go, even if they have to share? I'm progressive; you can have a poly-open relationship, but I still want grandkids. And if not a wedding, then some kind of commitment ceremony. I already have my mother-of-the-bride dress ready."

"No, Mother," I sigh. "I think you'll be a bride again before me. I've really screwed everything up. I could throw a 'Biggest Screw-Up Party.' It'd be well attended and loads of pictures posted. You could do a speech, and I could do a drunken interpretive dance."

She gives me that look – you know the one, part concern, part "I love you but you're being ridiculous"–and says, "You know I love a party. Don't tease me, or I'll start planning it! By the way, there's a kale smoothie in the fridge for you."

"Thanks, Mother," I mutter. Now my mother is more positive than me–*can it get any worse?*

My phone buzzes. For a split second, my heart does a little hopeful somersault. But nope, it's not Levi or even an Alex text. It's Brad, my ex-publicist that the tax lawyer threatened on my behalf. *I wonder how threatening a tax lawyer is?*

Time to start answering calls, before my mother does. The pit of my stomach churns as I answer. "Hello?" I try sounding like a functional human, not a sentient ball of self-pity.

"Meaghan, darling!" Brad's chipper voice assaults my ear. "How's my favorite yogi doing?"

Wow! Tax Lawyers must be really scary. "Oh, you know," I say cautiously to see where this is going, examining the couch creases pressed into my skin. "Just living the dream. If the dream is being a social media pariah and hiding out in my childhood home."

"Well, I've got news that might cheer you up," Brad says, practically vibrating with excitement. "Are you sitting down?"

I roll my eyes. "Brad, I haven't been vertical in days. Hit me with it."

"RuRuRamons officially dropped you as a sponsor, but I'm still your publicist and even bad publicity is good publicity when you're a social media influencer. I did have a new contract to review with you and I apologize for not giving you adequate time to respond and for not taking your cancer recovery into account when I communicated with you last week," he rattles off, as if it's written down in front of him. "I emailed a written, formal apology, too."

Now, I'm a little scared of Tax Lawyer John, I better stay in his good graces.

I blink. "And this is supposed to cheer me up, how exactly?"

"Because," Brad continues, undeterred, "we have a new offer! The Perfection Makeup Brand wants you as their new face!"

I sit up so fast I nearly give myself whiplash. "I'm sorry, what? Did you miss the part where I publicly trashed my last sponsor, got canceled by the health community, and drunkenly got a cat tattoo? Not exactly 'perfection' material."

"That's the beauty of it!" Brad exclaims. "They want to do a whole campaign about covering up imperfections. Scars, tattoos, all those quirks that don't fit the perfect influencer image. They're calling it 'Perfect You.' Since you're social media infamous, you're the perfect ambassador. Isn't it brilliant?"

A knot forms in my stomach. "They want to capitalize on the worst mistake of my life? And they expect me to cover my scar? The one I got from, you know, surviving cancer?"

"And that ridiculous tattoo!" Brad adds cheerfully. "They have this amazing concealer for tattoos. You'll look like a blank canvas. Fresh start, clean slate, all that good stuff."

I glance down at my arm, at the little cat in a musketeer hat doing a wobbly Warrior pose. It's embarrassing, sure, but looking at it now makes me smile. Especially knowing two other people also have terrible tattoos from that night. It reminds me of when I felt genuinely happy, like myself, for the first time in ages.

"Brad," I say slowly, "I don't think—"

"Oh, one more thing," he interrupts. "They think it's best if you distance yourself from your two gentleman friends. Polyamory doesn't really fit the Perfection brand image. They want you to look and be, you know, *traditionally* beautiful."

"Ah." And just like that, something inside me snaps.

"Are you serious right now?" I explode, jumping to my feet. "You want me to cover my scar – the one that reminds me I survived cancer – and pretend my tattoo doesn't exist? And now you want me to act like Alex and Levi don't exist either?"

"Meaghan, calm down," Brad scoffs, taken aback. "This is a great opportunity—"

"No, YOU calm down!" I'm on a roll, pacing back and forth. "Do you have any idea what I've been through? What I've realized this past week?"

"I—" He starts his marketing pitch to me.

"I've spent years trying to be a perfect yoga goddess. Always smiling, always positive, pretending like my biggest problem was choosing between almond milk and oat milk for my morning latte and matching my eyeshadow with my leggings. And you know what? It was exhausting, and I hated it!"

I pause, taking a deep breath. "I'm not perfect, Brad. I'm a mess. I'm a cancer survivor with a weird scar and a drunken tattoo. I'm in love with two men, and I don't know how to handle it. I ugly cry, and I snort when I laugh too hard. Sometimes I fart in yoga class!"

There's a choking sound from the kitchen. My mother is definitely listening and laughing.

"And you know what else?" The words tumble out of me like a waterfall. "I'm done pretending. I'm done trying to be perfect. To please everyone. I'm not Nutella. I can't make everyone happy. I'm done covering up who I really am just to sell leggings or makeup or whatever else you want me to push *this week.*"

"Meaghan, be reasonable," Brad pleads. "Think about your career—"

"My career?" I laugh, and it feels good. Real. "My career was killing me, Brad. It was making me hate yoga, hate myself. So you know what? I quit you. I'm not signing a new contract and you can log out of all of my social media accounts today. Thank you, and namaste, Brad," I say with a smile.

"You quit, me?" Brad sounds like he's about to faint.

"Yep. I quit. I'm done being an influencer. I'm done with sponsors and brands. I super-done by pretending to be someone I'm not. From now on, the only thing I'm influencing is my own kale-loving life," I say to reiterate and clear up any misunderstanding.

There's a long silence on the other end of the line. Then, in a small voice, Brad says, "So, I take it that's a no on the Perfection Makeup deal?"

I pause, and then I burst out laughing. "Yeah, Brad. That's a *no.* A big, fat, imperfect, Meaghan, *No!* Bye Brad. Lose my number, okay."

"I'm...you're...what?" Brad sputters.

"Should my lawyer John give you a call back or are we good?" I ask, my mother giving me a thumbs up from around the corner.

"Good. We are good. I understand. Thank you, Meaghan," he stutters back.

I hang up before he can say anything else or try to sell me on being a makeup model. I am feeling lighter than I have in years. My mother appears with my kale smoothie and a nod of approval.

"Oh, honey," she says and suddenly wraps me in a mom-hug that makes me feel like everything might be okay.

"I'm sorry, Mom," I mumble into her shoulder. "I know I've been a mess lately."

She pulls back, holding me at arm's length. "Meaghan, don't you dare apologize. I see now that I was adding to your stress of trying to be perfect and that wasn't my international. You are beautiful, strong-willed, opinionated, independent, and I love all those things about you, dear."

She wipes a tear from the corner of my eye. "I am so happy to hear you laugh and tell Brad off. He's such an ass and I'm sorry I didn't help you fire him earlier. You looked terrible with blonde hair in that RuRuRamons ad, too. Some people are much more attractive with their natural hair color," she says, smoothing down my frizzing brown hair.

I blink, frozen. "Really? You're not mad about anything or disappointed in me?"

She laughs. "Sweetie, I'm only surprised you admitted to farting in class. Does yoga give everyone gas? I'm always farting when I follow along to your classes online."

"Mom!" I gasp, but I'm laughing too. "Yes, yoga helps your overall health, including digestion."

"Well, now that I know, maybe I will start attending your classes in real life, when you start them up again. I'll be farting in the front row," she says with a smile.

"Oh Mom! Let's never discuss this aloud again, okay?" I say, shaking my head and realizing I have never heard my mother say the word "fart" before and knowing the reason she hasn't attended my classes suddenly makes me feel much better.

"I need to talk to Alex and Levi," I say with new resolve. "I need to fix this."

My mom nods. "I think that's a good idea. But Meaghan? Maybe take a shower first. And brush your teeth and wash your face. Self-acceptance is great, but hygiene is important too."

I roll my eyes, but I'm smiling. "Thanks, Mom. Maybe a little less realness next time."

After my shower and getting dressed, I sit cross-legged on my bed, phone in hand. My heart races as I hit Alex's number.

He picks up on the first ring. "Meaghan! Are you okay?"

"Hi, Alex," I say, my voice trembling. "I'm... I'm okay. Or at least, I'm getting there." I hear another voice talking to him. "Can you talk... is that Levi with you?"

There's a pause, then muffled voices. "Yeah, he's here. Hold on, I'm putting you on speaker."

"Meaghan?" Levi's voice comes through, gruff and uncertain. "Where are you? Are you safe?"

Tears prick at my eyes. He does care. They both do. "I'm safe. I'm at my parents' house in Lakewood. I'm so sorry I ran away. I just got freaked out and overwhelmed. I shouldn't have run away."

"We were worried sick, but decided to give you some time to recover" Alex says.

"Why didn't you call sooner? And why haven't you been doing your yoga classes?" Levi asks.

I take a deep breath. "Because I thought I'd ruined everything. Your lives, your careers. I thought you'd be better off without me and my followers didn't want me to teach anymore."

"That's the dumbest thing I've ever heard," Levi says bluntly, and I nervously laugh to break the tension. "Bliss and I will be at every class you do, when you start again. I'll even drag Doctor Hottie along with me."

"Ah, thanks, Levi," I say. "Look, I know I messed up. But I've done a lot of thinking this week, and I've realized something important."

"What's that?" Alex asks softly.

"I'm tired of pretending to be perfect. I'm tired of hiding who I am. The good, the bad, the ugly-crying, the snort-laughing, all of it. And I want to be with you. *Both of you.* If you'll still have me and you guys are open to allowing one more into your tight-knit relationship."

There's a moment of silence that feels like it stretches for eternity. Then, Levi speaks up.

"Well, it's about damn time," he says, and I can hear the smile in his voice. "We've been waiting for you to call all week."

"Really?" I ask, hardly daring to believe it.

"We are the three mus-cat-eers, after all," Levi says, and I hear Alex and him laugh.

"Cats hated by one, Cats hated by all," Alex adds with a laugh then says seriously, "Really, Meaghan, we're your friends, and we love you. All of you. Imperfections and all."

I'm crying now, but for once, I don't try to hide it. "I love you too. Both of you. So much. I've missed you guys."

"So," Levi says, "what's the plan, Yoga Hottie? You coming back to do classes and school us on how to be bendy or what?"

I grin, wiping away my tears. "Actually, I was thinking maybe you two could come here? I've got some ideas for a new kind of yoga class. Something a little more authentic *and more me.*"

"We're on our way," Alex says immediately.

As I hang up the phone, I shrug at my reflection in the mirror. My hair's a mess, my eyes are red, and my cat tattoo is on full display. And you know what? I don't care because I've never felt more beautiful.

Watch out, world. Meaghan 2.0 is coming, and she's *purr-fectly imperfect.*

I laugh, snort and warn my mother, "I invited the guys over to talk."

Chapter 20

CAFE REVELATIONS

I inhale deeply, centering myself as I mindfully wipe my hands on my wrinkled, organic cotton apron. The universe has guided me back in its infinite wisdom, working at Joy's Coffeehouse Cafe, my caffeinated sanctuary. I feel my chakras aligning as I sip the steamy, unique, sweet-smelling chai latte.

Mmm. This is perfection in a cup. Or should I say, im-perfection? My new life slogan should be *being imperfect is perfect.*

"Alright, spill it!" Tara asks, "What's in this magical latte you've concocted?"

I grin, striking a dramatic pose. "Behold, my dear caffeine baristas, I present to you, Meaghan's Mistake Chai Surprise!"

Demi gasps, pretending to clutch pearls on her chest. "You made a mistake? But you're like, always so perfect! Until…"

"The handcuffs come out," Hailey finishes with glee, and I shake my head at their attempts to derail my new drink special presentation.

"Even expert baristas make mistakes," I say, nodding sagely. "I accidentally made a cinnamon vanilla cappuccino with chai and macadamia nut milk for someone allergic to nuts. Oopsies! *But* as the ancient barista proverb goes, 'One person's anaphylactic shock is another's bestselling latte special.'"

"That is *so not a proverb,*" Sean chimes in, entering the room and rolling his eyes.

"Shh," I stage-whisper. "Don't anger the coffee gods. They're very temperamental and prone to bitterness."

Joy, materializing behind us, smirks. "Well, this 'mistake' is now our drink special for the month, it's so popular. Good job and welcome back, Meaghan."

"See, Meaghan? You always make lattes out of lemons!" Monica says with her quirky, confused metaphors.

This sets off a round of giggles with us all clutching our sides. As the laughter subsides, I realize how much I've missed this–the banter, camaraderie, and shared insanity from spending too much time around each other and free drinks.

"So," Tara says, leaning in conspiratorially, "how are you feeling about being back?"

I adopt my best 'positive' voice and respond, "Well, it feels like I've been gone for longer than two weeks. I'm still out of sorts. I think the path forward isn't always linear–like sometimes you have side quests. What I'm trying to say is, I'm glad to be back."

Joy interjects, "And we're glad you're back, Meaghan. This place hasn't been the same without your energy."

"Aww, you guys," I say, feeling a warm fuzzy feeling that has nothing to do with the three shots of espresso I've already consumed. "Group hug?"

Before anyone can protest, I've gathered everyone into a slightly awkward, very caffeinated group embrace. It's a mess of tangled limbs and giggles, and Sean is even giggling.

"Ow, that's my foot!"

"Whose elbow is this?"

"I think I'm wearing someone else's apron now."

"Is that the smell of new perfume, or did someone spill vanilla syrup?"

"Okay, you all saw her, Meaghan's alive. Now whoever isn't on the schedule get out of here," Joy announces dismissing the hug and Sean, Hailey, and Demo sneak out with a wave.

I'm so happy everyone came to see me on my first day back.

I'm feeling the cafe, fun vibes and glad to be here. This is where I belong–in this beautiful mess of coffee, friendship, and slightly questionable life choices.

"Oh, let her go, Tara," Monica chimes in, rolling her eyes but smiling at Tara who hasn't released me despite everyone else getting back to work. "We just got her back. Let's not smother her to death on day one."

Tara releases me and adds, "I'm so happy you came back. I kinda thought it was fifty-fifty if you'd show up today."

I laugh, helping her steady the tray. "My emotional breakdown with a side of self-discovery only took a few days in Hawaii and a week stuck at home with my parents. I'm ready for cafe reality, girls."

"Well, I am glad you're back," Joys says. "These girls keep over steaming and burning the soymilk lattes, and no one is able to sell the vegan muffin except you"

I gasp in mock offense. "Excuse you, I'm not pushing them. I'll have you know I actually like the vegan, chia seed muffins. They're delish." I give her a sheepish grin. "Hey, Joy. Thanks for, you know, for not firing me after I went AWOL and then had my public meltdown."

Joy waves a hand dismissively. "Please. If I fired everyone who had drama in their lives, we'd have no staff. Besides, your little drama has been good for business, everyone coming in to ask about you and which guy you finally chose." She raises a brow.

"*Both*! I choose both," I say, unable to stop myself.

"Can we keep it a secret for a week longer? I love all the business," Joy asks, biting her lip.

"How about we do a week of a Why Choose Special next week with a white and dark chocolate mocha mix? Why can't we have it all," I say with a laugh and a wink.

"Yes!" Tara agrees. "I mean girl power. You're a hero to us all."

I feel laughter bubbling up in my chest that I cannot hold back, and suddenly we're all cracking up–customers can wait. This is good. It feels real.

"Okay, okay," Joy says, trying to regain some semblance of professionalism but failing miserably as she wipes tears of laughter from her eyes. "As heartwarming as this reunion is, we do have a café to run. Meaghan, you remember how to make coffee, right?"

I straighten up, giving her a mock salute. "Yes, ma'am." I salute her and ask, "Would you like the 'Daily Meaghan Chai Special' or the 'Secret Meaghan's Why Choose Mocha'?"

She smiles, "I'll have the Why Choose but please hold the existential crisis and give me an extra shot."

"You got it, Boss," I say with a smile.

"I've had enough excitement with you coming back. I'll be in my office." Joy shakes her head and gives us—the group of giggling baristas—an amused smile, walking back to her office.

As we all settle back into our routines, I can't help but feel a warmth spreading through my chest that has nothing to do with the espresso machine I'm operating. These people are my cafe family and even if I never do yoga again, I have a pretty big community to lean into.

The morning rush comes and goes in a blur of orders, spills, and more than one customer asking me if I'm "that yoga girl from the internet" and "which guy did I choose?" I served her the "Why Choose Mocha" and let her come to her own conclusions on that question.

During the afternoon lull, Tara sidles up to me, a glint in her eye that usually means trouble. Or a really good gossip session.

Sometimes both.

"So," she says, dragging out the word like it's made of elastic. "We need to talk about your video."

I nearly dropped the mug I'm cleaning. "My... video?"

"Don't play coy with me, Miss Yoga Pants," Tara says, poking me in the ribs. "The one you posted last night? The one that's gone, and I quote, 'yoga-viral,' hashtag 'perfectly-imperfect'?"

"Oh, that video," I say, feeling a blush creep up my neck. "You, uh... you saw that, huh? I didn't think I'd get my followers back but apparently they like me, mistakes and all."

"It was so inspiring!" Hailey adds, her eyes wide with admiration. "The way you talked about embracing your imperfections and finding strength in vulnerability... I totally cried more, watching it than I did the time I saw a squirrel brutally get run over by a terrible driver on my way to work. The guy deserves prison for murdering an innocent animal like that." She says suddenly angry, discussing it.

My frozen smile falters as I pray, *please don't be me. Please be talking about someone else!*

"It was on the I-5 freeway heading to work, and no one was on the road. There was so much room to avoid Mr. Squirrel, but he aimed for it, like a murderous maniac," she elaborates, and I pat her arm and tut, my face burning.

"But, enough about that. He got a ticket, I saw a cop pulling behind him. Maybe he even got *jail time*. I should ask Officer Conner, if he knows about it. He does traffic sometimes, right?" She asks me with wide eyes.

"Um, no. He's usually doing special drug detection stuff with Rex. That sounds totally random. I'm so sorry you saw that," I quickly said. "You're *so* brave."

"Well, we stand by you and your brand, still, Meaghan," Tara says, steering the conversation back. "You're amazing and don't need all the fancy clothing or weird sponsors."

I have embarrassment and pride washing over me. The video was a spur-of-the-moment thing, just me, my yoga mat, and my phone propped up against a tree in the backyard. I talked about my journey, my struggles, and my newfound commitment to authenticity. And then, I did some light yoga stretches. Then–because apparently, I'd lost all sense of self-preservation–I invited everyone to join me for a forest yoga session tonight, followed by a cold lake plunge.

"So..." I say, trying to sound casual and probably failing miserably. "What did you think? I mean, *really* think? Are people going to show up for my first class, since everything went down?"

There's a pause, and for a moment, I'm terrified that they will tell me it was ridiculous, that I should stick to making lattes and leave the inspiring to actual inspirational people.

But then Joy steps forward, her face serious. "I think," she says slowly, "that we're all going to need to leave early today."

I blink. "What? Why?"

A slow smile spreads across Joy's face. "Because everyone's coming to your yoga thing, *obviously*. We can't very well plunge into a cold lake if I have everyone stuck here working, can we?"

I stare at her, then at my friends, all nodding and grinning like a bunch of caffeinated bobbleheads. "You... you're all coming? Really?"

"Duh," Tara says, throwing an arm around my shoulders. "You think we'd miss the chance to see our girl in action? Plus, I've always wanted to try yoga. It's like a mix of sleeping and dance, but with bougie outfits that show off our ASS-ets, right?"

I laugh, feeling a lump form in my throat. "It's a little more complicated than that. But don't worry, I'll guide you through it."

"You better," Monica says, narrowing her eyes. "Because if I pull something and can't work, I'm blaming you and expecting you have your personal doctor order me muscle relaxants"

"Noted," I say, grinning.

As we all laugh and start planning our yoga adventure—Tara's already talking about our 'fits and what types of matching hairstyles we should do—I don't have the heart to tell her that yoga is typically done in sweats and a messy bun—I feel a sense of peace wash over me.

This is what I've been searching for. It is not perfection, an immaculate Instagram feed, or a sponsorship deal. Just this.

Real people, real friends, supporting each other through the mess of life's adventures.

"Oh, one more thing," Tara says, interrupting my moment of zen. "This lake... it's not, like, leech-infested or anything, right? Because I draw the line at parasites. I mean, I have been on a few bad dates and I think I've seen enough parasites."

I shoot her a sly grin, shrugging innocently. "Guess you'll just have to come and find out, won't you? Maybe you'll find yourself a doctor?"

As my friends erupt into a chorus of groans and laughs and mild panic, I wink at them and enjoy the happiness and a surge of excitement. This is going to be an interesting class.

"Alright, Coffee Girls and Sean," I say, clapping my hands together. "Let's make it through this shift, and then we'll embark on our yoga adventure. Who knows? Maybe we'll discover our inner zen, allowing a release of our uninhibited self expression."

Sean raises an eyebrow. "Honey, I discovered that release years ago. It's called drag and involves flexibility *and lip syncing in sequins.* It makes wearing your RuRuRamons look like a cake walk, Honey."

We all burst into laughter again. This is definitely my cafe family, and my home. Somehow, despite all the recent chaos and confusion, I know everything will be okay.

Getting back to work, I catch sight of my reflection in the gleaming espresso machine. My hair's a mess, a smudge of coffee on my cheek, and my cat tattoo is peeking out from under my sleeve. My ponytail is not slicked back and there's no shimmery gloss on my lips–my image is far from perfect.

And you know what?

I've never felt more like myself and more perfect.

Chapter 21

THROUPLE WARRIOR POSE

"Okay, folks!" I call out, clapping my hands together. "Welcome to 'Namaste, Perfectly Imperfect–The Evening Forest Edition'! Also known as 'Let's See How Many Pine Needles We Can Get Stuck into Our Yoga Mats' and 'Surviving a Lake Polar Plunge'!"

A chorus of laughter ripples through the small crowd gathered before me. A grin plays on my lips when I spot my cafe crew–Tara, Monica, Hailey, Joy, Demi, and Sean–all looking slightly bemused and—aside from Demi—out of their element.

Poor Tara. She has already managed to get leaves tangled in her perfectly blown-out ombre hair.

She does not look comfortable.

However, to my amazement, Sean looks like he's successfully figured out how to incorporate rainbow sequins into outdoor yoga wear.

And then, I'm shocked to see my mother. She's in brand new yoga gear that still has the crease lines, looking like she's ready for a photo shoot rather than a forest yoga session.

"Mother?" I call out, my eyebrows shooting up to my hairline. "I didn't know you were coming!"

She waves enthusiastically, nearly whacking Sean in the face with her rolled-up yoga mat. "Surprise, honey! I thought I'd give this yoga thing a try. It's all the rage and good for overall health," she adds with a wink.

I stifle a laugh. "Well, welcome to your first in-person yoga class, Mom. Just remember, we're aiming for relaxation and only do what's comfortable for you."

"First things first," I continue, addressing the whole group, "let's all take a deep breath and connect with nature. Feel the earth beneath your feet, the gentle breeze on your skin, and try to erase the worries of the day and embrace the warmth of the group."

As everyone closes their eyes and breathes deeply, I let my gaze wander to the two men standing side by side at the edge of the group. Alex and Levi, my yin and yang, looking unfairly handsome in their workout gear. And closer than ever since our talk last week. They probably carpooled here and have planned a late dinner for me. It seems like not only do they meet my needs perfectly, but they complement each other.

I study Alex's lean runner's build and thoughtful expression. Alex is already in the perfect meditation pose. Conversely, Levi looks about two seconds away from challenging a tree to an arm-wrestling match and cannot seem to relax, even sitting down.

And there, sitting obediently between them is Rex—the bestest super dog. He's sporting a bougie service dog sweater that screams, "I'm not just a good boy. I'm a Gucci boy." It's a pastel cashmere number with "Rex" embroidered in gold thread, complete with a tiny pocket that I'm pretty sure is made for doggy breath mints. Despite his over-the-top outfit purchased by my mother's fundraising, this German shepherd looks far more zen than half the humans here, as if he's seconds away from leading his own canine meditation session.

"Alright, let's start with a simple Sun Salutation," I instruct, moving into the familiar pose. "And remember, if you fall over, it's not a failure—it's just an unexpected opportunity to embrace the earth."

Alex pokes Levi, and he almost loses his balance, even without being in a complicated yoga pose. Poor Levi! I'm going to have to give him some one-on-one lessons.

Moving through the poses, I marvel at the strange and wonderful twists my life has taken. A few weeks ago, I was spiraling into an existential crisis, and now here I am, leading my loving group of friends, family, and lovers in a forest yoga session. Life's funny like that.

"Great job, everyone!" I encourage them, trying not to laugh as I watch Levi attempt to contort his muscular frame into a Downward Dog. "Remember, yoga isn't about perfection. It's about progress, presence, and occasionally pretending you meant to face-plant."

I glance over at my mother, who's somehow managed to tangle herself up like a human pretzel. "Mother, are you okay over there? You look fierce, like you are ready to audition for Cirque du Soleil!"

"I'm fine, sweetie!" she calls back, her voice muffled as she speaks into her knee. "Just working on embracing the earth, like you said!"

"Hey, Meaghan!" Bliss, Levi's sister and my self-proclaimed biggest fan, lightly calls out from where she's set up her camera. "Can you do some downward dog again then move into a more difficult pose? It's great for the 'Gram!"

I shoot her a thumbs up. "Sure thing, Bliss, my publicist extraordinaire! Just remember, our new motto is 'Perfectly Imperfect', so if I fall on my face, make sure you get that on camera too!"

As I move into a more complex pose, I notice my mom has somehow extricated herself from her yoga knot and is chatting animatedly with Levi. I strain my ears to catch their conversation.

"Oh, Levi, dear," my mom gushes, "I had no idea you were into yoga too! You look like a young Sean Conner back in his 007 days."

I nearly fell out of my pose. I should warn Levi, but my mother is mostly harmless—*I hope!*

"Mother?" I call out, trying to keep my voice even to hide the bewilderment. "Focus on your core and balance."

She turns to me, beaming. "Oh, yes, dear!"

"Alright, everyone," I call out, "Let's move into Tree Pose. And remember, if you're wobbling, you're not unstable–you're doing a magical dance with gravity, like these pines around us."

As the class erupts in laughter and groans, I can't stop smiling and shaking my head in amazement. This perfectly imperfect yoga session is turning out to be a success, with all yoga skill level ranges represented. I have my expert yoga students, Demi and Bliss, in the front, who set an excellent example of what the poses should look like, and my carefree co-workers, trying hard but relaxing into poses that suit them.

Wait, is Tara napping? I pause and smile, watching her slow breathing and perfectly manicured fingers folded on her belly while she is oblivious to the class occurring around her.

I catch Alex's eye as I move into a more complex pose. He gives me a soft smile that makes my heart do a little backflip and causes a flush on my cheeks.

"Alright, friends," I say, straightening up. "Let's move into partner poses. Pair up with someone and remember–communication is key. Unless your partner is a tree, in which case, you might be doing this connection-thing wrong."

There's a shuffle as everyone pairs up. I watch my mother practically tackle Sean, declaring him her "stylish, tall yoga buddy," while Monica and Hailey giggle into a wobbly Tree Pose together.

"Hottie," Levi calls out, a mischievous glint in his eye, and both Alex and I look up at our pet name. "Should we show them how it's done? You, me, and the doc here?"

I feel a blush creeping up my neck. "I'm not sure there are any three-person yoga poses, Levi."

"Sure there are," he grins. "It's called 'Innovative Connection Yoga'. Very cutting edge. Right, Alex?"

Alex, bless his heart, looks amused and slightly flustered. "I suppose we could give it a try, and honestly, Levi needs both of us to keep him steady, so he doesn't fall this time."

I laugh, nodding, remembering how easily he gets unbalanced. And so, in front of God, Nature, and my entire yoga class, I find myself in a three-person yoga pose with the two men I'm hopelessly in love with. I'm a love-struck pretzel with Bliss taking pics.

"Okay," I say, trying to sound professional and not at all like I'm about to combust from the proximity of these two beautiful humans. "Levi, you are the strong base. Alex, you're the balance in the middle. And I'm on top, of course."

The words are out of my mouth before I can stop them. I hear a giggle from the class, and I immediately want to crawl into a hollow log and never come out.

"Kinky," Levi whispers, loud enough for most of the class to hear.

"I think what Meaghan means," Alex interjects smoothly, ever the diplomat, "is that we're going to attempt a multi-level balance pose, using our strengths. Right, Meaghan?"

"Right!" I squeak, my voice about three octaves higher than usual. "Exactly that. Very yogic. Using core stability and balance."

Somehow, miraculously, we form a human pyramid vaguely resembling a yoga pose. Levi's on his hands and knees, biceps bulging–*not that I'm noticing.*

Alex balances on Levi's back in a modified Plank, and I'm perched on top in what I hope looks like a graceful Warrior pose and not like I'm about to topple off at any second.

"Great job, team!" Bliss cheers, snapping photos like her life depends on it. "This is perfect for our 'Namaste, Perfectly Imperfect' campaign!"

Holding the pose, I feel a sense of balance beyond the physical. Here I am, supported by these two incredible men, surrounded by friends, doing what I love. It's messy and imperfect and probably looks ridiculous, but it *feels* right—*all good vibes!*

"And release!" I call out, half-collapsing into Alex, who somehow manages to catch me without letting go of our unbalanced partner, Levi.

I catch Demi's eye as we untangle ourselves, laughing and breathless. My fellow yoga follower and friend is grinning from ear to ear.

"Now that," she says, "is what I call innovative yoga. Maybe we should incorporate that into every class?"

"Sure," I laugh. "We'll call it 'Triple Tree Pose' or 'Meaghan's Messy Treesome.'"

Alex chimes in with "Throuple Warrior Pose!" followed by laughter.

When the laughter subsides, I notice the sun dipping below the treeline. "Alright, everyone," I announce. "Time for the grand finale–our cold lake plunge!"

Excited cheers and nervous groans greet my announcement. I notice my mom sneaking away with her yoga mat. She gives me a wave and a thumbs-up sign when I catch her eye. I feel a swell of love in my chest at her support during this harsh time. My mother means so much to me, and sharing yoga with her was fun.

"Remember," I say, making my way down to the lakeshore, "this is about embracing discomfort, connecting with nature, and pretending we're not secretly wishing for a hot tub instead."

Lining up at the lake's edge, I find myself between Alex and Levi again. The setting sun paints the water in shades of gold and pink, turning the whole scene into something out of a romance novel.

"On the count of three," I say, grabbing their hands. "One... two..."

"Wait!" Levi interrupts. "Don't we need to take off our... *you know,* clothes?"

I blink, suddenly very aware that we're all still fully dressed in our yoga gear. "Right. Yes. Clothes. Off. I mean, not off-off, but... you know what? *Dealer's choice,* folks! Whatever you feel inspired to do. Skinny dip or yoga clothed dip at your own risk!"

There's a flurry of movement as my class strips down to various levels of undress. I opt for a sports bra and shorts, trying hard not to ogle as Alex and Levi reveal their impressive physique, which is masked for everyone else farther away from them by the setting sun.

"Okay, take two," I say, grabbing their hands again. "Let's experience life. One... two... three!"

With a collective yell that probably scares every woodland creature within a five-mile radius, we plunge into the lake.

The cold water hits like a shock, sending adrenaline coursing through my body.

As we surface, gasping and laughing, I notice something. "Hey, look!" I exclaim, pointing to our arms. "Our tattoos look better wet!"

Sure enough, our little musketeer cats are on full display in the full moonlight taking over from the dusk–mine is doing a wobbly Warrior pose. Levi's tat is flexing its little cat muscles, and Alex's is looking scholarly with a tiny stethoscope.

"The *Three Mus-cat-eers,*" Alex chuckles, shaking water from his hair.

"Meow!" Levi and I do at the same time, resulting in giggles.

"United in ink and questionable life choices," Levi grins.

Rex, not to be left out, is paddling around us with a look of pure doggy joy on his face. I run my hands through his wet fur.

"Sorry Rex, next time we will consider a doggy tattoo."

"Weren't we doing hamsters next?" Alex jokes.

"No," Levi says. "And next time, maybe we could do hot yoga with a sauna after?"

I laugh, splashing them both. "Oh, come on! Where's your sense of adventure? We live in the beautiful Northwest, and icy plunges are all around us."

"I think I left my sense of adventure on dry land, along with the feeling in my toes," Levi grumbles good-naturedly.

Following the others returning to shore, the excitement for what's to come bubbles up in me. Sure, my life might be complicated. I might be in love with two *very different* men. I might be rebranding myself and only have a few hundred followers.

But you know what?

I wouldn't have it any other way.

"Remember there's Sunrise Yoga tomorrow morning!" I call out in my chipper voice to the group that groans and giggles in response. "I'll bring the coffee and kombucha."

"Girl, I'll be drinking coffee and questioning my sanity after this!" Sean calls out, linking arms with the other baristas as they walk back the path back to their cars.

"Let's head back to my place. I have a sauna calling our names," Levi leans into Alex and myself as we wrap ourselves in dry towels. We nod in agreement and follow him.

Perfectly Imperfect.

Levi shows us his phone. "Check this out guys."

The notifications catch my eye:

@MakutunaHoney: "We respect @MeaghanPerfectlyImperfect decision to stay true to herself and decline our sponsorship. We did meet a very special someone in her class that is saving lives, teaching others, and changing medical practices. We'd like to shout out that Meaghan has inspired us to donate 100k, in her name, to Rex's Canines in Cancer group for innovative, inexpensive cancer detection programs. #PerfectlyImperfect"

I feel tears prick in my eyes. "Guys," I say, showing Alex and Levi the post. "I think we might have started a revolution."

"A yoga revolution?" Levi asks, scratching his head.

"An authenticity revolution," Alex clarifies, squeezing my hand.

"A revolution of caring and being yourself," I add, looking between them.

Walking out of the park, hand in hand in hand, I know we're at the beginning of something unique and inspiring to so many others.

Sure, life is messy. Relationships are complicated. And sometimes, you end up with a weird cat tattoo, but also, that's perfect for me—and us.

I wouldn't have it any other way.

"So," Levi says as we reach the car, "same time tomorrow?"

Alex grins and nods at us.

I laugh, leaning in to kiss him on the cheek. "You bet. Now, let's go to your sauna and drink some of your famous kombucha!"

Chapter 22

—☕—

INFAMOUS THREE MUS-CAT-EER POSE

"Holy kale-eating, downward dog," I mutter, my eyes wide as I survey the sea of yoga mats stretching across the park. "Did I accidentally schedule this class during a tik tok flash mob event?"

Bliss, my self-appointed social media guru, and Levi's sister, pops beside me, grinning with energy like she's taken four espresso shots. "Nope! They are all here for you. This, my perfectly imperfect friend, is what we call 'going viral in real life.' Your evening yoga, skinny dip class video broke the internet last night!"

"I wasn't even trying," I say.

"Exactly!" Bliss exclaims, practically vibrating with excitement. "You were just you—real and authentic. People eat that stuff up like it's gluten-free, dairy-free, sugar-free cake that magically still tastes delish."

I glance down at my phone, which hasn't stopped buzzing since I regained control of my social media accounts. The notifications are rolling in faster than I can read them.

"You're trending, Girl," comes a familiar voice.

I turn to see Tara decked out in pink and gold yoga gear with matching jewelry. "You're like the Kardashians, but with more namaste and less contouring."

"Thanks, Tara," I say, unsure if I should be flattered or mortified. "I'm glad I can still motivate and inspire the masses. Aren't you working the morning shift in an hour?"

"Oh, I asked Monica to cover. I needed to see if this class draws in more hot men because my dating calendar is looking pretty sad." She lays out her nap/yoga mat. "Now, where are those two hunky men of yours, and did you tell them to bring all their hot friends?"

Alex and Levi materialize on either side of me as if on cue. Looking like he just stepped out of a medical drama in his yoga attire, Alex gives me a soft smile that makes my insides go to goo. Conversely, Levi looks ready to bench press a small car, his muscles threatening to burst out of his tank top.

"Ready to namaste and chill?" Levi grins with raised brows and munching on something crunchy.

"You can't eat during yoga," I scold, trying to sound stern but failing miserably.

Everyone knows I'm the most lax and accepting yoga teacher. All I ask is for people to enjoy and connect with the world and people around them.

"Oh right. Sorry, I'd offer to share, but these kale chips have bacon in them."

I groan, "Wait, what? You're actually eating kale chips?"

"Alex made them for me," Levi says proudly, puffing out his chest. "He knows I only eat bacon in the morning, hence my new favorite snack."

"I'm weaning him off bacon," Alex says with a shrug. "He's highly addicted so it's going to be a slow process."

"I don't think I can handle either one of you. You two are impossible. I may have to break it off and just date the most normal one of you–*Rex*." I smile and rub Rex's belly as he pants his excitement.

"No, you won't," Alex chimes in, his voice warm with amusement. "You love us too much. Both of us."

And just like that, with those simple words, I feel a wave of calm wash over me.

He's right.

I do love them–*all of them*. And somehow, miraculously, they love me too–imperfect, cancer, scars, over-the-top yoga enthusiasm, and vegan habits included. Our unconventional relationship is becoming a symbol of love and acceptance, inspiring others to embrace perfectly imperfect relationships that work for them.

Who knew we weren't that unusual after all?

"Alright, folks!" I call out, clapping my hands to get everyone's attention. "Welcome to 'Namaste, Perfectly Imperfect: The Park Edition'! Also known as, 'Yes, We Skinny Dip After Class.'"

A ripple of laughter runs through the crowd, and my nervousness dissipates. My classes are growing, and I'm not doing anything special, just being regular ol' me.

"Before we start," I continue, "I just want to say thank you. Thank you for being here, for supporting me through... well, everything. And for embracing the mess that is life. Because let's face it, if life were a yoga pose, we'd need each other to keep our balance."

More laughter.

Halfway through the class, a commotion at the back of the crowd catches my attention. I spot a familiar face pushing through—it's Brad, my former publicist, looking frazzled and out of place among the zen yogis.

"Meaghan!" he calls out, waving frantically. "If I start attending class, will you sign with me, again?

I pause, the whole class turning to watch the drama unfold. For a moment, I'm transported back to when I was desperately chasing likes and sponsorships and begging Brad to help me succeed. But that's not *me* or my yoga brand anymore.

"Brad," I say, my voice carrying across the suddenly silent park, "I appreciate the offer, but I'm doing better than fine on my own. I'm not for sale."

Spontaneous applause ripples through my massive class. I catch Alex and Levi exchanging proud glances, and my heart swells. Looking deflated, Brad retreats into the crowd, but I applaud him because he is staying to try out the class. Maybe I'll say hello after class and see how he's doing.

I take a deep breath, centering myself. "Alright, everyone. Let's redirect that energy into our poses. We're going to move into Sunrise Salutation. Remember, it's not about being perfect–it's about finding your own balance."

Flowing through the poses, I notice a woman hovering at the crowd's edge, clutching a clipboard and looking like she's on a critical mission. When we break for water, she makes her way over to me, a bright smile plastered on her face.

"Meaghan!" she trills, air-kissing both my cheeks. "I'm Veronica from Manuka Honey. We loved your video–so raw, so real! We'd love to offer you a sponsorship deal, again. Think about it: 'Meaghan's Perfectly Imperfect Manuka Moments.' It's gold!"

I blink, taken aback. "I... wow. That's incredibly flattering. But–"

"But nothing, darling! We'll plaster your face on every jar. You'll be the queen bee of authenticity, and we are happy that our honey helped heal you. Let's help each other grow."

I glance over at Alex and Levi, who are watching the exchange with amused expressions, knowing that I no longer want a sponsor or anyone managing me and my content. I don't need money or fame. I just want to be myself and spread joy and happiness.

"I'm sorry, Veronica," I say, surprising myself with how firm my voice sounds. "But I can't accept your offer. My journey isn't about selling products. It's about being true to myself, scars and all. And right now, that means focusing on my health, my relationships, and helping others feel less alone in their own messy journeys. I do think your product is amazing, and I know you'll find the right person for your company. It's just not me."

Veronica's smile falters before she recovers. "If you change your mind–"

"I won't," I say, then add with a grin, "But thanks for *bee-lieving* in me."

Levi and Alex laugh as she retreats, looking slightly shell-shocked. "That was quite the *sting,*" Levi quips, pulling me into a side hug.

"Very proud of you," Alex adds, taking my other hand. "You are really gaining your independence and confidence."

EPILOGUE: Icky Sticky Time

"No, Rex!" I call out as he bumps into the table, causing my mimosa to wobble precariously.

"Don't you dare be mean to this sweet dog!" my mother scolds, her voice full of loving protection.

Rex, our impossibly spoiled and loyal German Shepherd, slinks to his usual spot beside her. She bought him a real-fur lined dog bed. His tail wags so enthusiastically that I half expect him to generate enough wind to solve the world's energy crisis.

The sun bathes the patio in golden warmth, casting a dreamy glow over what feels like one of those perfect Sunday mornings you only see in commercials for orange juice or life insurance.

My parents' Sunday brunch, once a small gathering for four, now sprawls across the patio, with extra spots added for my guys, Bliss, and Rex, our furry family member.

It's like we're the cast of a sitcom, where nobody looks related, and everyone has their quirks. Somehow, we all laugh and come together for these elaborate breakfasts—sometimes on weekends, sometimes even on weekdays. The food budget for these get-togethers rivals that of a small country, thanks to my surprisingly large income as a social media influencer and my mother's cook's magic.

"You spoil her every time we come over," Levi teases, eyeing Rex's prime spot next to my mom. He tries to sound stern, but the smirk on his face betrays his amusement at the unlikely friendship.

My mother gasps dramatically, clutching her imaginary pearls like a Southern belle who's just been told sweet tea isn't the nectar of the gods.

"Nonsense! You can't spoil a dog! Isn't that right, my handsome furry grandchild?" she coos, slipping Rex another piece of bacon with the stealth of a CIA agent.

"Mom," I laugh, "if you keep this up, Rex is going to need his own nutritionist. And trust me, his daddies are already keeping a close eye on his diet."

Levi grins, reaching over to rub Rex's ears. The dog's eyes roll back in bliss, and for a moment, I'm jealous of his ability to find such joy in a simple ear scratch. "Well," Levi admits, "I guess Rex did get more work done than me this last week. Turns out, sleeping 18 hours a day and looking adorable in his cute uniform—Thanks to your fundraising, Sandy—is a full-time job for him."

"We all know who's working the hardest here," Alex chimes in, passing the plate of pain au chocolat.

The pastries look so perfect. I'm half convinced they flew here directly from Paris this morning. He turns to me, "I swear, between your yoga classes, social media empire, and saving the world one downward dog at a time, I'm not sure when you sleep. Do you have a secret clone we don't know about?"

"This world couldn't handle two of me!" I strike a yoga pose in my chair, nearly knocking over a pitcher of mimosas. "And sleep is for people who haven't discovered the rejuvenating power of sunrise salutations and green juice," I proclaim with all the zeal of a late-night infomercial host.

Everyone groans collectively, and my dad throws a napkin at me with surprising accuracy. "Sweetie, if you try to sell us on the benefits of kale smoothies one more time, I'm going to have to check your birth certificate and do a DNA test. You clearly can't be my daughter."

"Oh, come on, Dad," I tease back. "Don't knock it till you've tried it. Who knows? A little spirulina might be just what the doctor ordered. And you would know, being the doctor."

My dad shudders dramatically. "I'd rather perform my own root canal, thanks."

"Speaking of Meaghan's world domination," Bliss pipes up, rescuing my dad from the threat of green juice, "who knew having a furry yoga partner would be such a viral sensation? Your follower count is so lit, it's breaking the internet! You're basically TikTok famous without the cringey dances!"

I beam at her, feeling a rush of gratitude. "I have you to thank for getting all those great pictures. You've single-handedly made 'Doggy Downward-Facing Dog' the hottest trend since avocado toast."

"Hey, anything to keep my brother from scaring all my dates away," Bliss says with a devilish grin that perfectly mirrors Levi's. "We can't all grow up to be doctors and police officers who take on the world, you know. Or to date doctors and police officers, some of us must stay behind, serve kombucha, and ensure the Instagram filters are just right."

Rex barks his agreement and turns his best puppy eyes on my mother. It's a look that could melt the heart of even the sternest dog trainer.

My mother, already a pushover for anything that Rex does, doesn't stand a chance. She sneaks him a full sausage roll.

"It's his favorite, you know," my mother stage-whispers to Levi as she slips Rex food. He licks his lips and gives her puppy eyes. Both of them are about as subtle as a fireworks display.

"You know, I'm trying to get my family to become vegan or at least vegetarian," I say.

Alex attempts to rein in my mom. "Mom, if you keep this up, we're going to have to roll Rex home. Or worse, put him on a diet. Do you have any idea how sad a German Shepherd on a diet looks? It's like watching Dr Mitchel drinking a kale smoothie."

"Oh hush," my mother says, laughing and waving him off with the regal air of a queen dismissing a petty complaint. "I'm just making up for lost time. Who knew I'd end up with not one, but two strapping sons and an adorable furry grandchild? I have so many extra birthdays, fundraisers, and anniversaries, it's like I won the lottery with all of you, Bliss included."

I smile at her lovely remarks.

Alex, meanwhile, is deep in conversation with my dad about their upcoming Physicians Global Initiatives trip to Haiti. They're talking about clinics and vaccinations with the enthusiasm of kids discussing their favorite video games. It's like watching two nerds debate Star Wars versus Star Trek but with more talk of syringes.

"And get this," my dad says, practically bouncing in his seat like a kid with too much sugar, "Meaghan's Spreading Harmony fame has raised thousands in donations for the trip! We will be able to afford to hand out meals along with medication."

"Who knew that my ability to stand on my head while talking about inner peace would lead to actual world hunger?" I quip with pride and amusement. "If I'd known that, I would have started doing handstands years ago. We could have solved world peace by now."

The doorbell rings, cutting through our laughter like a hot knife through vegan butter.

I leap from my seat like I've been shot out of a cannon, nearly knocking over my chair in the process. "Ooh! It's here!"

"Oh no," Levi mutters to Alex and my dad, his voice a mix of resignation and amusement. "I don't like the look of this. Last time she was this excited, we ended up doing goat yoga in the living room. Do you know how long it took to get the smell out of the carpet?"

"You *loved* those mini goats," I retort as I get the door, returning with a Cheshire Cat grin. In my arms, I'm cradling a box decorated with "BeeWell Honey Rollers" and pictures of bees that look like they're doing yoga.

"I asked them to send some samples so we could get some family pictures trying out the new product," I announced proudly, setting the box down with all the reverence of a museum curator placing a priceless artifact.

"Meaghan, what a wonderful surprise," my mother exclaims, whipping out her lipstick faster than a gunslinger in a Western. "Now move out of my light, I need the direct sun!"

"Mom, it's just pictures with honey," I laugh, watching her prep like she's about to walk the red carpet. "Not a Vogue photoshoot. Unless Vogue has suddenly decided that 'Breakfast Chic' is the new black."

"Dear," my mother retorts, puckering her lips in the reflection of a spoon with impressive accuracy, "in your family, every moment could be insta-famous so it's best to be prepared and put together."

"Or maybe just be real and imperfect, right?" I say, setting up my phone and hitting record, feeling like a cross between a QVC host and a mad scientist about to unveil their most incredible creation. "Ladies and gentlemen, I present to you... Sticky for the Icky!"

There's a moment of silence, like the calm before a storm. Then, as if on cue, everyone bursts into laughter. It's the kind of laughter that starts in your belly and works its way up, leaving you gasping for air and wiping tears from your eyes.

"Sticky for the Icky?" Levi gasps, clutching his sides. "Please tell me that's not the actual slogan. Did you lose a bet or something?"

"It is!" I beam, undeterred by their reaction. If anything, it only fuels my enthusiasm. "Isn't it great? It's for all those icky situations where you need a bit of sticky sweetness. Like life, but with more natural sweetness."

"Like when you're trying to sweet-talk your way out of a speeding ticket?" Alex suggests innocently, his eyes twinkling with mischief.

I swat him with a napkin, trying to look stern but failing miserably. "No, you goof. It's for minor cuts, scrapes, and burns. You know, for when life gives you lemons, and you need some honey to make it bearable. It's like a first aid kit, but natural and tastier."

"Well, I think it's wonderful," my mother says, already applying the honey to her hands and smiling at Bliss taking pictures. She's rubbing it in with the intensity of someone trying to summon a genie. "My skin feels smoother already. Bill, darling, feel my hands!"

My dad obliges, probably more out of self-preservation than genuine interest. But as he touches her hand, his eyebrows shoot up in surprise. "Well, I'll be damned. It does work. Meaghan, you might have just put dermatologists out of business. I hope you're prepared to support Alex in his retirement."

Alex clutches his chest in mock horror, staggering back as if he's been shot. "Et tu, Dr. Mitchell? Betraying a fellow doctor? Next thing you know, Levi will be teaching criminals how to pick locks, and I'll be running a juice bar."

"You'd love to run a Kombucha bar, don't lie," Bliss teases.

We all laugh, the sound mingling with the clinking of glasses and the sizzle of the last few pieces of bacon on the grill.

I can't help but feel a wave of contentment wash over me, as warm and comforting as a freshly laundered blanket. Here we are, this mismatched, unconventional family, brought together by chance, choice, and a whole lot of love. It's like we're the Island of Misfit Toys, but instead of waiting for someone to love us, we went ahead and created our own family.

"You know," I say, looking around at all the smiling faces, each one dear to me in their unique way, "if you had told me a year ago that I'd be sitting here with my parents, my two boyfriends, a yoga-famous dog, and a box of medical-grade honey, I'd have told you to lay off the kombucha. I'd have said you were fermenting your brain cells instead of your tea."

"And if you'd told me I'd be willingly participating in family brunches, eat kale chips and yoga sessions," Levi adds with a grin that lights up his whole face, "I'd have arrested you for being delusional."

"And I," Alex chimes in, his voice warm with affection, "would have prescribed some serious medication if you'd suggested I'd find happiness in a polyamorous relationship with a yoga influencer and a gruff cop."

We all clink our glasses together, a motley crew united by love, laughter, and, apparently, honey. The sound is clear and joyful, like a bell heralding a new chapter.

"To family," my dad toasts, his voice filled with emotion. "The ones we're born with, and the ones we choose."

"To love in all its forms," my mom adds, her eyes misty. "Even the forms that involve fur and tails."

"To sticky situations," I say with a wink, "and the sweet solutions we find along the way."

"And to happily ever afters," Levi and Alex say in unison, sharing a look of surprise at their synchronicity before bursting into laughter.

Drinking to our unconventional happily ever after, I can't help but reflect on the journey that brought us here. It's been a wild ride, full of more twists and turns than one of my yoga classes. There were moments of doubt, fear, and confusion. Times when I thought I'd lost everything, only to discover that what I needed was waiting just around the corner.

Looking around this table, I see more than just a group sharing a meal. I know the love and support of my family and all of us together create a beautiful whole. My parents have shown me that love can grow, change, and adapt. Bliss, who's changed from my friend to become the sister I never had. Rex, our furry family member, reminds us daily of the simple joys in life. And my eyes rest on Levi and Alex, two men who couldn't be more different, yet both hold pieces of my heart.

As the brunch winds down and we start to clear the table, I'm struck by a thought.

Life doesn't always turn out the way we expect. Sometimes, it's messier, more complicated, and infinitely more interesting than we could have imagined.

And if we're lucky, really lucky, we end up with a family that we've hand-chosen and is as wonderfully weird and perfectly imperfect as we are.

I can't stop smiling while I watch Levi and Alex playfully argue over who will do the dishes. I glimpse my parents sneaking more treats to Rex, and Bliss snapping candid photos for my next Instagram post.

I know one thing for sure—I am really, really lucky.

I hold up my kombucha and make a silent toast. Here's to sticky situations and sweet solutions, choosing your family and a love that defies definition, and finding harmony in the chaos and beauty in the imperfections. And most of all, here's to happily ever afters that look nothing like we expected but turn out to be everything we ever wanted and more.

Namaste, friends.

If you loved Meaghan's why-choose romance, then you'll love Monica and David's fake engagement in *Coffeehouse Romance: My Accidental Christmas Fiancé*

CHECK IT OUT HERE or HarmonyNoble.com

Discover the heartwarming slow burn romances in the *Coffeehouse Romance* series.

CHECK IT OUT HERE or HarmonyNoble.com

Keep reading to enjoy the next book.

·♥·♥·♥·♥·♥·

Coffeehouse Romance: My Accidental Christmas Fiancé
Chapter 1: Monica's Cafe Christmas Surprise

Ugh. Christmas Eve. It's more like *Bah Humbug Eve*. Scratch that. *It's more like a Disasterpiece Eve.*

I sigh and glance at my eerily quiet phone while the pouring rain pounds outside echoing inside the empty cafe.

I'm stuck working the slowest shift *ever* at Joy's Coffeehouse while the rest of Lakewood, Washington, is snugly nestled by their fireplaces. They're sipping hot chocolates, surrounded by family, and tearing into early Christmas presents. Meanwhile, here I am with my Gingerbread Latte—*usually my absolute fave*. Today, it tastes more like a Letdown Latte with a side of bitter disappointment.

Glancing at my phone, I sigh at another Christmas Eve letdown. The holiday is overshadowing my birthday. Talk about a double whammy of suck. *No, wait, a triple whammy*—I'm pretty sure I just spotted a zit forming on my chin.

Happy freakin' birthday to me!

I blow a stray strand of dark hair out of my face, cursing my decision to skip the extra bobby pins this morning. "Get your birds in a row, Monica," I mutter, surveying the empty café. The cheeriness of twinkling lights and festive garland mock me. Even the dogs that usually fill our pet-friendly space, munching on free biscuits and lounging in the doggy beds under the tables, have abandoned this ship for livelier hangouts.

I'm contemplating whether dusting the already spotless espresso machine for the millionth time counts as productivity—or perhaps gazing at the local student's modern art hanging on walls?—the bell above the door jingles. My heart does a little flip, then a complete somersault with a triple twist dismount, when I spot who it is.

David. My geeky, funny regular customer. His Clark Kent looks make my insides feel like I've had a quad shot of espresso every time he walks in. And, of course, trailing behind him like a Victoria's Secret Angel who took a wrong turn on the runway is his stunning girlfriend, Monique.

"Hey guys!" I call out, plastering on my best *I'm-totally-not-crushing-on-your-boyfriend* smile. "The usual? Or are you feeling adventurous on this beautiful Christmas Eve?"

David locks eyes with me and gives me a shy smile, making my knees weak. I lean on the counter.

"You know it, Monica. I'd be in a *latte* trouble without my daily fix!"

"Ooh, good one!" I laugh a bit *too* enthusiastically. "You'd be in hot water without it... Get it? Because coffee—hot water..." But he is already looking away.

I finish, muttering, "Oh, never mind." *Smooth, Monica. Real smooth.*

Instead of laughing or giving me his playful wink, David looks away, suddenly fascinated by the chalkboard menu he's seen a thousand times.

Hum. *That's sus.*

He forgot to tell me what he *espresso-ly* wanted or his *ground-breaking* drink order. I shrug and get to work making their drinks: a simple Mexican mocha for him—*after I recommended it to him on his first visit*—and Monique's fussy concoction. The concoction offends baristas and coffee lovers alike, as she mixes green tea, coffee, cinnamon, oat milk, and an orange slice.

Pick a lane, Ice Princess!

I start frothing the milk—*oat? Hemp? Almond? Who can keep track?* Every week, she's on a different diet, requiring different ingredients for her drink. Monique doesn't notice or even drink the coffee I make her anyway. She uses the frothy latte as a prop for her pics.

I can't help noticing David's odd behavior. He fidgets more than a kid who's eaten all the low-hanging candy canes from the Christmas tree. Then, he alternates sitting and standing as he pulls a small red box out of his pocket.

Meanwhile, Monique's busy taking selfies in front of our sparkling Christmas tree, decorated in shades of lavender. Despite David's smoldering good looks, she rarely takes pics with him.

I side-eye him. He looks especially delish, with his adorably rumpled hair and that cozy yellow knitted scarf that is more his vibe than this expensive jacket and pointy leather shoes. *Monique probably picked those out.* He looks the part of the perfect, doting boyfriend, and I'm *totally* not jealous.

Nope. Not at all.

I glance down at my own too-tight black slacks—hugging my curves in all the wrong places—and an overly ruffly red blouse I found in the back of my closet. The laundromat is closed with the holidays, so I'm wearing my wardrobe rejects. *Maybe someone will buy me new clothes for Christmas.*

Ha! As if.

Who am I kidding? My dad is the only one getting me a present. His go-to gifts are flowers and chocolate.

Don't get me wrong—I love the guy, but picking gifts isn't exactly his talent. Someday, I'll buy myself the sequin dresses and impractical rhinestone heels I see on holiday displays. I'll rock the outfit with a cute boyfriend. For now, I'll settle for drooling over the holiday fashions—and other people's boyfriends.

I finished crafting the perfect rosetta on Monique's latte—which she'll love using for her Insta stories. Spotting movement, I see David slide to one knee with the mysterious red box now in his hand.

Holy gingerbread men on a stick. Is he...?

It hits me like a ton of gingerbread houses—*David is proposing. On Christmas Eve. In my café!* I'm watching while wearing the world's ugliest Christmas outfit, featuring a zit growing on my chin.

The universe hates me!

I glance back at Monique, who's filming her Christmas Eve greeting in front of the cutesy tree, utterly oblivious to the life-changing event about to happen.

My heart flutters as part of me heats up at this sweet, romantic moment. The other part of me wants to crawl under the counter with a tray of cookies and hide until New Year's.

Instead, I stand there, my heart pounding louder than the beat of Mariah Carey's "All I Want for Christmas Is You" as I watch David clear his throat to get her attention.

My fingers twitch towards my phone. *Should I?*

It's kinda creepy to film strangers, but David and Monique are hardly strangers. They're practically friends since I see them a few times a week at the cafe. And if someone were proposing to me, I'd want the magical moment captured.

Before I can overthink it—*a rare occurrence, let me tell you*—I've whipped out my phone quicker than you can say "peppermint mocha." Subtly—or what passes for subtle when only three of us are in the cafe–I start recording.

I have a clear view, and my phone picks up every sound—like David's shaky breaths. I'm in a front-row seat to this rom-com holiday realness.

David clears his throat again. I hear his heart pounding from here—or that's my heart doing the cha-cha and swooning.

"Monique? There's something I want to ask you."

I hold my breath, suddenly feeling like I'm an extra in a real-life Hallmark Christmas movie. Cue the snow, the sappy music, and the inevitable happy ending. I bite back my giggle, watching how adorably nervous David is. Even Monique looks surprised as she turns to him, probably ready to scold him for ruining her Instagram-perfect reel.

Who knew a Christmas miracle would happen in my small-town coffee shop? Well, besides every Hallmark holiday movie *ever.*

Looking up from kneeling, David makes eye contact with her, his eyes shining. I have to keep myself from clapping or hooting. *Sure, he's proposing to someone else, but a girl can be supportive, right?* Maybe someday, an adorkable guy will look at me like David's looking at Monique.

His brown eyes are wide, and his gaze is intense. He licks his full lips and remains bowed down in the romantic gesture.

My eyes fill with tears, and I blink to stop my "ugly cry." No way am I ruining my mascara over someone else's proposal, even if that someone is the star of approximately 99% of my daydreams.

"Monique," David's voice is soft but steady, filled with love. "From the moment I first saw you, I knew you were special. You've certainly lit up my life. You light up every room you enter. I'm honored to be your boyfriend. These past two years have been the happiest of my life." He pauses to slow the rush of words, and I see his hands trembling. "I want to spend the rest of my days making you as happy as you've made me."

Oh. My. Latte.

Is this real life? Or did I accidentally inhale too much cinnamon? I'm pretty sure my mascara is a complete mess as I watch from behind my phone.

Note to self—invest in waterproof makeup.

Who knew my pun-loving customer had such a way with words? If his whole computer genius thing doesn't work out, he's got a future in writing Valentine's cards.

"You're my best friend, my partner in crime, and the love of my life," David continues, reaching for the little red box. "Monique, will you marry me?"

He opens the velvet box, revealing a ring that catches the cafe's twinkling lights. It's vintage-looking, very heirloom-trendy, and gorgeous. It is the kind of ring that would make me say *yes,* even if it was from a drunken mall Santa.

I'm grinning like an idiot and silently dancing with excitement. I'm already planning on how I'll surprise them with this video. *Maybe I'll even get invited to their lavish wedding!*

I can see it now–"How did you meet the happy couple" "Oh, I just happened to be there for the most romantic proposal ever! No big deal—I'm their morning coffee friend."

But, faster than you can say "abso-brew-tely"—which is how David responds when I ask if he wants an extra shot in his mocha—my private Hallmark movie turns into a Lifetime drama.

Monique's delicate features scrunch up like she's just been served a full-fat, full-sugar latte in a to-go cup. *The horror!*

"No. No way!"

Wait, what?

I gasp so hard I inhale my tongue and cough-choke, but they don't notice as I try to regain my composure to hear the conversation.

"First, you can't propose at a café without warning me. I need to be picture-ready for my Cinderella moment," she admonishes, her voice rising with each word.

If she goes any higher, only dogs will hear her.

"And what is this ring? Is this pre-owned? This thing is the worst hand-me-down *ever.* No way! Just no, David!"

I know I should stop filming, but I'm frozen.

How could she say no to my wonderful David? She rejected the loveliest, most romantic proposal I've ever witnessed. *Okay, the only proposal I've ever witnessed, but still. What a spoiled diva!*

David wilts, looking like someone told him that Santa isn't real. "But... I have reservations at Sparrows to celebrate. I chose to ask you here, in our special morning spot. Sparrows is very posh, Michelin-starred, and it's a three-month wait for a reservation. I thought you could say yes privately and then you could film the proposal at Sparrows later. Can we at least talk?"

Oh, David. Sweet, naive David. He's not offended by Monique's response. Instead, he's trying to appease her. I want to shake him and yell, "Wake up and smell the coffee!" He's too good for her. But I'm behind the counter, holding my phone, being the world's worst undercover videographer.

I stare, transfixed on Monique. She stomps to the door with her designer boots clicking against the hardwood floor.

"Talk about it? There's nothing to talk about. This is so not Instagram-worthy! This whole set-up is *underwhelming* and *common.*"

The bell jingles as she storms out, sounding more ominous than the cheerful jingle when they entered. For a moment, the café is so quiet that I can hear a snowflake fall or the soft, crackling sound of David's heart shattering into a million pieces.

David remains on one knee with the open ring box, stunned by the rejection.

I realize I'm still recording and quickly shut off my phone. I shudder, feeling like a creeper.

Way to go, Monica. You've officially crossed the line from "friendly barista" to "potential stalker."

Standing there, wondering if it's too late to hide or pretend I didn't see everything, I can't help but think: *this is officially a worse Christmas Eve for David than for me.* And the thought of someone more miserable than me makes me bite back a little smile.

However—knowing my rotten luck—there must be a meteor headed my way.

·❤·❤·❤·❤·❤·

Chapter 2: Broken Man

Rooted to my spot behind the cafe counter, I'm dazed, reeling from the romantic trainwreck. David—my workplace crush with his endless supply of dad jokes and Clark Kent allure—just had his heart mercilessly stomped on by Maria, the Ice Queen herself.

Seriously, why do the sweetest guys always fall for the terriblest women? And here I am, an insensitive friend, capturing his heartache on film.

I'm failing at this whole adulting, nonchalant *I-don't-have-a-crush-on-you* thing. Maybe I should add "professional heartbreak documenter" to my useless skill list on my resume.

David moves, placing his head in his hands, and he leans heavily against the table. He's still on one knee, the rejected ring glittering from its red velvet box—a sad, sparkly reminder of the cruel rejection.

Suddenly, Mariah Carey twists the knife, belting out, "All I Want for Christmas is YOU," which echoes in the quiet cafe.

OMG!

I fumble with my phone, nearly dropping it to silence Mariah's poorly-timed serenade.

Stopping the music, I notice that my phone continues to be message-free, despite my birthday. Letting out a small sigh—not too dramatic, though, because at least *I didn't get dumped* by the "love of my life" during the holidays.

Chewing my bottom lip, I debate what to do, taking in the scene: the dark, quiet cafe with one awkward barista—me—and one broken-hearted customer. It's the saddest Christmas Hallmark movie ever.

I should do something, *anything*. Offer him my shoulder to cry on? Be his listening ear? Or perhaps, rub his broad shoulders and offer to be his rebound girlfriend.

I shake my head. *Down, girl.*

"Get it together, Monica," I whisper to loosen my tight chest. "You've got this. Just be cool. Be—"

"Are you talking to yourself?"

"Ah!" I jump out of my skin, nearly knocking the coffee off the counter.

David unfreezes, looking up from his hands, an eyebrow raised in a way that is too calm for someone who just got his heart shattered.

Busted!

"Me? Talking to myself? Psh, no way," I babble, waving my hands to swat away my awkwardness. "I was just, uh... practicing my ventriloquism. You know, gotta keep those skills sharp for my future career as a... coffee-making ventriloquist."

Smooth, Monica. Real smooth. *Why does my mouth always come back to life before my brain?* I need to install a brain-to-mouth filter.

Surprisingly, David chuckles. "A coffee-making ventriloquist, huh? That's a show I'd go to. Do the lattes tell jokes, too?"

"Only the really frothy ones," I quip. A warm flutter in my chest starts when I look into his soft, brown eyes, and his face resets into his easy-going smile.

"I always considered your espresso more the strong, silent type," he volleys back with the awkward vibe lifting.

"Well, you know me. Always brewing up ideas," I say. "Sorry, that was a terrible pun. I'll leave the coffee jokes to you."

"Nah, it was pretty good," he says, slowly bringing himself to his feet, only to collapse on the wooden chair next to him.

I giggle, feeling the tension dissolving like sugar into hot coffee. His casual humor is what I love about David. Even with his heart in pieces, he is cracking jokes.

"Speaking of sweet things," I say, mentally high-fiving myself for the smooth segue, "How about I bring you your mocha? And a gingerbread cookie, on the house, of course. It's the least I can do after... well, you know."

David nods. He looks like he's aged a few years over the last few minutes. I resist the urge to run over and wrap him in a big hug.

"Thanks, Monica. That sounds nice."

It's probably my imagination or wishful thinking, but he doesn't seem *too broken up* about Maria. His eyes meet mine with warm appreciation.

I fill the empty air with a whisper, "For what it's worth, I thought it was beautiful... Your proposal, I mean."

He pauses, turning to give me a sad smile that squeezes my chest uncomfortably. "Thanks. At least someone appreciated it. I'm pretty sure Maria wasn't impressed, and she isn't coming back."

Good riddance! David is too good for her. Instead of voicing my totally harsh opinion, I nod. I grab his coffee and cookie. "Your coffee and a consolation prize for surviving."

Handing him the steaming mug, my fingers accidentally brush against his. A spark between our hands sends a hot chill down my spine.

Maybe it's just static electricity.

David jolts slightly and looks down at his latte. He sips it and gives me a relieved smile.

I take that as my cue to linger a little longer, sliding into the seat beside him. A warm flutter of excitement courses through me, igniting my senses like the rich aroma of freshly brewed coffee wafting through the café.

He's single now—a fact that sends a thrill racing down my spine—and I can finally seize the chance I should have taken ages ago. The air between us crackles with an undeniable energy, a magnetic pull that is exhilarating and dangerously enticing.

Moving the ring box to the table center, David relaxes and sips his mocha thoughtfully. My heart does a little somersault of sympathy, threatening to leap out of my chest and directly into his hands.

"Thanks, Monica. It's all good," he says quietly, suggesting that everything is *not* all good.

I busy myself, moving the cookie in front of him and wiping my hands on my apron while sneaking a glance. He is a lost puppy. It's a far cry from the confident guy who walked in here ready to propose—making me, again, want to wrap him in a big hug.

He picks up the cookie, a trace of a smile on his lips, making my heart do a little tap dance. "Thanks, again. I—"

But before he can finish, the gingerbread man jumps from his hand and lands on the table with a *thunk*. Its head breaks off, rolling off the table in a trail of crumbs—a bad omen for sure.

We stare at it for a second, and I'm about to apologize—*for what, I'm not quite sure, but it feels right*—when David breaks the silence.

"Well," he says, the mood oppressive, again. "Guess he's broken. Just like—"

"Don't *you dare*!" I warn sharply. "If you say 'just like me', I swear I'll dump that Mexican mocha over your head. And trust me, nobody looks good covered in spilled coffee." I surprise even myself with my fierceness. "You are *not* broken, David. You're... you're..."

I fumble for words, trying to find the right thing to say.

What do you tell a guy who just had his heart handed back to him on a sterling silver platter? There are other fish in the stream seems too weak and too trite to say–also, I think I mangled the metaphor, *or is it a simile?*

"You're more like... like a gingerbread latte than a ruined cookie!" I blurt, gesturing wildly at our Christmas drink displayed on the table topper.

David blinks slowly, confusion written over his face. "I'm a cheap, unnecessary holiday drink?"

My cheeks burn hotter than fresh drip coffee. *Why, oh why, can't I think before speaking?*

"No! I mean, yes, but that's not—" I take a deep breath, trying to salvage my thought. "What I mean is, I love gingerbread lattes. They're unique and only someone who takes time to look at the menu would order one because it's not the classic Christmas drink. You're special, and you have more wonderfulness than what meets the eye. You are a gentleman, holding doors for people, a lowkey genius, and... and you make people happy."

He remains silent, looking at the Gingerbread Latte picture, then down to the floor at the cookie mess.

I forge on, filling the silence and putting my foot so far in my mouth I can taste my itchy synthetic pants, "You make *me* happy and smile. I hate the holidays and you made my afternoon better by coming in while everyone else is shopping and enjoying the holiday except me. I mean, when you walked in, I forgot that I'm stuck working alone with no holiday plans."

I shake my head and return to my flailing metaphor, "You're like my Gingerbread Latte. You are sweet, underappreciated, and anyone with taste would fall in love with you."

OMG! Did I just announce my love to him? *What just happened?!*

David stares at me with wide eyes, and I'm mentally preparing my resignation letter to Joy. I can *never* come back from this. I'll relocate, change my name, and pretend this never happened.

But then, slowly, a genuine smile spreads across his face, lighting up his eyes and giving him his spark back. He chuckles, taking my hands in his.

My heart races, and I lick my lips with the sudden tenderness he's beaming at me. I open my mouth, but there are no words.

He leans forward, and I lean into him, automatically.

"Monica, that's—"

The jingling of the door cuts him off, and he flinches, sending the mug by his arm, crashing. He leaps to mop it up with napkins before I can move.

I turn to see who's crazy enough to be in a cafe on this dreary afternoon.

Oh.

My.

Gingerbread.

Head.

The weirdest workday just got *more bizarrer.*

Standing in the doorway, looking like they stepped out of a holiday Vogue photoshoot, is a dazzling group of people I've never seen in my cozy cafe. *Most likely, no Washington cafe has ever seen these supermodel-posh people layered in cashmere and jewelry, looking ready to walk a holiday runway.*

Leading the charge is a woman swathed in luxurious silver fox fur, sparkling like she'd just stepped off a red carpet, with diamonds glittering on every exposed inch of her skin—if Martha Stewart had a bougie sister who moonlighted as a fashion icon, this is definitely her. Right behind her is a hunky European man who looks like he bench-presses his Ferrari for fun; honestly, I think I've seen him in an expensive cologne ad. And trailing joyfully after him is a stunning young woman radiating major Norwegian princess vibes—her graceful style making it seem as if she's strutting her elegant attire for the invisible cameras.

I blink, wondering if I'd accidentally slipped into an alternate universe where only supermodels live and everything sparkles with diamonds.

And they're all staring at me, like I'm the main attraction at the Woodland Park Zoo.

Look over here - a rare specimen, native to the greater Seattle area. This is the elusive working-class barista wearing a box-store outfit, and spotted during an ill-fated mating ritual.

"David?" the stylish woman inquires, her British accent wrapping around his name like a silk scarf. Her gaze locks onto David, who's currently down on one knee, surrounded by shards of a shattered mug.

"Is that you, darling?"

I can practically see the gears turning as his eyes go wide with a mix of shock and confusion. A look on his face—pure alarm—makes me think he's as bewildered by this unexpected situation as I am.

He scrambles to stand up, sending the table teetering. In a split second, I instinctively catch the ring box before it tumbles onto the messy floor.

"Mother?" David squeaks out. "Mom? What are you—how did you...?"

Chapter 3: Not Gay, Mom

Wait, what? This is David's mother? And the others must be...

Oh boy. Suddenly, my brain whirls into overdrive, trying to compute how my adorable David is related to these posh foreigners. I glance at the chiseled Nordic features and perfect hair, trying to spot any family resemblance to David. It's like trying to find a decaf drinker at eight AM—*impossible!*

David leans in close, his breath warm against my ear, sending a shiver down my spine that has nothing to do with the winter chill. "I'm so sorry, Monica," he whispers, his contained panic and pleading. "I had no idea they were coming. I'm kind of the family disappointment, so... brace yourself for some upper-class rudeness. Just... Please don't hate me after meeting them."

His puppy dog eyes could melt a snowman's heart, and I find myself nodding before I can even process what I'm agreeing to.

"Surprise, big *little* bro!" the suave guy booms across the café. I half expect the windows to rattle.

David's mom clasps her hands together, tears in her eyes. "Oh, David! You didn't tell us you were proposing *today!*"

And that's when I realized what this scene looks like. David is on his knees, picking up ceramic pieces. I'm standing over him with the ring box I'd instinctively grabbed when he bumped the table.

Oh no. *No, no, no.* This is not happening. This *cannot* be happening. I suddenly have the spotlight back on me. I don't know how to *do* family stuff. I don't know my lines. I blush so hard my eyelashes must be sweating off the last of my mascara.

I open my mouth, ready to explain the misunderstanding, but then I catch sight of David's face. He looks *defeated*. He's back to the guy dumped by his girlfriend and ready to be the family's disappointment. The words dry up, and I'm silent.

"I—" David starts, but his brother cuts him off, dismissing him faster than Maria did.

Mr. Muscles steps forward. And holy peppermint sticks, he steps into my personal space bubble.

"Enchanté, bella," he purrs, taking my hand and bringing it to his lips. His eyes, the same warm brown as David's, hold a mischievous glint, locking onto mine. "I'm Edward, the better-looking brother."

"You could have ordered us some sunshine or at least snow for the holidays," his brother scoffs toward David, releasing my hand to smooth over perfectly sleek hair.

David's sister—I presume—rushes forward, her eyes sparkling. "Oh my gosh, did we miss it? Did she say yes? Where is she?"

"You idiot. This *worker* is her," his brother says, dismissing her and me with a wave and saying the word "worker" like it's foul-tasting.

"Oh, sorry," she says, warmly smiling. She shrugs and sets her leather purse and jacket on the table beside us. "Nice to meet you. I'm Emily. I can't wait to hear all about you."

"Oh, how wonderful!" David's mom exclaims, rushing to envelop me in an odd hug since I'm ultra-petite compared to the regal lady. The embrace smells like Chanel No. 5 and money—lots of silver fox fur-buying money. This is the most expensive, plush hug I've ever had.

"I'm Victoria, David's mother. This is Edward and Emily, my youngest," she explains with an over-enunciation due more to her accent than rudeness–*I hope.*

"Way to go, nerd! We actually thought you made her up!" Edward laughs, slapping David hard enough to make him almost fall as he is trying to stand up. "I mean, come on, a girlfriend? You?"

Edward gives me a once-over, sizing me up to see if I'm worth his time. I blush at his condescending stare, feeling out of place with their impromptu family reunion.

"Not bad, bro. " He whistles at me, and I resist the urge to touch my zit or fix my messy hair with his eyes on me.

Emily, on the other hand, looks ready to explode from excitement. She's almost dancing as she leans to kiss my cheeks and vibrates with joy. "I can't believe we're finally meeting you! David didn't say much but we knew he was dating someone special. Now I see why he didn't say anything. *You're gorgeous!*"

My blush increases. *Me, gorgeous?* Has she looked in a mirror lately? Besides David's almost-fiancée—Maria—Emily is hands down the most gorgeous woman in Lakewood. She is statuesque, blonde, blue-eyed, stylish, and with a casual girl-next-door smile.

"Oh, um, thanks," I stammer, suddenly very aware of my coffee-stained apron and zit throbbing on my chin.

David finally finds his voice and a pause in the conversation to say, "Guys, this isn't—"

"Well, I simply thought you were *a gay*," his mom says with a dismissive shrug. "Which is fine with *the family*. It explained why you've never dated girls or *had* a girlfriend, and you spent so much time on the computer. Dating your elusive model, Maria, seemed like a ruse to me to stop asking for grandkids."

David's face turns an impressive shade of red that would make Rudolph's nose look dull.

"Mom! Who can date attending a boys' private school? And I've been finishing my graduate school and working as a computer programmer. Being a GIS programmer is—"

"Yes, yes, dear. No need to bore us with your mundane life. I know, your maps are *very* important," his mom says, waving a perfectly manicured hand with rings that catch the light and sparkle more than our entire cafe's holiday decor. "*Now*, introduce us to your beautiful fiancée!"

All eyes turn to me, and I suddenly wish I had Maria's ability to look glamorous and aloof. I open my mouth, ready to explain the misunderstanding, but David's face shows that this is the final straw in a day that's been one giant kick to his emotional groin. His family's words cut him deeper than Maria's rejection. I feel my pulse quicken with a fierce protectiveness.

He doesn't deserve his family's judgment and more embarrassment.

And before I can stop myself, my brain makes the connection that his family doesn't know Maria, I'm holding a ring box, and my name is *quite* similar. I hear my mouth blurting, "Hi, I'm Monica. It's so nice to meet you all. David told me a lot of wonderful things about you."

Liar, liar, clothes on fire.

"Sorry, Monica. David's hardly mentioned you," Emily says sheepishly with a smile. "He's quite secretive, living on the other side of the globe from us."

David's head snaps up, his eyes wide in shock, meet mine. I give him a tiny nod, hoping he understands what I'm doing. *I've got your back, buddy. We'll sort this out when they leave.*

"Isn't it wonderful?" Victoria interrupts, ignoring her son and smiling at her two other children–her clones. "Our David is finally settling down. And on the holidays, no less!"

I catch David's eye, silently asking if he wants me to come clean. But there's something in his gaze–*relief? Gratitude, perhaps?* I hold my tongue and smile.

"Yeah," he says softly, reaching to take my hand. His palm is warm against mine, and I try to ignore the little flutter in my stomach and the spark ignited with his touch. "It is pretty wonderful."

And just like that, the lie is born. I'm fake engaged to my dreamy customer on my birthday.

What have I gotten myself into?

David's family crowds around us, and he squeezes my hand for support. I squeeze his back as his family congratulates us.

Even though it's wild–*right? I mean, pretending to be engaged to a guy I'm saving from more embarrassment*–I'm laughing with them and accepting their compliments.

I look at David, seeing the tension easing from his shoulders as his family fusses over us, and I know I made the right choice.

After all, isn't that what Christmas is all about? Helping others out of ridiculous family situations, or at least that's what everyone always says. I don't have the two parents, siblings, or big family to compare notes on what a family should look like.

"So, when's the wedding?" Edward asks bluntly, his grin too calculated to be friendly.

"Oh, we haven't really—" I begin, but Victoria cuts me off faster than I can say, *venti double shot no-foam latte.*

"Nonsense! You must have *some* idea. Spring weddings are lovely, you know. Or perhaps a destination wedding? The family has a lovely villa we're redecorating in Tuscany, with a divine vineyard, that would suit a wedding perfectly."

My head spins fast to keep up. *Tuscany? Villas?*

First, who are these people? Secondly, what's wrong with a good old-fashioned backyard wedding with a barbecue and a retro 80s DJ?

I'm pretty sure our ideas of what a dream wedding is, are galaxies apart.

"Mom," David says, a stiff warning in his tone with his slight British accent seeping through talking with his family. "Monica and I haven't discussed any of that yet. We've only been engaged for a few minutes now."

Victoria waves her hand dismissively, nearly taking out a nearby Christmas candle. "Oh, darling, there's so much to plan! We can't waste time. Now, Monica dear, tell me about your family. What do they think?"

I hesitate–*I'm walking into a trap.* "It's just my dad, and I haven't told him yet."

She waves off my answers like they're pesky flies. "And what does he do?"

I pause, as I'm not used to lying, and there's an undercurrent of judgment. "Oh, um, well."

"Mom," Emily interjects with a hidden wink only I see. She comes to my rescue as if we are already friends. "Maybe we should let them breathe for a minute? They just got engaged, after all."

Bless you, Emily. I could kiss her plump, shiny lips—*platonically, since I'm fake engaged to her brother, of course.*

"Of course, of course," Victoria says, unapologetically. "We're all so excited! There's so much planning. It's all very exhilarating, isn't it, David?"

Oddly quiet and even more shy with his family, David nods. "Yeah, Mom. It's... *great.*"

He sounds about as enthusiastic as someone headed to a root canal. *Or maybe someone who's realizing they're engaged to a barista.* Either way, he's not exactly playing the part of a happy fiancé.

Victoria launches into a detailed description of our wedding—*doves are non-negotiable*—and I catch David's eye. He mouths a silent 'thank you' and grimaces at his mom's outrageous wedding plans.

A giggle bubbles up inside me, threatening to spill. And there's a warmth in my chest that has nothing to do with the gallons of coffee I've consumed today. It's more like belonging and being part of a family. *The feeling is hard to pinpoint but oddly satisfying.*

This fake engagement could be fun, and I do need a dash of holiday family realness anyway. I'm not doing anything fun for the holidays.

I'm sure the charade will only be long enough for David to break the news to his family. But I might as well enjoy having my fake engagement and fake family while they are here. I smile, holding back my giggle, which makes my smile brighter.

Listening to Victoria debate the merits of white versus ivory for my wedding dress, then lace versus hand-beaded pearls, makes me smile even more. Omg, Maria would have loved this. David's mom should be having this convo with his actual girlfriend, fashionista Maria.

Maybe Santa heard my secret Christmas wish. Perhaps I'll be getting a crazy, wealthy family for Christmas?

"Oh, and Monica," Victoria says, snapping me back to reality. "You and your dad simply must join us for our elegant holiday dinner tomorrow. I won't take no for an answer!"

I look at David, panic rising in my throat. *The situation is escalating too fast.* But he shrugs, with a quirk of his brow, saying, *Why not?*

"Umm...Lovely," I hear myself say, wondering who this polite lady is. "I'd be honored."

A dinner with his family will probably be at a luxurious restaurant. *Wait. I bet they rented out a big Seattle mansion overlooking Puget Sound with bathrooms bigger than my apartment and a private chef.*

This makes me ponder the most important question, what *am* I going to wear to our pretend engagement, family dinner?

David's hand squeezes mine gently, a silent signal to not worry. I hope he's saying, "I'll buy you a sequin holiday dress and you can pretend to be my fiancé for tomorrow's family dinner."

Squeezing his hand back, I gaze into his chocolatey eyes, inches from mine. I inhale his masculine cologne, and suddenly, I wonder if this is all an insane daydream. My heart gallops, and I bite my lip.

'Tis the season for miracles, right? And if he needs me to rescue him from his family and embarrassment, I will gladly hold his hand and have dinner with my cafe crush's family.

If this isn't a *Christmas miracle, I don't know what is!*

Find out what happens next in Monica's engagement adventure in
Coffeehouse Romance: My Accidental Christmas Fiancé
CHECK IT OUT HERE or HarmonyNoble.com

Coffeehouse Romance: The Wrong Bride Romance for Christmas

One white lie, two hearts, and a dash of amnesia... Can a lonely barista turn a fake engagement into her real-life fairytale?

Monica's been brewing a crush on David, her adorably handsome cafe regular, for two years. But when a twist of fate lands them on a ski trip together, one little white lie about being engaged suddenly snowballs into the Christmas chaos.

David takes a tumble on the slopes and wakes up with amnesia, leaving Monica living her best life–complete with a doting almost-mother-in-law, a would-be sister, and the man of her dreams, who looks at her like she hangs the moon.

There's just one problem... none of it is real.

Will Monica come clean and risk losing everything, including the family she's grown to love? Or will she say "I do" to a man who has no idea their engagement is fake?

One thing's for sure–this holiday season is about to get a whole latte complicated.

Coffeehouse Romance: Love, Joy & Lattes

Will the police, a drag queen, an anonymous online friend, and a faithful customer help Joy to save her cafe and her love life?

Join cafe owner Joy, who is unlucky in love, on a caffeine fueled adventure to rescue her beloved dog and save her cafe in this enemies-to-lovers rom-com set in the beautiful backdrop of a small town in the Pacific Northwest.

A coffee entrepreneur with a banging boyfriend and an adorable Labradoodle, Joy's life is perfect. . . until a Sex-presso stand opens nearby, threatening her business.

Just when things couldn't get worse, they do! Joy's cafe is in ruins, her boyfriend's infidelity is revealed, and her online confidante ghosts her. With her heart searching for a happily ever after fate brews up a twist as Joy finds herself teaming up with her charming nemesis to rescue her beloved Coco Puff from the clutches of a dognapper!

Discover your next favorite story at <u>HarmonyNoble.com</u> & sign up to receive the e-newsletter for exclusive news and giveaways from authors Harmony Noble and Melody Best.

Coffeehouse Romance: Test Driving a Millionaire

Join me, Tara, as I trade in my barista apron at Joy's Coffeehouse in quaint Lakewood, Washington, for a chic Gucci gown to party in dazzling New York City. Buckle up for this exhilarating romantic adventure where a millionaire—scratch that, a billionaire—sweeps me off my feet undeterred by my fake fiancé.

I'm a small-town girl with big dreams of sophisticated soirees, wealthy men, and driving posh sports cars. Serendipity strikes when a lost puppy leads me into the arms of his dashing owner: a powerful tycoon who can cherish and indulge my millionaire fantasy.

Just as my billionaire beau rescues me from my mundane life and introduces me to his glamorous world of luxury, with his massive yacht, private jet, and New York City penthouse, my past threatens to ruin my dazzling new reality with a shocking revelation.

Will I succumb to the seductive allure of wealth and the glamor of New York City? Or will I discover that true happiness is closer to home in my small town cafe?

Discover your next favorite story at HarmonyNoble.com & sign up to receive the e-newsletter for exclusive news and giveaways from authors Harmony Noble and Melody Best.

Coffeehouse Romance: Shattering Crystal
a Bully Romance

Can a secret and an unexpected reunion shatter Crystal's dreams, or will faith and forgiveness brew a second chance at love?

Nursing student Crystal thought she'd found her happily ever after, until heartbreak from a secret relationship with her college professor ended in heartbreak. But everything changes the moment Dr. Thomas walks into Joy's Coffeehouse—the high school bully who once tormented her, now a compassionate doctor stirring feelings she never expected.

Crystal fights to keep her most guarded secret—her pregnancy—from unraveling her carefully constructed world. Thomas, battling his own guilt, finds himself drawn to the resilient woman he once hurt, struggling to prove he's more than the boy she feared.

Will Crystal risk trusting a man who once broke her heart? Or will the weight of lies shatter any chance at the future they both crave?

A tender, tension-filled romance about faith, forgiveness, and finding love where you least expect it.

Discover your next favorite story at <u>HarmonyNoble.com</u>

COMING NEXT

AURORA'S WILDERNESS LOVE:
HOT GIRLS SUMMER LOVE

HARMONY NOBLE

Where the odds are good, but the goods are odd—welcome to Alaska, where finding love is wilder than the wilderness.

Aurora knows two things for certain: dating in Alaska is a contact sport, and survival isn't just about navigating frozen tundra—it's about navigating the heart. Broke, desperate, and one dating disaster away from giving up, she's determined to rewrite her story, one hilarious misstep at a time.

With more men than women in this last-frontier dating landscape, Aurora is about to discover that finding herself might be the greatest adventure of all. Armed with nothing but her wits, a killer sense of humor, and an uncanny ability to turn romantic catastrophes into comedic gold, she's ready to prove that sometimes love finds you when you least expect it—and usually when you look absolutely ridiculous.

Get ready for a heartwarming Alaskan rom-com where hunting for love is the ultimate wilderness sport, and Aurora is determined to bag her happily ever after.

In Alaska, the ice is cold, but the workplace tension is scorching

Download at <u>HarmonyNoble.com</u> & sign up to receive the e-newsletter for exclusive news and giveaways from authors Harmony Noble & Melody Best.

Coffeehouse Romance Series:

Love, Joy & Lattes (Joy's Story)
Test Driving a Millionaire (Tara's Story)
Shattering Crystal a Bully Romance (Crystal's Story)
Choosing Love, Namaste (Meaghan's Story)
The Wrong Bride for Christmas (Monica's Story)

Coffeehouse Romance Short Stories:

Joy's 4th of July Holidate
Tara's Valentine Holidate
Crystal's Easter Holidate
Meaghan's New Year Holidate
Monica's Halloween Holidate
My Accidental Christmas Fiancé
Joy's Coffeehouse Romance

UNLOCK YOUR GIFT

Snag the latest swoon-worthy reads and stay tuned for upcoming stories at www.HarmonyNoble.com.

About Author –
Melody Best & Harmony Noble

Meet the unstoppable twins from the rugged wilds of Alaska, the writing duo, Harmony & Melody. Fueled by endless lattes, their character-driven stories brim with authenticity, humor, and heart—featuring Alaskan grit, journeys of self-discovery, and swoon-worthy happily-ever-afters.

When they're not crafting adventure romances, these twins can be found hiking trails with breathtaking views, enjoying charming coffee shops, or exploring new worldwide destinations together.

Join the e-newsletter for exclusive content and giveaways at
website: https://harmonynoble.com
Email: TrueLoveWriters@gmail.com
Instagram/Facebook/TikTok: @truelovewriters

www.ingramcontent.com/pod-product-compliance
Lightning Source LLC
Chambersburg PA
CBHW051334020726
47501CB00007B/2076